for Barbara,

Enjoy the story ..
& I hope it motivates

you.

Saachi

Pari

A Quiet Journey of Perseverance

PARVANEH SAATCHI

authorHOUSE®

AuthorHouse™
1663 Liberty Drive
Bloomington, IN 47403
www.authorhouse.com
Phone: 1 (800) 839-8640

Published by AuthorHouse   08/15/2017

ISBN: 978-1-5246-8606-2 (sc)
ISBN: 978-1-5246-8605-5 (e)

I dedicate this book to two incredible women in my life: my maman, who inspired me to write it, and my daughter, who makes me proud every day to be her maman.

Prologue

My mother was a neighbour to the Piruz and Pushtekar families. From before she was school aged she would listen as her mother and Pari chatted by the running water outside their gates. They met there periodically while each gathered water for her pond. Pari good-naturedly would tell of her latest life situation. My mother became a witness to Pari's life while playing nearby her mother. Being a natural story teller, my mother retold Pari's story to her children. She shared many stories from people she knew, books she read, and folklore. Always, the stories were captivating and with moral endings. I heard Pari's story when I was very young. It was not until I overheard Pari's story from my mother as she told it to my daughter that I decided to share it as a novel. It is my sincere wish that Pari's story touches the hearts of my readers.

by Parvaneh Saatchi

Contents

Part 3

Part 1

Before death takes away what you are given, give away what there is to give.

—Rumi

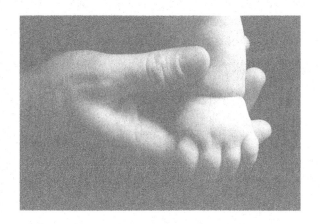

Chapter 1

Losing Baba (1309 SH)

I was alone with my father, and my screams reached no one. I sat on the first of three wide steps that led to the front entrance of our house. The sun was not yet overhead, but the Tehran heat was already strong. I cradled my father's head in my lap, stroking his cool, damp forehead. The blood flowed down from the wound in his head and soaked my white cotton dress. I held my skirt bunched against his open wound, but the blood pushed stubbornly past.

One month ago, on my eleventh birthday, my father brought this dress home for me. His grin and enthusiasm may have exceeded mine. He sat on the Persian carpet cushions in the family room while I ran upstairs to try the dress on. My bedroom was on the second floor along with my brothers' rooms. Two more rooms were on the third floor, but we used them for storage. My father's bedroom, which was more like a library with shelves full of books, was on the main floor. The cot he slept on disappeared into the background.

My father was a tall, slim man. He grabbed his knees to his chest when he sat on the Persian carpet cushions in the family room. His dark curls were showing specks of white on the temples. He had me believe the white specks were from the plaster he worked with, until the day I saw him dry his hair with a towel, leaving the specks intact.

My father gasped when I entered the family room. I twirled around to show him the full skirt. His green eyes, something I was proud we had in common, were two bright lights in his tanned face, and they followed me around the room. We laughed deliriously when I collapsed into his arms in a cloud of white cotton.

My father never hid his biased affection for me from my two older brothers, even though my birth had caused the death of his beloved wife, Nargis. I asked my father if he was sad about the way I had come into the world. He assured me that if my mother had to leave, at least she left the best part of herself behind. He said having me made him miss her less, and his only regret was that she did not get to meet me.

I came to know my mother through the wonderful stories my father told me about her. My brothers, Ali and Amir, never interrupted him, and they never spoke of her either. They must have had many memories to share, because they were in secondary school when she died. They chose to step aside and allow our father to tell the stories.

Now, dying in my lap, my father selflessly reached out to comfort me.

"Ali ... Amir ... they will care for you, Pari *joon*," Baba said, trying to smile.

He was so weak that the smile turned into a grimace.

I watched the life leave his body and the light go out of his eyes. Still, his head in my lap comforted me. I continued to stroke his forehead. I stared at his gentle face, remembering how often I had heard someone comment on how handsome he was. They felt it was strange that after all these years, he had not remarried.

* * *

"Mohamad Pushtekar," Khale Sara, my mother's younger sister, scolded Baba playfully, "you have to get on with your life."

"Sara joon, remarrying is for those who are still looking for love," my father answered with an emerald wink. "I have already found it, although she left me some time ago."

Khale Sara persisted.

"You need to give that meaningful name to another lucky girl."

"A girl can have perseverance without being called *Khanum* Pushtekar."

* * *

Hours passed unnoticed. I spent the time gazing at my

father and around the yard that only he cared for. Since the garden had been important to him, I gave each item my full, deliberate attention. The mustard brick ground had a three-foot-deep pond with a stone pedestal fountain in the middle, spouting water. A tall brick wall and an iron gate, lined with copper and brass flowers on the top edge, enclosed the yard. The inside border of this yard, in contrast to the bricks, was a lush garden. There were bushes of roses, jasmine, and honeysuckle embracing each other, making it difficult to tell where one ended and the other began. Emerging from these bushes in tall splendour were fruit trees: mulberry, quince, fig, and walnut. My father loved tending to them, keeping the yard colourful on a backdrop of shimmering green foliage. It was his paradise.

Today it was where we waited together for one of my brothers to return from work.

Amir was the first to come through the gate. He took a few steps and halted when he saw the scene my father and I had created.

It was early evening, but Tehran's summer sun was relentless.

"Amir, Baba is dead," I said in a groggy voice.

New tears flowed down my face. Amir looked from me to Baba and back to me. Then his eyes lifted to the tall ladder still leaning against the wall. It reached the third floor, where Baba had been washing a window. He scowled.

"I said I would take care of those damn windows on Friday," he mumbled, warily walking over to us.

Baba had recently lost his job working as a plaster layer. With no work, he wanted to be productive. That morning he had decided to wash the outside of the windows himself.

Amir tried to lift Baba off my lap, telling me in his usual annoyed voice to go clean myself. A stale, metallic smell rose into the air.

"*Nooooo!*" I wailed, holding tightly to Baba.

Amir adopted a gentle voice. It took me by surprise.

"I will take care of Baba, Pari, until you return."

The thought of Baba not being alone was comforting, but I still did not want to leave. Amir tried gently to take Baba out of my lap, but when I still held on, he used force. I threw my torso over Baba and did not let go. Amir raised his voice, and my body became instantly limp. I became aware of my fatigue from the weight of Baba on my lap all day. Amir lifted me to stand on the top step, defeated. I dragged my feet to my room.

My dress was covered in dried blood that made the soft cloth brittle and brown. I tried to move quickly so I could return faster. My limbs felt as if the bones had left them. Letting my cotton dress drop to the floor, I let another drop over my head and land at my knees. I hurried to the front of the house. When I arrived, I found only the blood-streaked steps. I ran through the house calling Amir and Baba, but there were no answers.

I suppose I should not have expected to hear Baba's voice, but still I did. In fact, I felt his presence in that house for a long time after he left us.

I ran out the front gate and saw only the street lined with sycamore trees reaching up to the sky, forming a shady canopy. Normally the branches coming together and the leaves shading us against the sun made the neighbourhood look friendly and welcoming. Tonight they looked menacing, looming over me as I stood there, betrayed.

Baba was gone.

Words are a pretext. It is the inner bond that draws one person to another, not words.

—Rumi

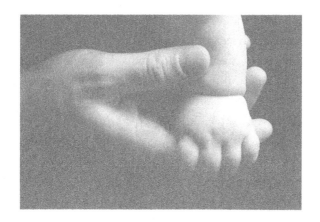

Chapter 2

Solace (1309 SH)

The next few days were a blur. Family, friends, neighbours, and shopkeepers that Baba had readily befriended all dropped by with food and white flowers. The house was filled with men's cologne, women's perfume, and a mixture of stews and *shirini*. Everyone wore black, and the women were in tears.

I felt angry with them. They had no right to cry for Baba. He was my father, not theirs. Besides, he was not really gone. I felt he was still with me. I wanted to escape all those people.

I would stand in one spot until I saw someone coming

towards me, and then I would escape to another spot. Sometimes I would be quick enough, but other times they would catch me off guard. I would have to listen to them talk about Baba as if he were not there.

I decided I needed hiding spots. Standing behind a tall chair in the dining room, I filled my time with observing every detail of my surroundings. Above the front door was a framed *vanyakad* – a passage from the Quran meant to keep one safe. Inside the front door was a single statue – my favourite one from Takht-e-Jamshid. It was a tall pillar with a two-headed bull on the top. I liked it because I felt the bulls would always have each other and never be lonely. Baba said they were the guards at the gate.

I remember visiting people whose homes were filled with so many things that the value of each one seemed diminished. Every wall, shelf, and counter was covered with trinkets. I did not know where to look. My senses were invaded.

I preferred our home, with its occasional vase or piece of furniture.

Our cherry wood dining table, my mother's taste, was in a corner of the living room, but Baba preferred to eat at a *sofreh* in the family room.

In another corner of the living room was a piano that I had played for a year. My piano teacher, Hamid Agha, was teaching me how to read music. I had pleaded with him to show me how to play "Gole Gandom," Baba's favourite. Hamid Agha had told me that the notes were too difficult. After persistent pleading on my part, he patiently showed me the finger movements, one measure at a time, and I memorized them. It demanded my full focus to coordinate both hands on the keyboard. I kept the piece a secret until I could play it fluently. When I did play it for Baba, his wide eyes and gaping mouth took away the weight of the effort.

Hamid Agha came to pay his respect to Baba with an armful of fragrant white tuberose.

The day of the funeral was the last time I saw Hamid Agha.

I looked down at my feet. I stood on our wool Persian carpet that covered the wicker sheets that went over the dirt floor. The wicker kept the dirt from rising and away from the wool carpet. Baba had said wool is more durable than silk. I had heard Amir say it was Baba's humility, and Ali say it was his frugality, that made him avoid silk in carpets.

A woman I did not recognize and a friend of Baba's named Rahim Agha were walking towards me. Rahim Agha was a sayyid, and Baba had great respect for such men who wore the black turban.

I ducked behind our olive velvet curtain that hung to the floor. The sheer lace lining brushed softly against my face and was easy to breathe through. The curtains, usually held back with golden fringed cords, were respectfully drawn and hid me perfectly.

"It seems odd that he would fall off of a ladder, since he was on a ladder every day for work," said the woman.

"It was his time," Rahim Agha answered. "Not a leaf falls to the ground without God's will."

"Did you hear Piruz fired him once his boys were competent at the job?"

"His *roozi* laid elsewhere."

The voices continued for a while and then began to fade as the couple walked out of the room.

Baba had said that my mother admired the olive-green curtains in the shop, but she felt they were too extravagant. One day Baba surprised her by coming home with the entire velvet curtain and lace ensemble. He liked telling me of the times he had made her happy.

I rolled out from behind the curtain, ending up behind the cherry wood sofa. There was no one in sight, so I lay there, staring at the ceiling. I heard a loud sob and someone's comforting words. I forced myself to focus on the ceiling with its white plaster mouldings of flowers and fruits. Baba had created the mouldings as a gift before he brought my mother and baby Ali home from the hospital.

From behind the sofa, I could hear Ali answering the door and greeting everyone. He liked to grease back his thick, dark hair to show his piercing dark eyes and wide grin that he reserved for the public. He was handsome and stood a couple of inches taller than both Baba and Amir. I used to think he was too tall, but girls admired and complimented him for it. They would walk up to him in public and start a conversation. Like Baba, Ali attracted people to him, but unlike Baba, he was unable to keep their interest. Ali's curt and often unguarded manner alienated people.

That night, Ali tried to rise to the occasion. I could hear him indulging the guests in the traditional expressions of salutation, gratitude, and farewell that Iranians hold dear.

I received mixed messages about these expressions. Baba had painted them as endearing ways to bring the people of Iran together like a cosy blanket. Ali felt they were pretentious and insincere. Baba did not argue with Ali, but when we were together, Baba became animated as he explained each expression to me. He gave their origins and their literal and figurative meanings.

* * *

"*Mamnoon*' is the original Persian word for 'thank you'," Baba explained. "'*Moteshaker*' and '*merci*' are Arabic and French."

"Why do we use them?" I asked.

"Language travels with the people who speak it, and some of the words take root in other languages."

"What do you mean?" I asked. "How can a language travel?"

"Remember how Khanum Piruz planted *kedu* and one of her vines climbed the wall and produced a kedu vine on our side?"

"Oooooh, yes. Khanum Piruz got none on her side. She came to our gate angry, wanting her kedu."

"We had already made a pot of *khoresht-e kedu* with it," Baba chuckled.

I nodded, giggling. We had offered to share the stew, but she refused and stomped home.

"Is the vine the person and the kedu the words?" I asked, trying to solve what Baba liked to call his puzzle story.

"Yes. Some words get used so frequently that people think the word is from their own language."

"How about '*ghorban-e shoma*', '*lotf darin*,' and '*bozorgitun-o miresune*'?" I wanted to know why I heard those in the place of "mamnoon".

"Those are the beautiful ones. 'Ghorban-e shoma' means 'I would sacrifice myself for you.' 'Lotf darin' means 'You have kindness.' 'Bozorgitun-o miresune' means 'It shows your greatness.'"

"How about all the goodbye words?"

"'*Khoda negahdar, hamrah, pushtepanah*', for example, means 'God keep you, be with you, and be your shield.'"

"Why do you call me *jigar tala*, but you call Ali and Amir *azizam* or *joon*?"

I was searching for something different here.

"'Jigar tala' has the same meaning as 'azizam' or 'joon'," Baba said.

When he saw I was not satisfied, he explained further.

"They are boys; jigar tala is reserved for girls."

"Oooooh," I said, contented. "It is because they are boys."

Baba loved us equally.

* * *

"I was sorry to hear of your father's passing," said Armon Agha, the baker. "Agha Pushtekar was always kind to me. When my son, Moji, needed surgery and I could not afford it, your father generously paid for it. May light shine on his grave."

"Mamnoon," Ali recited to Armon Agha and every other guest, "Ghorban-e shoma, lotf darin, bozorgitun-o miresune, khada hamrah."

"Here is some *ghorme sabzi,* Ali," said Khanum Piruz, our neighbour from next door. "Tasliat migam. Akharin ghametun bashe. I am sorry I cannot stay. The babies, Mina and Sana, need me at home."

Khanum Piruz was nine months pregnant with their

tenth child. Her husband, Agha Piruz, had already decided to call the baby Darius, after the great Persian king. When pregnant, Khanum Piruz's already short, chubby figure almost became a sphere with dark-rimmed glasses.

* * *

Since Agha Piruz and Baba were boys and their parents had passed long ago, they lived next to each other in the affluent northern district of Tehran called Shemiran. Every home had an iron gate and a tall brick wall surrounding it. Tehran had been the capital city of Iran for the past 135 years. Many other cities were the capital before Tehran, such as Tabriz, Shiraz, Persepolis, Mashhad, and Isfahan, to name a few.

Baba had worked as a plaster layer for years when Agha Piruz showed interest in the trade. Baba accepted his friend as an apprentice and taught Agha Piruz the trade. The two friends worked well together, so their reputation grew to make them trustworthy masters of their trade.

A client asked for their business name so he could refer them to his friends. Baba saw an advantage to having a title and suggested they start an official company. Agha Piruz made the trip to the business licence office. Since he was the only one present to sign, his name was the only one written on the licence. When asked for the company's name, he made up the name *Piruz az Pushtekar*, meaning "victorious from perseverance".

One afternoon, Nargis was visiting Khanum Piruz and the two women were chatting while weeding around her fragrant tuberose patch. Khanum Piruz needed a shovel to take out a stubborn root, so Nargis volunteered to get it from their shed. Inside the shed, on the wall, Nargis saw the business licence with only Agha Piruz's name on it.

"Why did you accept that?" Nargis questioned Baba that evening.

Baba enjoyed recounting clever conversations with my mother, and I enjoyed listening to them.

"We are friends."

"You have no security in a company that does not have your name on it."

"I have known him all my life. That is my security."

"He owes you an apology!"

"'Even after all this time, the sun never says to the earth, 'You owe me.' That one is from Hafez."

"You forgive him?"

"'Forgiveness is the fragrance that the violet sheds on the heel that has crushed it.' That one is our good friend Agha Twain."

"'If you allow harm to come to you knowingly, God will turn aside and let you perish.'"

"Wow, who said that?"

"Nargis."

The two men worked side by side as equals for almost thirty years. It seemed natural when Agha Piruz hired his fourteen-year-old sons, Farid and Saam, as apprentices. Baba welcomed and mentored the twins. Ali had not shown interest in Baba's trade. He established his own electrical company, Amir being his first employee.

After three years, when Farid and Saam were proficient

at the plaster moulding trade, Agha Piruz fired Baba and renamed his business *Piruz-o Pesarash*, meaning "Piruz and Sons".

* * *

It was sympathy or guilt that drove Khanum Piruz, unescorted by her husband, to her neighbours' door with food and condolences. She handed the pot to Ali and left.

"Mamnoon," Ali recited to her back. "Ghorban-e shoma, khada hamrah."

Khanum Piruz was in a hurry, and she knew Ali was not fond of socializing. Her relieved thanks punned her condolence wish.

"*Khoda pedaresho beyamorze*," she said to the newly arriving guests as she passed through Baba's gate.

Amir was quiet as usual and said very little. He could not stay out of sight as I did, because he was too big. He relied on the fact that he was easily missed with his ordinary features and uninterested eyes. When noticed, he would accept the condolences with a thin smile. A conversation with him would end quickly no matter what the topic was.

"How is the business progressing?"

"Fine," Amir would block.

"Tell me about your girlfriend, Nasim."

"Not much to tell."

"Is your little sister coping with her baba gone?"

"Yes," Amir would lie.

* * *

17

The day Amir returned, after stealing Baba, he ignored my questions and pleas. I followed him around the house while he got a bucket and a scrub brush and headed for the front yard. I began whining my questions as he took the hose from its hook and started filling the bucket with water.

Frustrated that he was always so cold with me, I raised my voice to him for the first time. He did not react. Perhaps he thought I was trying to be heard over the running water. Amir walked towards the blood-streaked steps, bucket in one hand and scrub brush in the other. I halted, eyes fixed on the bucket. I realized what he was about to do. A chill ran through my body.

"No! Leave him alone!" I screamed, running at him, only to be swatted away.

I threw myself at him again, pounding on his back. He tipped the bucket over the blood anyway. I began to pull at his arm holding the brush. Amir scrubbed at the blood despite me. My hands were now over the brush, but it continued its back-and-forth motion. The idea that I was helping him startled me into taking my hands off the brush. I returned to his body, punching and kicking him.

I screamed louder. He scrubbed harder. I was skinny but strong for my age, yet he was taller and stronger. Effortlessly, he pushed me away with an arm or a leg while finishing the job of erasing Baba.

He stood up, expressionless, one hand on my head while I punched through the air with both of mine. With his free hand, he picked up the bucket, fingers gripping the edge. With a flick of his wrist, he poured the last of the water over what was left of Baba.

When Amir went inside, I crumpled on the steps over

the wet spot, weeping. It felt as though I had lost Baba all over again.

I must have fallen asleep there, because when I awoke, I was in my bed and it was a new day.

Why are you knocking at every other door?
Go, knock at the door of your own heart.

—Rumi

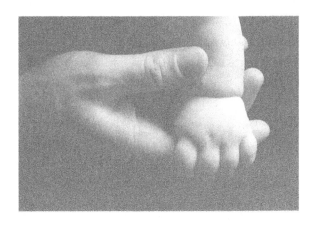

Chapter 3

Nuptials (1309 SH)

The rest of the summer was filled with chores and reading Baba's books from the shelves in his room.

After Baba's accident, my brothers began inviting two sisters to our home. The familiar way they spoke to the girls made me think they had known them for a long time.

I found the difference between these sisters interesting. Shole was slim, and Nasim was chubby. Shole was talkative, and Nasim said very little. Shole wore fashionable clothes, and Nasim hid in her clothing. Shole was short, and Nasim was shorter.

On days when the girls were going to join us for

dinner, Ali would call me to ensure I made enough. The candlestick phone would ring soon after I arrived home from school.

"Make *fesenjoon* tonight, Pari. That is Shole's favourite."

Fesenjoon is a stew made primarily with walnuts, and we had several bags from the previous year's harvest. Our trees would not yield again until the fall.

Baba had loved cooking, and I had loved being around him, so I learned how to cook his dishes. Learning from Baba was like an adventure in discovery. He would show me something, and next time it needed to be done, he would remember to let me do it. He would give me time to come up with the next step, which made me feel proud when I figured it out. No job was too big or too small. I would be expected to rinse produce as well as cut meat with a cleaver. Baba believed I was capable, so I believed it too.

Preparing the nuts for fesenjoon was the most work, but it was fun with Baba. We would finish harvesting the nuts over several days. One day we would pick the walnuts off the tree in our yard. I would climb the tree to get the higher ones and toss them into a burlap sack that Baba was holding on the ground. Sometimes he would dance around and dare me to miss the bag. He was great at making me laugh.

Another day, we would peel off the thick green layer on the outside of the nut while sitting under the trees. When the green skin was broken, the strong scent of walnut filled the air. In the spring, when the walnuts were not yet ripe, I would long for that smell of walnut. Baba showed me how to rub the walnut leaf between my fingers and then smell my fingers. There was that fresh fragrant scent of walnut, right inside its leaves. The next layer was the wrinkled woody shell. We stored the nuts in the burlap sacks until we were ready to shell them.

The process of shelling meant one of us would hammer the nut until the shell was cracked in multiple places, and the other would take the nut out with the aid of a fork. Sometimes the walnut would come out as two halves, and sometimes it would crumble. We would sit on the floor on a thick canvas sheet, hammering the walnuts on a large brick.

*   *   *

"Did you hear what the radio announcer said, jigar tala?" Baba asked, pausing in the middle of pounding the walnut.

Baba had built a wooden battery-operated radio that was sitting on the kitchen counter. It had three dials and five tubes. Baba had let me help him build it. He had called my brothers too, but they had been busy.

I stopped poking the fork at the walnut in my hand and focused on the announcer's words. The topic had already changed to football.

"He said Reza Shah has a secular government."

"What is secular?" I asked.

"Officially neutral in terms of religion," Baba said. "Sure, it is fine to keep religion out of politics, but the announcer did not mention that the Shah is not allowing women to wear the hijab."

"That is not nice," I said.

Baba laughed, but he looked sad.

"No, it is not nice at all. It is not even officially neutral. The announcer said it is wonderful that Reza Shah has brought telephone, radio, and cinema to us, but he left out the fact that he uses these devices for propaganda."

"What is propaganda?" I asked.

"Making you think what they want you to think."

Baba wanted me to think for myself.

* * *

"How about Amir's friend Nasim?" I asked Ali. "What dish is her favourite?"

"Who cares? If Amir does not know how to speak up for her, then forget him."

My brothers had been working as electricians for a large construction company in Sa'adat Abad, the most affluent district in Tehran. Two years ago, Ali opened his own electrical company and hired Amir. Soon they were receiving large contracts and had to hire more people.

When Baba lost his job with Agha Piruz, he began looking for a job that he was qualified for: mason, metalworker, gardener, or cook. There was no demand for any of those jobs. Baba heard from his friend Rahim Agha that there was an opening for someone in construction. He decided to pursue that.

Ali offered him a position in his company, but Baba turned him down, saying he knew nothing about being an electrician.

* * *

"You know just as much about construction," Ali said tactlessly. "Besides, it is better than being idle at home."

"Ali joon, you know I love you and I appreciate your offer, but only some can tolerate your condescending manner, and I am not one of them."

* * *

Ali and Amir decided to have a joint wedding with the girls. Their garden wedding at home began on a hot Friday afternoon and continued late into the night. They waited exactly the traditional forty days after Baba's accident to have their ceremony.

As it grew dark, the trees were lit with candles inside white paper lanterns that I had made. I had learned the paper folding at school through an assignment and enjoyed making use of it. The cool night air was filled with the scent of jasmine. A few aunts – actual ones like my mother's sister, Khale Sara, and honorary ones like our neighbour, Khanum Nosrat – had come to help with the food preparations.

After the meal was ready to be served, Khale Sara picked up her purse to leave. We paused at the front door while she tied her shawl around her shoulders. I did not want her to leave.

"Where did they pick up these two?" she said to herself. "It seems they could not wait for the poor man to leave before they began their lives."

She walked to the gate, and I followed her. She had parked her Peugeot outside of the gate so the elderly relatives could park inside. I unwillingly opened the gate as she slipped he hands into her driving gloves. I did not want her to leave, but I was not accustomed to asking for what I wanted.

She kissed me on the forehead.

"Say goodbye to them for me, will you, Pari joon?" she requested.

"Please stay, Khale," I blurted.

Finding my voice at the last second, I had made my plea.

Khale Sara looked very sad as she stared at me.

"All right, Pari joon," she said with a weak smile.

I could not believe my ears. I had asked, and now she was staying.

"Why look so surprised?" she said with a wink as she walked back inside.

As I was closing the gate, a skinny white cat sneaked in. I picked it up by the loose skin on the back of its neck and tossed it back out. I had seen Baba do it numerous times with stray cats in our neighbourhood. I took too long to close the heavy gate, and the cat ran back in. I thought that if it had that much gumption, it was worthy of my attention.

I went to the kitchen, and it followed me. I placed a small saucer of milk and a few breadcrumbs dunked in it outside on the top wide step of our yard. The skinny cat meowed pathetically and cowered on the step. I sat beside it and petted its white fur.

"Why are you not eating, little one?" I asked, not expecting an answer.

As I petted it, I felt something small like a lentil and saw in the parted fur a shiny silver end of a pin. There was rust around where the pin met the skin of the sorry cat. Clearly the pin had been there for some time, but I knew I had to remove it. I cooed to the cat as I pulled it out. To my surprise, the cat did not pull away but made a tiny cry. I found more pins and removed them, cringing with each one.

At first I thought some cruel children had done this, but as I removed more, I began to think this was too organized for children. There were pins on its back in a straight line like a cobbler would make on a boot. There were more pins surrounding its genitals in a perfect circle. The pins were all inserted to the same depth.

Once I had felt around the entire body and was sure there were no more pins, I petted the cat with empathy for what it had endured. I went inside, hoping it would eat now. I threw the pins into the trash and returned to the celebration with a feeling of angst towards the human potential.

The meal was served and the dishes washed and put away. I lit the samovar for tea, and Khale Sara set the tea tray with sweets and glasses.

It was comforting to have Khale Sara in the house. She stayed with me in the kitchen except when she took tea for the guests. I appreciated listening to her speak. She did not talk, like everyone else, only about people and things. She spoke like Baba, mostly about ideas.

The women gathered on the sofas in the living room, drinking tea with shirini and talking about the latest fashion, newly discovered recipes, and whatever gossip was in circulation at the time. The brides stayed close to their respective grooms for the duration of the evening, which was fortunate for them because the women's conversation included the brides' ill-chosen hairstyles and unflattering dresses and makeup. The girls had two uncles, though they were no support, because they were seated with the men. A neighbour, Khanum Nosrat, knew the girls, but even she was disloyal to them.

"God matches people to their like," I heard Khanum Nosrat say. "They each reflect their mate. Shole is outspoken and controlling, and Nasim is quiet and mean."

The room fell quiet as Khale Sara entered with the second tea tray and held it in front of each woman to take a glass and a sweet.

The men gathered in the garden, smoking, drinking, and talking about Iran's latest football game. Two years before, a team from Baku had been invited to play on a newly seeded state-owned grass field. There had been great excitement, but when all three games were won by the visitors, Iranians were humiliated and no longer showed enthusiasm for football. Future games were rarely reported on until the monarchy changed.

The topic switched to the new reign of Reza Shah Pahlavi just as Khale Sara brought in another round of tea and set it on the table.

"The king has made Iran proud," one of the men said.

"You like paying such high taxes?" asked Khaleh Sara.

A hush fell on the garden; the crickets' chirping seemed to scream. Khale Sara stood even taller among the seated men.

"Everything costs money, Sara Khanum," said a brave young guest. "New highways, universities, hospitals. What do you expect?"

"The Shah has made superficial changes," Khale Sara argued, "not long-lasting improvements. He insists on Western clothing and no hijab. A law for no hijab would be as ridiculous as a law for mandatory hijab. His propaganda is spreading."

"Sara Khanum is right," said Rahim Agha. "My poor

wife was jeered at today in the bazaar over the scarf she was wearing. Imagine what they would do to the poor woman who wants to wear a manteau or a chador?"

Ali and Amir remained quiet. To their credit, the girls followed my brothers' example.

After Khale Sara left, the men's and ladies' circles grew animated, and the participants became captivated. No one noticed when I slipped away to my room and went to sleep.

*There is a voice that doesn't use words.
Listen.*

—Rumi

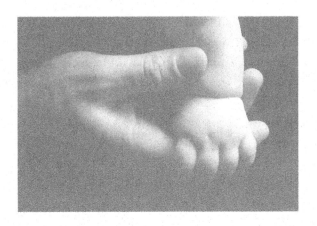

Chapter 4

Khanum Piruz (1310 SH)

The woman's shrieks were blood-curdling. The little ones could hear their mother in labour with their tenth sibling all the way across the house and two floors up. One-year-old Darius was surrounded by his two-year-old sister, Mina; four-year-old sister, Sana; seven-year-old sister, Saba; and ten-year-old brother, Curosh. They were balled together on Saba's cot in a comfort-seeking huddle. Twelve-year-old Shakiba and I had been playing *ye-ghol-do-ghol* in the hallway outside the girls' room. The wave of this turn of events brought us into a corner of Khanum Piruz's room, where we witnessed the birth of an eleventh child into this family. The two older sisters – Malize, sixteen, and Soghra, fourteen – were assisting the midwife. The eighteen-year-old twin brothers, Farid and Saam, were taking refuge down the street at the convenience store with their friends.

"One more push," said the midwife as Malize and Soghra flanked the bed, one wiping her mother's drenched face and the other offering her hand to be almost crushed.

One last scream came from Khanum Piruz, and the next one was the infant's.

It was a boy.

When the children were given the news, the boys cheered and the girls groaned.

The baby was cleaned and handed to his mother. Khanum Piruz, hair matted around a grey complexion, smirked weakly at the baby's face.

"Looks just like his poor father," she sighed, turning her face away from the baby and handing him to Malize.

"Do you have a name picked out, Khanum?" asked the midwife.

"My poor husband always named the children," Khanum Piruz groaned, facing the wall.

Agha Piruz had died seven months ago in a traffic accident on his way home from work. He had stayed behind to finish the plaster mouldings on the last room of a house that they were working on. He insisted that his sons leave earlier with his car. He planned to finish the job and use Farid's motorcycle to get home.

"How could either of those poor boys refuse that man?" Shole had said. "If he stood anywhere close to me, I would cower too."

Agha Piruz had become desperate to regain the reputation that the company had while Baba was with him. Job assignments for *Piruz-o Pesarash* had decreased in number after Baba's accident.

With the mouldings done on the last room, Agha Piruz had hopped on Farid's motorcycle and driven it directly into an oncoming truck going the wrong way on the freeway. The driver had fallen asleep behind the wheel and survived to live with the knowledge that he had killed a man.

Khanum Piruz had been deprived of telling her husband the news of her eleventh pregnancy.

It was soon evident that Khanum Piruz was to be confined to a wheelchair. The eleventh child's birth had left her legs weak and useless.

It was a week into the three-month summer holiday from school. All the Piruz children were home and willing to lend a hand according to their ability.

"I do not know what I will do when the children return to school and I am left with three little ones plus the baby," Khanum Piruz told Shole and Nasim over tea and raisins. "My Malize needs to study and will not be able to do the necessary work around the house."

The girls were visiting Khanum Piruz's home more regularly now that she was in a wheelchair. The three of them had in common the lack of chores and the abundance of boredom. They sought each other's company to fill their days. The conversation was usually between Sholeh and Khanum Piruz, with Nasim quietly listening. The two ladies did not seem to mind Nasim's silence, as it allowed more time for each of them to talk. When they took me along, I was required to sit beside them during their visit. I would have preferred to go play with the other children, but that was the girls' rule.

On this day, the girls' visit was to congratulate the family on the arrival of their new baby. Tea was served in the family room. The living room was furnished in mahogany wood and lace. Khanum Piruz kept that furniture covered in white sheets and reserved it for important guests.

Shakiba came and sat with me for the duration of this visit. I appreciated her sacrifice. She had brought five stones, so we played ye-ghol-do-ghol quietly in a corner.

The girls lounged on the carpet cushions, sipping tea from small, curvy gold-trimmed glasses. They modestly tucked their legs underneath them because they were in dresses – Shole in a pretty yellow dress with a bow at the waist, and Nasim in a plain beige dress with no waist.

Khanum Piruz sat slumped in her wheelchair, looking mournful, in contrast to her usual proud posture and confident manner. She was a short, wide woman who had become the sole commander of her children.

Despite housing eleven children, four under the age of five and the youngest three in diapers, Khanum Piruz's home smelled of fresh flowers – usually tuberose, since she grew them in her garden. She had told the girls in detail about a time when a passer-by had stopped at her gate and asked if she was interested in selling her tuberose plants for extracts. He wanted to use them as a note in his perfumery. The girls had laughed behind Khanum Piruz's back at how naive she had been to believe so easily the words of a stranger at her gate.

"You could get a maid," Sholeh offered as a solution.

"My God, no!" Khanum Piruz gasped. "I would not ask my dear Farid to spend money on something that is my responsibility."

The baby had been swaddled and brought into the room by Malize for an outburst of compliments. The girls had brought an obligatory gift stowed in one of Baba's cloth grocery bags. Shole ceremoniously handed over the unwrapped blue blanket to Malize, who tucked it under her arm as she walked out of the room with the baby. Long after Malize was gone, Shole continued to explain the high quality of the blanket, where it had been made, and how difficult it had been to find. Nasim had picked it up at the local bazaar, where there were bins full of them, but she allowed Shole to tell her own version.

The clicking sound of the stones as they hit the ground finally exhausted Khanum Piruz, and Nazim whispered to me to go home. I heard the rest of that fateful conversation from Shakiba several years later.

"I thought Farid was doing well as a plaster artist," Shole said, admitting to hearing the gossip.

"Yes, but it has to serve twelve people."

Maman acknowledged Farid's success proudly but defended him at the same time. All three women stared at the glasses of tea in their hands for a moment.

"How about Pari?" suggested Nasim.

With a sudden jerk, Maman and Shole turned to look at Nasim. She had come out of her silence without any preliminaries. Not only was she speaking, but she was also giving a suggestion. Shole grew angry watching Nasim, who calmly sipped her tea, eyes focused on something inside her glass.

"What has Pari got to do with anything, *jari*?" asked Shole with irritation in her voice.

Nasim, acting out of character, ignored her sister.

"Simply marry Pari to Farid," she said, addressing Maman. "She runs our household flawlessly, so she would make a great maid for you."

Maman looked pensive while Shole glared at Nasim. Nasim kept her eyes downcast, as she knew better than to meet her sister's daggered eyes.

Shole came up with an excuse, and the sisters took their leave, thanking Maman lavishly.

"Mamnoon, dast-e shoma dard nakon-e, khoshbakhteem," Shole recited.

Maman seemed only partly aware of the sisters' parting ritual. She seemed mostly lost in thought.

"Congratulations on your baby boy," Shole called over her shoulder as the two sisters skip-walked the few steps to their gate.

I saw the cloth grocery bag left by the tea tray, so I ran after the sisters to return it. I halted at our gate because I heard Shole talking angrily to Nasim.

"For a guest of few words, you sure can put your foot in your mouth when you finally do speak!"

"I said nothing wrong. Sounds like Khanum Piruz needs our Pari more than we do."

"Oh, you are so innocent, so charitable," Shole said sarcastically. "You would rather do without Pari's help than have her around the house to show you up in front of your Amir."

"You must be joking," Nasim said, feigning a chuckle.

"She is taller and prettier than you."

"Than *us*," Nasim corrected.

"She can carry on a conversation better than you."

"Just because you can always find something to say does not mean you are speaking intelligently."

"Do you mean me or Pari?"

Shole wanted to know if she had been insulted.

They arrived at their gate, and Nasim reached up to open it. Shole grabbed Nasim's wrist and pulled it down hard. Nasim stood there unmoved, staring at the gate.

"I only know one person nastier than you, Shole, and that is the Piruz woman. Pari deserves to go there."

Shole pulled Nasim to face her.

"Well at least I can bear children." Shole scowled, their faces inches apart.

If Nasim was pained, she did not show it. I suppose she had learned to remain steadfast in the face of her sister's cruelty.

"And even so, there are no babies that I can see," Nasim said, enviably aloof.

Maman had told us that when Nasim was very young, she suffered from a serious case of the mumps which left her infertile. Childbearing was very important to Maman, so she stated Nasim's condition as the ultimate flaw in a woman. Through the mercy of God, Maman had said, neither brother wanted children.

"You know I do not want brats any more than Ali," Shole spat. "Even so, *khahar* joon, I will bear a brood of them to spite you!"

Shole tossed aside her sister's arm, and they both entered the house, dejected.

I walked back into our house, cloth bag in hand, in possession of a secret I did not know what to do with.

*Why are you so enchanted by this world,
when a mine of gold lies within you?*

—Rumi

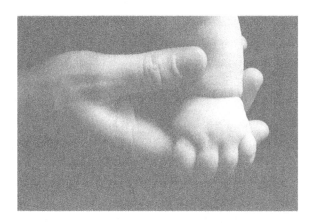

Chapter 5

Guard or Guardian (1310 SH)

School was a welcome blessing for me. It held more challenge than housecleaning and cooking. Outside of school, Kuchulu, as I named the stray cat, was good company. I had to beg to keep him. Amir was the one who gave permission on behalf of the others. I wondered if his generous gesture was a result of his guilt over stealing Baba.

Kuchulu was eating better, and it showed in his face and in his coat that he was recovering from his trauma. I was not sure how much was muscles and how much was fur, but the whole package was fun to cuddle.

After my brothers' wedding, the girls continued to be

guests in Baba's house – guests with demands. I did not seem to mind. The house was not as empty, and I was no longer the only female. The laundry was increased, but the aluminium tub was large enough. The meals required only more of each ingredient.

The girls' criticism was ever present. I had just read the Grimm fairy tale "Cinderella" and fancied pretending the girls were my two stepsisters. The tale did have a happy ending. I knew the girls would rather I did the work, so I ignored them.

As it turned out, ignoring them was a mistake. The next thing I knew, they had convinced my brothers to have me married to the neighbour's oldest son, Farid.

"Imagine, Amir," Nasim said, "how much more privacy we would have without your little sister around."

"Pari is a lot of help *here*," Amir said.

I was carrying the dirty laundry tub past their room and stopped when I heard my name.

"Yes, but she often gets things wrong," Nasim lied. "Let her go and mess things up for Khanum Piruz. Shole and I can handle things around here."

What was this? I was supposed to go live with Khanum Piruz? For how long? I decided to stay and find out.

"Khanum Piruz has so many children and so much more housework," Amir said. "She would never get to her schoolwork."

"Who said anything about school? Pari joon does not need school if she is to be a housewife."

The shock of her comment almost made me drop the tub and give away my position. Amir was quiet, so he was either considering or ignoring Nasim's suggestion. She gave him one more push.

"I recall you saying that your father gave all his attention to Pari." Nasim stung her husband with his own words from the past. "You do not owe her anything. That spoiled girl has been a thorn in your side ever since she was born. Why, was it not her birth that caused your mother's—"

"Enough!" Amir interrupted.

It seemed that never speaking about our mother was still a rule in Baba's house. Perhaps they had only tolerated Baba. Now that he was gone, I suppose no one could speak of her again. I felt sad for my brothers until I heard that they had accepted the arranged marriage between Farid and me.

I had completed one month of school at the local public school, Movafagh Secondary, when they told me I was to be married and moved out. I felt my world collapsing around me. I had lost Baba, and now I was going to lose my brothers. Although they had not been affectionate, they were still the only family I had. I felt I was repeatedly going down the steepest drop of a roller coaster – the wooden type at Tehran's amusement park that Baba had taken me to. My stomach clenched each time I began the descent. The dread before each fall continued as I went through the motions of my daily routine leading up to the wedding.

I rose just before the sun, washed, and prayed. I had been reciting the namaz with Baba since I turned nine years old – the compulsory age for a girl to pray. Memorizing the prayer in Arabic had been so much easier than any assigned memorization at school. Baba explained that God makes it easy if you try.

There was a large amount of smoke from the oil lamp, as it used animal fat. I used kindling to start a fire in the wood stove to boil water for tea. Moji would deliver bread each morning, along with milk and cheese from the store next to their bakery, in honour of Baba's memory.

I poured a saucer of milk with chunks of bread for Kuchulu. I set the breakfast table with *naan taftoon*, goat cheese, and milk, plus mint, basil, walnuts, and preserves from Baba's garden. The house would be filled with the smell of fresh bread and herbs. I ate alone and walked to school, meeting some of my friends along the way.

After classes, I stopped and bought the meat and produce needed for dinner. We did not have a refrigeration system, so nothing could be stored for more than a day. Even the legumes would be stored in small quantities; otherwise, I would find worms in them.

At home, I changed out of my school uniform, washed, and prayed. In the kitchen, I prepared the food for dinner. Outside, on the top wide step, I washed whatever was in the laundry tub. Sweeping the house was easy because the wicker sheets between the dirt floors and the carpets kept the dirt under control. The tea tray was the last chore, with dates for Ali and *noghl* for Amir.

When I finished early, I was able to play with Kuchulu in the yard. That was the condition under which the cat was allowed to stay – that he live outside. Mostly I would pet him, but sometimes we would play games. Just out of his reach, I would dangle a wooden airplane with only one wing. I had found it in the ditch on my way home from school. I washed it clean and tied a long string to it. This enormous cat would pounce at it tirelessly for as long as I was interested.

Kuchulu liked to rub his side and cheek against me,

arching his back and purring like a soft motor. I had to be careful to shake my clothes free of his white fur before going inside. Cat fur found around the house was a cause for alarm from the girls. Cat fur on my clothes made my prayer *batel* – unacceptable to God.

By the time the tea tray was set, the girls would return from their outing or emerge from their rooms and have tea until their husbands arrived. After dinner, dishes were cleaned and put away. If the girls did not have any requests, I went to my room and, after my evening prayer, worked on my school assignments. I stayed awake until all of my work was done, to avoid the teacher's punishment.

The punishment in elementary school was to stand in the corner of the room with one knee and one arm up. Years ago, I had gone to my first talking picture with Baba and come home too late to complete my assignments. My primary teacher sent me to the corner and forgot me there when everyone left the classroom for recess. My friend Kobra Sultani, a stocky girl whom no one dared cross, glanced at me sympathetically as she left with the others. People feared her because of her attitude, and they feared me because of my height. It was this mutual attribute that initially bonded us in friendship.

I needed to use the washroom but had not been excused from the corner. Exhausted, I could not wait until everyone returned from recess. They found me drooped over, crying, with a puddle beneath me. After I was cleaned, the teacher whispered in my ear that while in the corner, I had automatic permission to use the washroom.

Having permission was a relief, but I did not need it after that incident. I worked so hard that not only did I avoid ending up in the corner but also that they advanced me until I was sitting in the ninth grade when I turned twelve years old. The first time I was advanced, Kobra was too, and we ended up in the same classroom. I was advanced again, but Kobra was not.

In Movafagh Secondary School, students of the same grade shared a classroom for all their subjects, and the teachers moved from one classroom to another, according to their teaching schedule.

When Baba was a young boy, there were no schools like mine. A mullah, a theologist, would open one room in his house and call it a *maktab* – a place of study. Children of the neighbourhood would come and learn from him. Baba had joined in the instructions of reading, writing, and Islamic studies in the maktab in his neighbourhood.

* * *

One day, a frail man came to talk to the mullah. Baba and the other children were working on an assignment, and the mullah was translating the Quran from Arabic to Persian. After the long ceremonial salutation and inquiry into the health of everyone, the frail man made his request.

"My son moved to Mashhad," he began, "and I have not heard from him in months. My friend is travelling with a caravan to Mashhad in two months. I want to give him a letter to give to my son. Will you write it for me? It does not need to be long. I just want to ask how he is doing and if he needs anything."

"What is a caravan?" I asked.

Baba interrupted his story to answer my question. "Well, there were no cars or buses in those days, so people travelled by caravan. There would be a guide that they would pay, and the number of people who joined varied from tens to hundreds. People either walked or rode donkeys or camels. They had saddlebags, which were really two wooden boxes flanking the animal. One or both boxes held people or cargo."

Before the maktab, the frail man had knocked on several literate people's doors. One had gone to *deh bala*, Northern Village; one had gone to buy a cow; and one had moved to another town. The mother of the man who had moved to another town told the frail man about the maktab.

"I do not have time either," said the mullah. "Mohammad jaan," he called to Baba, "do this man a kindness and write his letter for him, will you, *pesaram*?"

The frail man turned to Baba and made his plea again.

"What is your skill?" asked Baba.

"I lay fresh white plaster and mould it on the ceilings of homes," said the frail man, somewhat offended by the boy questioning him so boldly.

"Your friend does not leave for two months, you said. I could teach you how to read and write in a month, and you could write your own letter," Baba proposed.

"What? That fast? I cannot pay you."

"I do not ask for money, but I cannot teach just one. Go find four other men who want to learn how to read and write and bring them here. Ensure each has a skill. I want each person to teach me his skill in return."

The frail man saw initiative and a desire to learn in Baba. He wasted no time in bringing four men to the maktab: a metalworker, a mason, a gardener, and a cook.

Baba taught all of them how to read and write and in return gained five trades. He enjoyed all of his talents: in his workplace, laying plaster; at home, welding decorative copper and brass flowers on our iron gate; in the yard, carving our stone pedestal fountain; in the garden, tending to the trees and flowers; and in the kitchen, cooking for his family.

* * *

My maktab improved when I entered secondary school. I fit in more because of my size. The teachers expected more focus, organization, and maturity. They inspired me to become efficient with the household chores so I could finish my assignments on time. This way I avoided being the topic of criticism from my teachers at school and the girls at home.

My mathematics teacher, Agha Nemat, was a short man with an uncertain manner. He wore reading glasses that did not fit well, so he continuously pushed them up as they slid down his round nose. I had heard this was his first teaching job since he finished his studies. He seemed to care about us. He did not give up until everyone understood every concept.

Unfortunately, I was in his class for only one month before I was married to Farid.

The day of my wedding arrived. Shole and Nasim carried our cherry dining table outside to the grassy section of our backyard. My wedding reception was going to be outdoors. Only a year had passed since their double wedding with my brothers in this same garden. As I watched them holding each end of the table, manoeuvring through the glass doors to the backyard, I felt moved that they were making an effort for me.

"Those clumsy old men", Shole grunted from her end of the table, "will spill their food and tea all over my Kashan carpet before the night is over. Safer to serve them outside."

Nasim nodded without needing to comment on the ownership of the Kashan carpet. The girls each held two corners of a white linen tablecloth and placed it over the table, making it parachute down.

"Pari," Shole called to me as she walked in from the garden. "By the front door, there is a large carpet bag packed with your belongings. Take it to Khanum Piruz's house now, before it gets dark."

"Will it not be rude if I show up with a bag in my hand?" I asked, stalling.

"You can get settled in now so after the wedding your things will already be in place," Shole reasoned. "It is more practical that way – right, Nasim?"

Nasim nodded.

I went upstairs, and sure enough, my school uniform was still in my closet. I picked up the folded pile and came downstairs to the front door. The bag was large and so it was only half full, and my uniform easily sat on top. The carpet bag had come from one of the storage rooms on the third floor.

In the yard, I bent down and absent-mindedly petted Kuchulu. He was always in the mood to be adored. My mind was busy contemplating all that I would miss from

Baba's house. Just then, my white fluffy friend was added to the list.

I walked over to our neighbour's house as I had done so many times before, but this time with a carpet bag in hand. It was fun playing with Shakiba, who was my age. It felt strange that I would now be living with her and all her siblings.

Soghra, her older sister, opened the front gate and led me to a room on the first floor. She wore a simple housedress, a pair of flip-flops, and no smile. Like her sisters, she was short, olive-skinned, and had straight black hair – the complete opposite to me. They often teased me that I had been adopted, since my hair was so much lighter and curlier than my brothers'.

* * *

"Your hair is exactly like your mother's, God rest her soul," Baba said when I returned from the Piruz yard.

Baba's comment both embarrassed and thrilled me. He had overheard the girls taunting me, but I had my mother's hair.

* * *

The Piruz house was three floors. Each floor had two bedrooms, and each bedroom had several cots. On the first floor, one bedroom belonged to the parents and the other was reserved for guests. The second floor belonged to the brothers, and the third floor belonged to the sisters.

I was led to the guest room, which had one cot, a closet, and a window. I stared at the cot, finding it difficult to imagine myself in it with Farid. I wanted to go to the third floor, where Shakiba would be.

Khanum Piruz had wanted me to sleep with the girls as well. The previous day, I was making awsh in the kitchen when I heard Shole tell Nasim how she had talked Khanum Piruz out of it.

"Can you believe that woman?" Shole said as they sipped tea in the family room. "I warned her that it would not look good in front of a guest when one of the children gave away where Pari sleeps. She thought about that and agreed with me, that donkey."

Soghra waited until I put my bag on the floor and then hurriedly ushered me out. Oddly, I did not see anyone else on my short walk through the house. There was the faint whispering of children and another voice hushing them in a distant room. Could they be hiding from me? Suddenly I felt like an intruder in this house that had once been full of playmates.

Back in Baba's house, I went to my room and found that someone had laid a plain white dress on my bed. I picked up my hairbrush and my yellow ribbon and sat on the edge of my bed, feeling numb and staring into space. I brushed my hair and tied it with the ribbon. Baba had said yellow and orange compliment my green eyes.

My mind had lost its focus, and my thoughts meandered from one peculiar thought to another. I was thinking about the length of my hair. My brown curls hung down to my shoulder blades, but when my hair was wet, they reached my waist. I had heard that a person's hand is the same length as her face. I decided to try it. When I placed my hand flat against my face, it reached from chin to forehead exactly. I reached under my bed and took out the small tin box that held Baba's notes to me. The notes were reminders of things to do, but he had drawn funny pictures on each one, so I had kept them. I also had a few handmade birthday cards in there from Khale Sara. I shook my head to clear it and tried to focus on something concrete like the things around my room.

My sparsely furnished room was not as plain as the one I had just left in the Piruz house. I had a white vanity and stool that belonged to my mother. It was for applying makeup, but I used it as a desk for my school assignments. There was a small Persian carpet on the floor beside my bed. The bed sheets and comforter were more of Baba's gifts. They were white with pink rosebuds.

Ali appeared in the doorway. He threw a red velvet pouch so it landed next to me on the bed.

"These belong to you," Ali said with a blank face. "You can wear the earrings when you get your ears pierced. Shole can help you with the makeup."

I pulled open the drawstring of the pouch, wondering where it had come from. I looked up to ask, but Ali was gone. I did not think the pouch belonged to the girls, since I had not seen them wear any of these treasures. I wondered if they belonged to my mother – or maybe I was just hoping.

Inside the bag was a silver case with roses carved on the lid. I opened the lid to discover rouge inside, so I began there. I had seen Khale Sara apply makeup, and it looked straightforward. I sat at the vanity, ready to use it appropriately for the first time. After the rouge, I applied eye makeup and then lipstick – a subtle shade of orange. I fastened the clasp of a single strand of pearls behind my neck and pulled onto my wrist a wide gold bangle with a scene of birds and flowers carved into it. I returned the rouge and lipstick to the pouch and added my hairbrush. I slipped into the white dress, which came to my toes. I went to the kitchen to help set the table in the garden.

"Well look who found Nargis' precious loot," Shole sneered sarcastically as she poured *shirin polo* onto a tray.

Nasim was counting dishes. She looked up for a moment with disinterest and then returned to counting. The house was filled with the smell of saffron rice and lemon chicken.

"So that is why Ali was holding on to that worthless pouch," Shole said, her eyes fixed on the pearl necklace around my neck. "To give it to his little sister."

"If it was worthless, why did you beg Ali for it so often?" Nasim asked, walking into the backyard with the stack of dishes.

"*Khafesho!*" Shole snapped, losing her fixed stare on the pearls.

You are not a drop in the ocean. You are the entire ocean in a drop.

—Rumi

Chapter 6

Imminent (1310 SH)

Khanum Piruz stayed home with a feverish baby so as not to spread germs. To avoid undue chaos at the wedding party, the little ones stayed home under the care of their oldest sister, Malize. A job came up for Piruz and Sons, so Saam volunteered to go on site and allow his older brother, by fifteen minutes, to enjoy his wedding ceremony.

The twins were fraternal, so they looked different. Saam was taller, and Farid was heavier. Farid's features were round like his mother's, and Saam had narrow features like his father's. Today the biggest difference was that one was trapped and the other was free.

I opened the front door, and there stood Farid, hair neatly combed and handsome in a dark suit. He looked older than his eighteen years. He wore a pink rosebud boutonniere on his lapel and held a matching bouquet of pink roses in his hand.

Beside him, Shakiba wore a blue summer dress.

Farid held the bouquet out to me. It was for me. I had never received flowers before. I reached to take it, but my arm was grabbed and pulled into the house. Shakiba was pulling me through the hall, talking in a stream of continuous words, but they were not registering with me. My thoughts were consumed with whom we had left at the door.

The cleric read from the Quran while Farid and I sat across from him on the sofa in the living room. There was no wedding sofreh like the one the girls had with the decorative mirror and candlesticks. I did not mind, since I did not want any of this. The cleric asked repeatedly whether I wanted to marry Farid. I said *baleh* after the third time I was asked. Shole had told me that it was the customary number of times to make the groom wait in anticipation.

Once Farid and I were officially married, our few relatives applauded and we moved to the garden for dinner. Shakiba was seated on one side of me, and her brother sat on the other. I took Farid's silence to mean that he did not have a choice in this marriage. That made me feel uncomfortable.

Khale Sara busied herself with helping the girls serve the food and, later, the tea. She was never in my view for very long, but her smiles and quick winks were reassuring.

The rest of the evening could have been any other family gathering. Our guests ate and socialized with each other. No one spoke to Farid or me. They did not fuss over me as they had with the girls a year ago. Knowing my relatives' attention to the girls had not been genuine, I was grateful for the lack of it that night.

The air was autumn cool and smelled of jasmine, but it did not fill me with the same joy as it had before. This day was going to change my life. I would do housework for someone other than my family. I would leave the comfort of Baba's home. This change frightened me, but I did not know how to stop it from happening.

During dinner, I had ample time to think, as Farid had taken a vow of silence, and Shakiba spoke incessantly with no apparent care to who was listening. Perhaps she was nervous, but I was glad she was beside me. Her company was comforting. Farid, sitting on the other side of me, so close, made me increasingly nervous. The feeling was not completely negative.

I had seen Farid come and go when I was at the Piruz house playing with Shakiba. To him I was just another friend of one of his siblings who appeared and disappeared at their house, but I admired him from a distance, as young girls sometimes do. Now he was eighteen and sitting next to me as my husband.

Unlike my brothers, I had never heard the twins speak in harsh tones with their siblings or with me when I visited. When they entered the room, the little ones would run to them and hug their legs. I remember wishing I could show my affection in the same way, but I knew it was inappropriate. Sometimes Farid would lift one of his siblings, hold him or her over his shoulder, and run so he or she flew like an airplane, the way Baba had done with me.

I missed Baba.

Sitting next to Farid now, I had a sudden urge to reach over and touch his arm. The urge turned into regret when I saw his expressionless profile staring ahead like a statue. I felt a strange sense of envy towards the other guests, who seemed happy and carefree. I was tired of sitting. I would have liked to go to my room and sleep, but I felt my absence may have been noticed this time.

Dinner was over, and to my surprise, the women, including the girls, headed to the kitchen with dishes in hand. This was routinely my task, so I gratefully filed in to help.

"Oh, Pari joon, you do not need to help in your pretty white dress," said Khale Sara, taking the pile of dishes from my hands.

I knew my dress was plain, but it felt good to hear Khale say it was pretty. She had good fashion sense.

Khale Sara had never married but had devoted herself to her successful law firm. Despite the vicious gossip I heard, I liked her the most, because she was the most kind to me.

"You can go get changed, Pari joon," Shole suggested.

All the aunts turned to look at Shole with disapproval.

"She does not have any clothes to change into, jari," Nasim reminded her sister. "Have you forgotten? This afternoon you packed her belongings and sent her with them to our dear neighbour, Khanum Piruz."

This caused some gasps and whispers among the aunts. Shole stood red-faced and dumbfounded but recovered quickly.

"That is all right," Shole said. "She can wear one of my dresses. Go ahead, Pari joon. Help yourself."

I was relieved to take my cue and ran out of the tense kitchen. Upstairs, outside Shole's room, I realized I had never been allowed into this sanctuary. I immediately felt unwelcome as I stood in the doorway. A hand on my back pushed me in, sending me stumbling forward. Nasim walked by me and flung open the closet doors.

"Let's sssseeee," she hissed, flipping through the dresses on their hangers. I had never seen so many dresses except at the bazaar. "How about … this one?"

Nasim held Shole's favourite dress by the hanger for me to see. When I began to object, she tore it off its hanger and threw it on the bed.

"Put it on and hurry down to help. If you dawdle, everyone will think you are lazy."

I did as I was told. Before leaving the room, I glanced at myself in the full-length mirror. The dress was a little loose and hung above my knees instead of below like on Shole. It was made of two layers: a solid yellow layer topped with a sheer layer. The sleeves and the bottom of the dress ended in waves of sheer fabric. I tied the sheer sash to one side of the waist in a puffy bow like the one I had seen on the front cover of Shole's *Cosmopolitan*.

When I entered the kitchen, everyone gushed over the dress. One woman clumsily admitted that it was prettier than the white wedding dress. Her grin turned into regret when she received disapproving glances. Khale Sara commented on how stylish the bow looked, tied to one side.

I saw Shole's horrified expression only for a moment before the aunts whisked me away to the living room. They sat me down on the sofa, and showered me with attention. From the kitchen, the girls' argument could be heard over the voices of the aunts adoring me in that dress.

"You know that is my favourite dress, and yet you let her wear it and possibly get it dirty."

Shole was seething.

"Then you should be relieved", Nasim said in her monotone voice, "that she is settled in the living room instead of helping in the kitchen."

Late in the evening, the guests left, shaking the hands of my brothers and thanking them for ensuring that the poor youngster was settled down with a respectable boy.

"Your father would have been proud of you boys," the aunts said, congratulating my brothers and kissing them on both cheeks.

Khale Sara gave me a firm hug. I noticed her glare at my brothers before kissing my forehead and walking out.

I busied myself with collecting the last few dishes from the garden. Ali grabbed the dishes from me before I reached the kitchen.

"You need to go to your new home," he said with a scowl. "Farid has already left. What kind of a wife are you going to be if you cannot keep up with him?"

I was embarrassed in front of my older brother. He was disappointed in me, which was rare because I worked desperately hard to avoid falling short of his expectations.

"Go on," Ali said with a wave of his hand. "Do not stand there like a child."

"She *is* a child," Amir said, coming in from the backyard.

His head was down and his shoulders rounded – not a common posture for him.

"Do not start again. We made this decision together."

"If by 'we' you mean you and your wife, then I agree," Amir said, sinking into a chair.

"Shole told me it was Nasim's idea, so stop accusing the innocent."

Even though in my mind I was soaring down the steep drop of a roller coaster, I could not stand seeing my brothers angry at each other. This was the incentive I needed to leave Baba's house.

When Baba was alive, our house was always peaceful. I thought that meant we were all at peace. Now I realized that it was Baba who had been keeping the peace.

With my brothers arguing in the living room and the girls arguing in the kitchen, I sneaked upstairs and changed. I put on my white dress and replaced Shole's dress on its hanger in her closet. I grabbed the velvet pouch and left through our front gate.

Khanum Piruz's house was dark and quiet. The front gate and door had been left unlocked for me, so I slipped inside and locked both behind me. I knew where my room was, since I had walked this route with Soghra that afternoon. Shole's idea had proven practical. I found the room in the dark and edged inside. The moonlight through the window illuminated everything in a mild blue hue. I was grateful because I did not want to bump anything and wake Farid. He was already snoring softly with his back to me and filling the cot. This gave me the perfect excuse to find a small spot on the floor and gladly make my bed. From my carpet bag, I pulled out a sweater to use as a pillow and a long coat to climb into. I did not bother changing out of my white dress, as I felt exhausted and shy in a room with a man.

I longed for my own bed in Baba's house next door, but it was no use wishing. I had to make the most of it here. My last thought as I fell asleep was how I was going to earn the affection of my ten new brothers and sisters.

Where there is ruin, there is hope for a treasure.

—Rumi

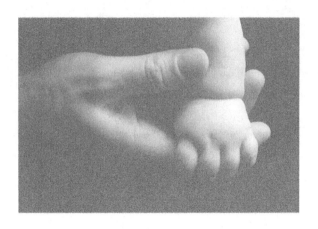

Chapter 7

Married or Maid (1310 SH)

I opened my eyes and was confused by my surroundings. I had never slept anywhere but my own bed in Baba's house. My eyes darted around the room in a panic until they landed on my open carpet bag. I calmed down as I recalled the events of the previous night. My head swung towards the cot, but Farid was gone. He must have left for work already. With a sigh of relief, I got up.

Farid and Saam laid soft white plaster, *gache zende,* and moulded it into fruit, flowers, angels, geometric shapes, or any design the homeowners desired. They stood on ladders holding a palate full of soft plaster. They threw a chunk of plaster where the wall met the ceiling or where a chandelier would be hung. Before the plaster hardened, they would carve a design into it. The trade was passed on to them whether or not they wanted it. Since their father's death, they were expected to run the company on their own.

I had heard Shole repeat to Nasim the gossip that Farid had soon surpassed Saam and had become the best plaster artist in Tehran. It was said that Farid secretly turned down solo job offers and stayed devoted to his brother and their late father's company.

The sun had not risen yet, so the room still glowed white. I washed and prayed. I changed out of my white dress and into my school uniform. The uniform consisted of a plain black sarafan dress and a white blouse. In our hair was a standard white ribbon, and on our feet we wore white socks and black shoes. Makeup and jewellery were strictly forbidden, which for me had not been an issue until now. I placed my golden wedding band inside the red velvet pouch and replaced the pouch in my carpet bag.

I went to the kitchen and lit a kerosene lamp. It was white in colour and burned cleanly. The oil lamps, which burned animal fat, were not being produced any more because their smoke was found to be poisonous. I lit the wood stove to boil water for tea.

A knock at the front gate yielded Moji, delivering fresh naan taftoon. I thanked him and apologized for not having money to pay him.

"Khanum Piruz always takes care of it at the end of each week," he said, still standing at the gate with a silly grin on his face.

I thanked him, took the bread, and almost had to

force the gate closed. As if awakened, he jumped back and apologized. With a limp wave and a trip over a rock, he was gone.

I set the table for breakfast and was about to leave for school when Khanum Piruz yelled my name. The alarm in her voice sounded like an emergency. I ran to her room, which was adjacent to the one I had slept in. I found her in bed with a face strikingly red against the white sheets.

"Good morning," I said, a little startled.

She did not reply but sat in her bed, staring at me with what appeared to be disgust.

"Would you like some tea?" I asked, attempting a pleasant tone, but I still got no response. "It is ready."

I turned to go pour her some tea, but she yelled so loudly that I stumbled as I faced her again.

"Who do you think you are?" she said through gritted teeth.

I was sure I was not supposed to answer that.

"You – impertinent child," she said, lowering her voice, but her face was still flushed with anger. "Did your brothers teach you to walk into someone else's kitchen without permission and do anything you like?"

"I am sorry that I upset you. I thought I would help by—"

"Do not think! Ask everything and, *panah bar Khoda*, go change out of that ridiculous outfit. You will need work clothes today."

"It is a school day," I reasoned.

"Not for you," she announced, barely audible.

I warned myself that a person who yells one sentence and whispers another is volatile and can't be trusted.

"Get the children fed and send to school. You will need

to make their lunches, too. Their school is Pishraft School, the all-day private school, not like the half-day public school your Baba sent you to. When you are done in the kitchen, you need to help me."

She looked away in anger at the last comment. I assumed that her use of the past tense about my school was in reference to Baba.

"What about the little ones who do not go to school?" I asked, wondering who was going to care for them during the day.

"Malize will give you directions." She sunk into her pillow and turned her head to the wall.

That was it; no school for me. I was to follow her orders.

The house was filled with the smell of fresh bread, but it brought me no joy. I went into the next room, changed into a housedress, and left my school uniform in a neat pile on top of my carpet bag. I wondered when I would be allowed to go to school. I knew Baba would have wanted me to continue my education. A tear found its way down my cheek, but I wiped it away with one angry swipe. I became determined to run the household so efficiently that Khanum Piruz would see that I could handle my chores as well as my studies.

My days soon fell into a smooth routine. Farid and Saam were gone before I got up to pray at dawn. I made breakfast for the school-aged children and laid out their lunches for them to grab as they headed out the door. Malize and Soghra did not acknowledge my presence. They ate in silence, picked up their lunches, and from the front door called Shakiba without hiding their impatience. Shakiba would have to interrupt our conversation to hurry after them. They had a long bus ride to the private school.

"They criticize me for talking to the 'hired hand'," Shakiba whispered secretively one morning.

"I am your brother's wife," I reminded her indignantly, but it was hard to believe it myself.

"I know, but they think your marriage was to make you our maid."

I suppose I looked hurt, because Shakiba apologized for telling me and hurried out the door.

Saba and Curosh lagged behind their three older sisters on their walk to catch the bus. The two of them would be arguing about something as I handed them their lunches and guided them out the door. They took their lunches without a break in their conversation, oblivious to me. I could hear them beyond the front gate as I tidied up whatever was out of place in the front yard.

I walked back in and began clearing the breakfast dishes from the kitchen table. It was uncanny how Khanum Piruz managed to scream my name each morning just as I dried my hands on a towel. The three toddlers – Darius, Mina, and Sana – would crouch and cover their ears at the sound, but then they would continue their play as before.

The scream would bring me to attention in Khanum Piruz's room to help her start the day. I would begin by pushing her to the bathroom in her wheelchair. Getting her out of bed and into her wheelchair was a challenge that we perfected. With arms across each other's shoulders, she leaned on me, and I supported her until she stood up from the bed and crumpled into the chair.

The bathroom consisted of a room apart from the house with a brick floor and a pear-shaped hole in the middle. On the wall there hung a long hose for washing afterward. The rest of the family squatted over the hole, but Farid and Saam had built a stool for their mother, which had a hole in the middle. I placed the stool over the oval hole and sat Khanum Piruz on it after stripping her of her skirt and panties.

"Now turn around, you insolent child!" she would snap at me every time, even though I knew the routine.

In the beginning, I felt assaulted by her manners, but in time I decided it was her way of feeling less helpless and more in control. I imagined she felt ashamed for needing help with things she used to do by herself.

I would wheel her into the kitchen, where I would sponge bathe her and serve her breakfast. After breakfast I would fetch baby Akbar, whom the midwife had named after her own grandfather, for Khanum Piruz to nurse. I would change his diaper, pull on the wool soakers over the cloth, and place him in his cradle, where he would coo and gurgle until he fell asleep. Akbar was an easy baby with no fuss. He made up for his mother's disposition. When he was playful, I asked Khanum Piruz if she wanted to hold him, but she shook her head and looked away from us every time. I stopped asking.

Aside from missing school, I missed reading Baba's books. The girls refused to allow me to bring any of his books, even though I never saw them read from those shelves. They even kept my mandatory purchased textbooks.

"The books belong to this house," Shole had declared, hands on hips.

I did not know how to argue that point.

Not only did Khanum Piruz's house have no books, but it also had no newspapers, magazines, or even a Quran. It was as if the house belonged to a family of illiterates. With nothing to read and no radio to listen to, I felt isolated. I longed for a poem by Saadi, Hafez, or Molana. I would have settled for a child's picture book or a comic book, but most of all, a textbook.

Sana, Mina, and Darius laughed easily and gave their affection readily, but they were not stimulating for me. As soon as the school-aged children returned, I was eager to hear about their lessons and assignments. They, on the other hand, wanted to talk about anything but school. I envied them their books, pencils, erasers, and the school bags that carried all those treasures. Soghra was in the ninth grade, so her assignments were the most interesting to me. When the children began working on their school assignments, I tried to get a glimpse of Soghra's. She would hide it from me when she noticed I was looking.

"Malize," Soghra asked, holding her math textbook open for her sister to see, "how do you do this problem?"

Malize looked for a short time and offered a suggestion.

"I already tried that; it did not work," Soghra said, frustrated.

Malize looked a little longer and then gave up.

"I do not have time to help you," she snapped. "I have my own work to do."

Soghra dejectedly turned back to her spot on the carpet. I used great caution in approaching Soghra and offering to look at her problem. Soghra's initial indignation turned to desperation, and she let me look. I figured it out and showed her the solution.

"Oh, that old trick," Soghra humphed.

I let her preserve her dignity. Eventually Soghra asked me every time she got stuck. I would do all the problem sets with delight, reasoning that this way I would be quicker to help her.

Once Khanum Piruz noticed I was doing schoolwork, she demanded I return to the kitchen and start dinner.

"It is simmering on the stove, Khanum," I called from beside Soghra.

"Then do the laundry or sweep the floor," she called back.

"I did both before lunch today, Khanum," I said, remaining hopeful that she would see I had time to do schoolwork.

I looked at Soghra pleadingly, hoping she would speak in defence of both of us. Fortunately, she understood.

"Maman, Pari is helping me."

"What? You need help from someone younger than you?"

"Uh … no. Of course not," Soghra said, looking ashamed. "I was just being nice to her."

"In the kitchen, you – impertinent child. And stop interfering with my daughter's work."

There was an unmistakable warning in her tone.

I rushed back to the kitchen, noticing along the way that Darius, Mina, and Sana had cowered close together. I felt responsible. I knew that I could keep Khanum Piruz from upsetting the children.

I kept the toys off the floor and the children occupied with play, naps, or chores. The chores were delegated according to the children's abilities. In the true spirit of childhood, even the chores given to them were taken as play.

To prevent disturbing Khanum Piruz, we played games two floors up in the opposite corner of the house. In the

Pari

same room, I hung Akbar's *nani*, a small hammock, on a couple of hooks so he could be close to us.

"Let's play *Atal Matal Tootoole*," Sana squealed in a shrill voice.

Akbar was undisturbed in his nani, and Darius and Mina watched me innocently with wide eyes, waiting for my decision.

"All right," I said, bracing myself for Sana's second screech of delight.

This was a children's elimination game, for which they knew the routine. We sat in as well-formed a circle as possible, with their outstretched legs to the centre. I bent my knees so my feet would meet theirs. I tapped each little foot plus mine to the beat of a chant that made very little sense.

Atal Matal Tootoole,	Atal Matal Tootoole,
Gave Hasan chetore?	How is the cow of Hasan?
Na shir dare, na pestun.	Has no milk, has no udder.
Shiresho dade Hendestun,	Sent his milk to India,
Yek zan-e Kordy bestun.	To get himself a Kurdish wife.
Esmesho bezar Anghazi.	Name her Anghazi.
Dor-e kolash ghermezi.	Around her hat a red trim.
Hachin-o-vachin,	Hachin-o-vachin,
Yek pato varchin!	Pull one leg back!

On the last word, "*varchin*", the foot I tapped was pulled back. Then the chant was repeated with the remaining feet. The owner of the last foot remaining was the winner. I made a point of starting on a different foot each game to allow for different winners.

The reaction to "*varchin*" progressed from light laughter to groans and finally an exhilarated scream. It was an effortless game to play but was taxing on my ears. Admittedly, I was drawn into their delirium most of the time.

After each game, they would throw themselves on me, hanging off my shoulder or back like chimpanzees from a vine. Next there was a period of hugs and lounging in my lap as they recounted the game. Once rested, they would ask for another game.

Baba and I had been great playmates. Among our games were chess, chase, or ye-ghol-do-ghol – a schoolyard game played with five stones. The game began with the first player letting the stones roll off the back of one hand and land where they fell. A turn consisted of picking up the outlier stone, throwing it straight up into the air, picking up a second stone from the ground, and catching the falling stone with the same hand before it hit the ground. There were many variations and levels. I had become coordinated from playing with my schoolmates, but no matter how many times Baba lost, he never tired of the game. In fact, he looked content whether he was winning or losing.

Raise your words, not voice. It is rain that grows flowers, not thunder.

—Rumi

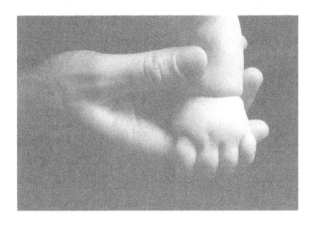

Chapter 8

Unforeseen (1310 SH)

One afternoon while the children were napping in the family room and Khanum Piruz was lying down in her bedroom, a man appeared at the gate.

Dinner was made and stewing on the wood stove. I was lying on my makeshift coat-and-sweater bed and reading Soghra's history textbook, which I had found lying around. I felt only slightly guilty for taking it without permission. I rationalized that Soghra could share with the student seated next to her. When I finished one textbook, Soghra would find it back among her belongings, but curiously, another textbook would vanish. If she guessed that the textbook was with me, she did not say so. In secret, she began asking me for help with other subjects besides mathematics, and coincidentally she would pick the subject whose textbook I had just finished reading.

I placed a sock as a bookmarker in the textbook and hid the book under my sweater-pillow. I walked stealthily, so as not to wake anyone. Shortened naps meant shortened reading time for me.

I opened the gate and found a beggar holding a bowl. Beggars usually did not stop at the Piruz house because they would be yelled at. From over the wall that joined our yards, I had heard Khanum or Agha Piruz be disrespectful to the beggars. In the month that I had been with them, no beggar had dared knock on this gate. This beggar must have been new to the neighbourhood. His clothes were old and out of style, but they were clean and mended. His posture was that of a businessman – tall and confident. His face was covered by a thick moustache and beard, but below his single bushy eyebrow, I saw Baba's green eyes. He talked to me in the same playful tone as Baba had.

"Now what is a delightful girl like you doing home in the middle of the day?" he grinned. "You should be in school, learning how to straighten out this country."

I was caught off guard, so I smiled at this stranger. At the mention of school, however, I looked down at my hands. I worried that I would give away my longing for school. From the bowl in his hand, I knew what he wanted. I asked him to wait there and took his bowl to the kitchen. I filled it with food from the pot and returned to the front gate. He took it from me with both his tanned, leathery hands and bowed his head in thanks. His eyes twinkled with gratitude, and I wished it had been a bigger bowl.

"I am Pari," I said, knowing it was inappropriate to introduce myself to him.

This man had stripped me of my inhibition. I felt a familiarity with him that I could not explain.

"Ahmad is the name, Khanum. Mamnoon," he said, giving a quick lift to the bowl in his hands.

His face turned sad as he bowed deeply, walking backward a few steps and then turning and walking away. I could only guess at how many bellies that bowl was going to fill.

Baba had routinely fed beggars who came to our gate. He would have interesting conversations with some, but others were unwilling. He would defend them to me by saying they needed to rush off to their loved ones, who were also waiting for the food.

* * *

"If this is to feed more than you," Baba offered to a beggar, "then let me fill a bigger bowl."

"Oh, no, *agha*," the man refused. "This size of bowl is more modest, and we all do get fed."

* * *

I was watching Ahmad Agha through the front gate when I heard Khanum Piruz yell my name. I hurried to close the front door so he would not hear her angry voice. I ran to her bedroom, weaving through the halls and jumping over the occasional toy on the floor. I told myself to remember to pick those toys up before Khanum Piruz saw them.

"You called me, Khanum?" I said in her doorway, trying to breathe evenly so she could not tell that I had run from a distance.

"You – insolent child," she growled. "How dare you give away the food that is to fill the bellies of my babies?"

Too late. She knew.

"Do not worry, Khanum," I replied, feeling an unfamiliar confidence. "I gave him my share."

I continued to feed beggars who came to the gate, despite Khanum Piruz's protests. I suppose word travelled, and beggars heard that the Piruz household was under new management. I tolerated Khanum's angry words and reminded myself not to have dinner that night.

During one of these exchanges between Khanum Piruz and me, Farid came home unnoticed. I served dinner and went to my room so I would not make the others uncomfortable by not eating. This was another opportunity for me to read the "borrowed" text of the month. I was accustomed to being asleep in my spot on the floor before Farid entered the room. Just before I rolled the wick down in the lantern to extinguish its light, there was a knock on the door.

That was unusual.

Farid had developed the routine of coming in after I was in my makeshift bed so he did not need to knock. I opened the door, and Farid pushed a plate of food into my hands and walked past me to his bed. His thick black hair had white flakes of plaster in it. I thought of Baba and his greying hair that he had pretended was plaster. Farid's button-down blue shirt and beige trousers had a thin film of white powder covering them.

"That is your dinner," he said in his deep voice as he sat on the cot, facing me.

I did not hear his voice often, but I liked its deep resonance. Tonight it had a hint of gentleness that touched me. He was unbuttoning his blue shirt and taking it off. I looked away.

"I am full," I lied.

"It is my share I am giving you," Farid admitted, without making eye contact. "Let me feed that poor beggar tonight."

I was startled. He knew what I had done, but he was not angry.

"I cannot let you do that."

"Yet you are willing to go hungry yourself?"

"I was home all day. You worked."

"Your work is just as demanding," he said, lowering his voice to a whisper, "I could not do it."

Only Baba had said words of admiration to me. In my surprise, I glanced in his direction and noticed that he had sweated in such a way that his white undershirt clung to his chest in the shape of a heart. His arms were bare, and I felt a strange delight in seeing him like this.

It still felt wrong to take his food.

"We can share it," I said, thrilled that I had come up with a fair solution.

"Eat and say no more about it," Farid said, climbing into bed with his pants still on and his back to me. "I lied to Maman and told her that I am eating in my room tonight. She looked displeased."

I saw his shoulders shrug. I felt moved. He had acted against his mother's will for me. I suppose I should have preferred him telling her the truth and accepting her disapproval.

I watched his back lift and fall, first quickly then slowly. His back muscles stretched the material of his undershirt showing contours. Eventually his gentle snore drifted to me, but it did not bother me. The Farid that sat beside me like a statue at our wedding dinner had been replaced by a new Farid. This Farid could feel and think and express himself to me.

That night, I slept as well as I did in Baba's house.

The next morning, I got up before Farid and Saam. I prepared their breakfast and placed it on the kitchen table. I made two lunches and set them on the counter by the door. The two brothers walked into the kitchen bleary-eyed, but their eyes popped open at the sight of breakfast already on the table. Without questioning it, they sat down, almost knocking over the chairs, and ate their fill ravenously. With both cheeks bulging with food, they chatted about what was on the agenda for the day. They gave no attention to me as I busied myself at the sink.

Unbeknownst to them, I was pleased with their reaction. I was accustomed to my brothers, who sat in silence and left without a word to each other or to me.

Saam brought his dish to the sink, peeked into his lunch bag by the door, and smirked at his brother.

"It certainly looks better than any I have made, and even better than any you have made for us."

"Take it and let's go," Farid said, feigning a serious tone, but I noticed his crooked smile.

"Thanks, Pari," Saam called over his shoulder as he hurried to catch up with Farid.

Later that morning, when Moji delivered our naan taftoon, I told him to bring our bread an hour earlier so Farid and Saam could enjoy fresh bread for their breakfast.

That night, after everyone was settled down for the evening and nothing more was needed of me, I went to my room to sleep. I halted inside the doorway and noticed the room had been tidied up. Not only were Farid's clothes hung in the closet instead of strewn across the floor, but my large carpet bag was closed and placed inside the closet. I noticed hangers holding Farid's clothes had been pushed to one side of the closet, and the other side held empty hangers. Where my sweater and coat had been, there was a mattress and bedding – a matching white blanket and pillowcase with tiny embroidered pink rosebuds!

There was a knock, but before I reached the handle, Farid's head popped through the door. His eyes were wild with excitement, and his mouth held that familiar crooked smile.

"Do you like it?" he asked with great anticipation.

I nodded. This was the first time he had kept eye contact long enough for me to see his face – the balanced features and the dark, gentle eyes. I almost felt like reaching up to touch him but did not dare.

"Do not tell Maman I spent the money," he whispered, looking quickly over his shoulder. "She would not understand."

I nodded again, wondering what had happened to my tongue. I was confused by how nervous and excited I had become. Fortunately he left, closing the door behind him. I exhaled with such force that I realized I had been holding my breath. I shook my head as if that would clear the confusion.

I did my part by unpacking my carpet bag and placing my clothing on hangers in the space Farid had cleared for me. I looked around our room and felt a deep pride of ownership: a cot, a mattress, and a closet – but it was ours.

Don't you know yet? It is your light that lights the world.

—Rumi

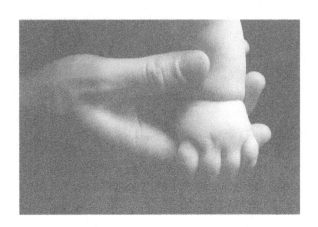

Chapter 9

Fereshteh (1310 SH)

I was walking home from the market with everything I needed for the week. There was a refrigeration system in the Piruz kitchen, so I did not need to get perishables daily. I used the naptime of the children once a week to do this chore. As in Baba's house, money to buy food was left for me, weekly, in a tin on the kitchen counter. I had to time the shopping to avoid the two hours they closed in the afternoons.

The construction of the shops varied, as did their owners and their inventory. Some were made of bricks, and some had rounded surfaces of *kagel* – a mixture of mud and straw.

The interior had chandeliers if the product was jewellery or fabrics, and a light bulb hanging from the ceiling by a cord if it was produce or meat.

There were cleaned and plucked chickens hung in a row above everyone's head at the entrance of the meat shop. The chickens were complete with nails at the end of their dangling feet, their limp heads hanging to one side from their wrinkly necks. Lobsters and crabs in crates were slathered in crushed ice. Sides of veal and lamb hung from thick metal hooks. Every purchase was custom cut. The butcher would cut and wrap whatever section the customer named.

The produce was not to be touched, but pointed to, and the shopkeeper would bag and weigh it. Packaging was paper bags or newspaper for green leafy produce. Baba had sewn cloth bags to make carrying parcels easier. I did the same for myself in the Piruz house, using old housedresses.

Tea was served like salutations – generously and abundantly. A samovar sat near the doorway on a crate or table with tiny glasses and sugar cubes. The floor under the samovar usually had a Persian carpet to make the presentation welcoming. This natural service was for the benefit of the owners as well as the customers.

The common thread through all the shops was the level of politeness. Even when people argued, they used the traditional polite expressions. Whether it was the farmer delivering the eggs and milk or the banker stepping out of his office, every man wore a suit and spoke with a bow.

In many of the stores I frequented, the owners were huddled around a radio, listening and discussing current events. I would pause a while after my purchase to hear the end of what the announcer was saying. Some shopkeepers allowed me to stay as long as I wanted. They even took time to discuss the news with me. Others were displeased and wanted me to leave as soon as I paid. I chose the shops according to which shopkeepers were most flexible.

There were good and bad feelings about Reza Shah. Those who accepted him were glad for the improvements he had made, and those who were against him were appalled by the imprisonments and the propaganda.

The dirt road I walked home along had stores and short, newly planted trees on either side. A long ditch full of water ran the length of the road. The water was to supply each building it passed. When a car or truck went by, a gust of dirt rose into the air, settling too slowly for the pedestrians, who ended up breathing it. Periodically, store owners would spray water from a hose over the dusty road. The dampness weighed the dust down, and the air filled with the smell of wet earth. Some of the water landed on nearby flowers, bringing their scent to life.

A young girl stood on the sidewalk, spraying water from a hose. I walked in an arc to avoid her range, but she lifted her hose and sprayed my dress anyway.

"*Akh*, sorry!" she called to me, but her giggles gave her away.

I was wearing my housedress with a light cardigan. The cardigan made my dress look more respectable for the market, plus it kept me warm in the cool autumn weather. I took a handkerchief from my pocket and patted at my wet dress. Normally the Tehran sun would dry my dress in minutes, but today I became chilled. The girl's sense of humour did not change with the seasons.

I passed Armon's Bakery, and through the window, Armon Agha and Moji waved to me. I nodded my head in a polite reply and carried on. Moji, standing almost as tall as his baba, was the age of Curosh. Unlike Curosh and the rest of the Piruz children, he wore an infectious smile.

I used to accompany Baba to Armon's Bakery early each morning to buy fresh bread, right out of the tandoor, for our breakfast. Moji could have delivered it, but Baba insisted on the walk with me, for which I was grateful.

"Let the boy have extra time to do his other deliveries," Baba had reasoned.

The clay tandoor opening had round edges and glowed red and orange from the coals below. Moji was as good as his father at flipping a ball of dough from hand to hand until it became so thin that it laid flat on a round, firm pillow. The pillow was picked up and hit against the inside wall of the tandoor. The hot brick wall held the dough to itself. I used to stand close to the opening, despite my face turning red from the heat. I had watched as bubbles formed on the dough and the colour turned golden. The timing was crucial: if picked too soon, the bread would not be done; if left too long, it would fall into the glowing coals below and be ruined.

Our naan taftoon had always been ready to take as soon as we arrived, but Baba and Armon Agha were great friends and would chat during the duration of our stay in the store. In fact, Baba had chatted with all the shopkeepers. I was proud to stand beside him and listen – especially since he would ask for my opinion on the topics, which varied from politics to sports to local business.

* * *

Amir was with us on one of our errands because he needed a pair of sneakers.

After we left the pharmacy, he said, "Baba, do you have to talk to everyone like they were Khale Sara?"

"They are all like Khale Sara," Baba replied earnestly. "They are all from God, and God makes no mistakes."

I squeezed Baba's hand and gazed up at him for the words he used. Amir's sullen expression told me that Baba's words did not affect him in the same way. That made me sad for Amir.

* * *

I turned off the street with the stores and walked along a road lined with mud houses surrounded by wooden gates. The walls and floors were made of kagel. Sweeping did not eliminate the dust on such floors. There would be plenty of dust in the air to breathe, and even more settled on everything in the house. When I visited my friends in these homes, we would inevitably come across a snake that had made its way through the kagel. My friends were used to it. They would pick it up with a stick and throw it outside. I wondered if that snake would find its way back in through the same hole it had dug, but I said nothing.

The water system here was the same as those in the commercial districts. It consisted of ditches along the homes where clean water would flow. People could take water for their use from the ditch and fill their pond in their yard. Boys and men were hired to do this heavy work for those who could afford the service. They would walk up and down the streets carrying a clay pitcher, yelling, "Ab hosi, ab hosi!"

Sometimes people would forget that the water in the ditch belonged to everyone along the road. They would dump their garbage in the ditch with a clear conscience, since the flowing water would take it out of their sight. When a section of the ditch got blocked by garbage, the water would find an alternate route and flow outside of the ditch and into houses. When this happened, the kagel walls of houses could become soggy and collapse.

"Among other news, a wall collapsed on Fereidun Street and killed three people," the radio announcer would report casually.

Baba had become angry that the ditches were abused and not monitored. He would say we needed policing of the dumping, and fixing of the collapsed ditches before people got hurt.

This was a poor part of Tehran. There were other routes home, but I chose this one because more children were out playing. I had known most of them all my life and liked to visit them, even for a moment. At this time of the day, the school-aged children were all girls. In public schools, classes for girls were in the morning and those for boys were in the afternoon, six days per week. Friday was the weekly holiday, and the summer holiday was three months long. Baba did not approve of private school.

"This way your classmates are the children in your neighbourhood," he had told me. "Besides, students learn more from their own effort than from the teacher's effort."

I rounded a corner, and there they were – the girls

from the morning school, out playing in the street. The younger children ran to me as soon as they saw me. I always had something for them in one of the grocery bags I was carrying. Today it was pistachios. My classmates would saunter over more and more slowly as the weeks went by.

"So how is married life, Pari?" asked a girl behind me.

I knew that voice. I gave the bag of pistachios to eight-year-old Sophia, who I knew would share fairly. I turned around, and it was Kobra Sultani, my best friend. We were the two that all the other students respected – or feared. Every year, we had sat together and shared our love for poetry and our talent for memorizing verses. My favourite poet had been Molana, and Kobra had preferred Saadi.

My life had taken a different turn to hers, and our friendship had suffered as a result. First I was advanced beyond her grade, and then I was married and quit school. She may have felt abandoned by me, but what she may not have known was that I felt alone too.

"It is like a long sleepover," I answered her and everyone else who had gathered.

The little ones were busy munching on pistachios, but the older ones were looking at me from head to toe. It made me uncomfortable. I wish we could have gone back to being neighbourhood friends and skipping rope or playing ye-ghol-do-ghol.

"You do not look any different," Homa observed, hands on hips.

"That is because I am not any different," I assured her.

"Agha Nemat keeps asking where his prized student went," Kobra ridiculed.

"What did you tell him?" I asked, not wanting to know.

"That you met with an untimely death," Sekine answered, emphasizing the last word.

"And he believed you?" I asked, knowing she would never say that.

"Of course," said Homa. "He sends his condolences to your brothers and their toys."

I never thought of the girls as toys, but the description was amusing.

I wished them well in school, secretly envying them, and continued down the road. I looked over my shoulder once. They were again in the same formation as when I entered the road. It was as if I had never been there. Then I saw Kobra turn and look at me. I recognized the expression as the one she had in elementary school when I stood punished in the corner of the classroom while she had to go outside for recess. Maybe she did understand.

As I walked towards the end of the road, I heard the soft weeping of a girl. When I reached the house, the wooden gate was open, so I went in and stood outside the curtain entrance. The door behind the curtain was closed. That was odd. The gate was usually closed and the front door left open, making use of only the curtain as the entrance.

I stood there wondering what the appropriate thing to do was.

"Salaam," I said, daring to say hello.

The weeping stopped momentarily and then resumed. Perhaps the girl thought the greeting was meant for someone else. I repeated myself. This time the silence was followed by feet shuffling towards the entrance. The door opened, and the curtain pulled slightly to one side. A small, tear-smeared face with unruly dark hair appeared in the open slit. Her eyes calmed when she saw it was me.

"I am Pari," I said, deciding an introduction was a good start.

"I am Fereshteh," she answered with a shaky voice.

"I pass this way often, but I have never seen you before."

"I am new here. I was just married."

"I am married too," I said, not sure if it was a positive status that we had in common.

Fereshteh looked surprised, but I think the commonality made her comfortable enough to invite me in. I wanted to take my shoes off, but she insisted that I keep them on. A few kilims covered the dirt floor. The room looked bare of furniture except for two wooden chairs at a wooden table where we both sat. On the table was an oil lamp, and in the corner were some cupboards with a wood stove. The walls were bare except for a framed photograph of an older couple. Fereshteh told me that they were her grandparents and her new husband had put it up to make her feel more at home.

Her parents had died when she was a baby, and she had lived with her grandparents for the last sixteen years. They had promised that her life would be better married to this man.

"Maman-bozorg said Shahram is a good man and will take care of me," Fereshteh said. "He was born in my village, but now he teaches here. I met him twice at my grandparents' home in Karaj. Both times he was kind to me. He promised that he would take me to school with him and I could continue my lessons. I do like him."

I felt a sudden stab of envy that Fereshteh would go to school despite being married.

"Then why were you crying?" I asked, puzzled.

"This morning a cleric read from the Quran and married us in my grandparents' living room. Shahram immediately left for work and will return here tonight. My grandparents brought me here and went back to Karaj. I did not have a ceremony with a wedding dress or cake like I had dreamed of. The house is empty of food. Shahram left money for me, but I do not know where to shop. What does Shahram expect when he comes home tonight?"

She began to sob again.

Despite the swollen eyes and red nose, Fereshteh was beautiful. Her eyes were golden, and they brightened her face. Her hair was unruly but long and thick. Her slender body was like a rag doll draped over the chair. Her shaky hands quivered, and she folded and unfolded them as if unsure what to do with them.

I wanted to help her. I got up, patted her on the back, and handed her my handkerchief from my pocket. I had an idea.

"I will be back soon," I said, picking up my grocery bags and leaving through the curtain before she could respond.

The dirt road ended, and I turned onto our street, where the houses were made of bricks. I passed by Baba's iron gate without pausing and opened the neighbour's iron gate. I stepped inside and was grateful for the silence. Everyone was still napping. I went straight to the kitchen with the bags of groceries and unpacked them. I set out to cook the *adas polo* with dates that I had planned.

As it steamed on the wood stove, I poured kerosene into a tin and set it by the front door, along with a full kerosene lamp. I stuffed a matchbox into my pocket. My carpet bag served to carry the white wedding dress and the hairbrush in my mother's velvet pouch. I snapped it shut and placed it next to the tin and lamp. Back in the kitchen, I filled some tins with food and a bag with fruit, vegetables, and nuts. I managed to carry it all to Fereshteh's home and set it down outside of her curtain. I called her as I rubbed the strain out of my red fingers. This time she came to the curtain and whipped it to the side with an excited laugh.

"Where did you go?" she asked brightly as her eyes curiously scanned the supplies I had brought. "What is all this for?"

"Help me carry them inside and I will explain," I said, excited myself. "You bring the carpet bag; I have the rest."

I put the tin of food on the kerosene stove and lit it so it could steam and stay warm. I gave Fereshteh the kerosene lamp and handed her the matchbox to light it.

"This tin has kerosene to refill the lamp," I said, handing it to her. "Your oil lamp is not healthy and must be thrown out."

I opened my bag, took out the hairbrush, and motioned to Fereshteh to kneel in front of me. Fereshteh had been following me like an enthusiastic puppy, watching with intense focus and obeying directions. I noticed her eyes were darting now between the brush in my hand and me.

"What are you going to do with that?"

"You have never seen a hairbrush?" I asked. "Come here."

Fereshteh knelt in front of me, and I tried brushing her hair. I immediately understood her hesitation about the brush. It was a long and painful task getting the tangles out of her hair, but Fereshteh was brave. I could hear the tiny gasps being stifled with every tug on a tangle.

Once I had brushed her hair and tied it with the yellow ribbon, I applied some rouge, eye makeup, and orange lipstick. I showed her the finished product in my compact mirror. She was silent, but when I withdrew the mirror to put it back in the pouch, she grabbed my wrist and continued to stare at her reflection.

"Is that really me?" she asked with a quivering lower lip.

"If you cry now, you will smear your makeup," I warned.

Fereshteh bit her lower lip, tasted the lipstick, and thought better of it. When she released my wrist, I put the mirror, brush, and makeup back into the pouch and pulled out the wedding dress. I handed it to her and turned my back.

"Put it on," I told her. "We are about the same size. It should fit."

I heard her shuffling around, and then it was quiet. I turned around and saw that she looked complete. Her long, dark curls made the ribbon look pretty. The eye makeup made her honey eyes exotic. She was taller, so the dress came to her ankles. She looked like the bride she had dreamed of.

"You have plates and cutlery in the cupboard. I checked. You will serve Shahram the meal tonight, and he will be stunned by how beautiful you look."

"Will he?" Fereshteh asked shyly. "Do you think he will like it?"

I nodded.

Without warning, she threw her arms around my neck and squeezed so hard that I grunted. I hugged her back and congratulated her on her marriage.

"May you have many years of happiness, Khanum …" I said, pausing so she would tell me her new last name.

"Khanum Nemat," she said, dramatically standing up straight, chin in the air and eyes closed.

Not being able to control herself, Fereshteh doubled over and burst into laughter, covering her mouth like a child.

It took me a moment to regain my composure as I realized I was standing in the house of my old math teacher, helping his new wife.

"And you are Khanum …?"

"Khanum Piruz," I said, embarrassed by my name.

Fortunately, Fereshteh did not pick up on any of my reactions. She was in her own world of bliss. I was glad for her. It had cost me a day of reading from my "borrowed" textbook, but I thought it was worth it.

What you seek is seeking you.

—Rumi

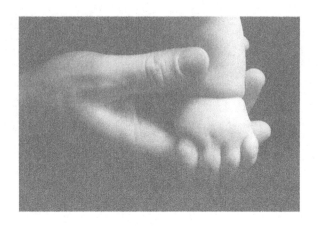

Chapter 10

Revelation (1310 SH)

I started bleeding just before my eleventh birthday and thought that was the prerequisite for becoming a wife. I had overheard Khanum Piruz discuss it with Shole on one of her visits to our home. Shole assured her that I was not bleeding and that there was no possibility of "it". I could only assume "it" meant marriage. I was not sure why Shole was lying, but I was grateful to her for getting me out of the marriage. Khanum Piruz had been consoled by the information too, but for some reason, the marriage had proceeded anyway.

For days after returning from Fereshteh's home, I imagined what had happened that night when Agha Nemat returned from work. I pictured them eating together at the wooden table – something Farid and I had not done since our wedding dinner. I thought of how he may have thanked her, perhaps hugged her, kissed her, and maybe had sex with her. My visualization ended there, as I was not sure how the rest looked. I had overheard Ali and Shole in the night as I lay in my bed. Shole's voice always held so much pain that I covered my ears with my pillow and prayed that the torture would soon be over.

I received a different image from Fereshteh. I stopped in to see her on my next trip to the market. She told me that she actually enjoyed it. To my relief, she was too shy to say more.

So far, Farid had not shown interest, and I had been grateful to him for that. Now I was curious.

I found myself looking at him as he ate his breakfast. I would try to imagine what he liked and what he did not like. What was he thinking about? How was his work? Were things going well, or did some things bother him? On Fridays, when he was home all day, I watched him play with his younger siblings or quietly sit outside in the garden, looking at nothing in particular. I noticed at these times that he looked peculiarly sad. I pointed this out to Shakiba as I read her dictee to her. I asked her if she knew why Farid looked so sad.

"I think he misses Baba," she said, preoccupied with her writing assignment.

"I can sympathize," I said, "but I have never seen either of my brothers look so sad at the loss of our father. I have not seen Saam look this sad either."

"Farid is more sensitive than Saam," Shakiba said, putting her pen down. "It was Farid's motorcycle that Baba was driving, so he blames himself."

"Oh, that is awful!" I exclaimed, wanting to take his pain away. "It was an accident. I cannot believe he would consider himself responsible."

"It did not help when Maman yelled at him after she was told the news of the accident."

This I could believe.

"She told him that he should have stayed to finish the job. Baba was not as comfortable on the motorcycle as Farid was. She said it was his fault for not offering to stay instead."

"In that case, Farid would have been hit by the truck in the wrong lane," I reasoned.

"Maman thinks Farid would have swerved and avoided the collision, since he is younger and more agile."

"She does not know that for sure. An accident is no one's fault."

I wanted to take Farid's sadness away. I knew how Khanum Piruz's wrath could be hurtful. I looked over at him through the glass doors to the backyard and noticed he had been watching me. He quickly looked away as if caught doing something wrong.

"We are married!" I wanted to call to him. "Look on!"

That night I went to bed ahead of Farid as usual, but I intentionally did not fall asleep. I waited nervously for him to enter our room. I did not have a plan, but I knew I did not want to continue rooming with him in silence. Impulsively, I jumped off my mattress on the floor, rosebud pillow in hand. I rolled the mattress with my free hand into the corner and climbed into Farid's cot. Once I was lying there, I was full of regret. I felt as if I had entered a forbidden space. I scolded and reminded myself that I had a right to be in this bed.

I lay on my back, changed my mind, and turned to face the wall, but I then turned onto my other side, facing the door. I thought having my back to the door sent the wrong message. When Farid entered the room, I wanted to be facing him.

The longer he took, the more nervous I became, wanting to jump out of the bed and back to the floor. I willed myself to stay. My thoughts took odd turns. Suddenly it seemed most important that I have on a prettier nightgown. I was wearing a light green cotton nightgown with no lace or pretty prints.

*   *   *

Baba had bought this nightgown for me at the market on a busy evening when people had to shout to be heard. I was walking beside him with my hand in his, picking up on the scents that changed by the second from saffron ice cream, car exhaust, and wet earth to eau de cologne, grilled corn sold on the street, and heavy body odour when someone bumped into me. Baba was there to buy plaster and a new palette. It ended up being his last trip to the market.

We passed a store which had a bin full of clothes outside its door. My eyes settled on the pale green nightgown, and I did not notice I had stopped. Baba's hand had slipped away from mine. He came and stood by me, following my eyes to the nightgown. He picked it up and let it dangle from his hand.

"This one?" he said with a smirk.

I looked at him, puzzled. He arched his eyebrow with amusement, so I managed a nod. Baba and I went on errands often, but he had never bought anything for me, and I did not expect it. I wore hand-me-downs of the Piruz

Pari

girls until even Malize's clothes were too small for me. I began wearing their brothers' clothes, which were oversized but comfortable. Baba did not believe in wasting money when there was an abundant supply of clothing right next door. Yet, that evening, he purchased this nightgown for me.

I did not mind hand-me-downs, but Malize relished embarrassing me in front of the neighbourhood children and her siblings. She would point out that I was so big I had to wear her brother's clothes.

I remember one evening after dinner we were all playing in the street and Farid showed up. He heard his sister taunting me. Malize was facing away from him and did not see him approach. He picked her up and flipped her over one shoulder like a sack of potatoes. Everyone laughed when she hollered for him to put her down. He lowered her to the ground, gave me a wink, and walked to their gate.

"See?" he said to Malize over his shoulder. "If you were as big as Pari, I could not lift you so easily."

The children laughed while Malize turned red in the face and stormed into her house.

* * *

This green nightgown was more feminine than anything I had got from the Piruz children, but suddenly, tonight, it felt not pretty enough.

The doorknob turned, and Farid entered. He closed the door behind him, and I noticed he was careful not to be too loud. My heart melted with affection. Once his eyes adjusted to the darkness, he stopped where he stood and stared into my open eyes. My elbow sunk into my rosebud pillow, and my hand propped up my head to give the clear message that I had been waiting for him. I was determined to hold his gaze and force him to speak first. He looked handsome in the moonlight: his eyes, his lips, his arms – his eyes. He broke into a smile, dropped his eyes, and moved to the closet. He began to undress, so I looked away, my shyness returning. I was glad he smiled. He climbed into bed next to me wearing a long white cotton shirt with three buttons at the top. This was the first time I saw him change clothes for sleeping. The small cot forced us to lie close to each other. He faced me and propped his head up with one arm. Was he mimicking me? I wanted him to take me seriously. I could not stand the silence any more.

"I wish I had a prettier nightgown for you." I heard my pathetic words and immediately wanted to take them back.

"I wish I had a prettier nightgown to give you," he said, still smiling, letting his eyes join in. "One of Saam's, perhaps."

We burst into laughter. My nerves calmed until he reached out and stroked my cheek with his free hand. I felt excitement rush through me. I lowered my head onto the pillow and touched his arm – something I had longed to do. The contact sent my heart beating as if I had carried the wet tub of laundry around the yard several times for no reason.

I resigned to having my body betray my emotions. Farid took both of my shaky hands in one of his and squeezed them. I loved that he knew how to calm them. I was awestruck when my hands disappeared in his.

"I was teased about having large hands," I rambled.

"Better to reach the piano keys with," Farid offered.

"How did you …"

"I could hear you practicing. What was that piece – 'Gole Gandom'?"

I was amazed. I had not realized he was listening. His head came close, and his lips grazed mine. I was not sure if I had just been kissed for the first time.

"I do not know what I am supposed to do," I confessed with a hoarse voice.

"This is my first time too," he admitted, looking away shyly, but then his eyes locked with mine again. "We can figure it out together."

We became two children finding a new game. Every evening, I looked forward to playing this game with Farid, and he returned to our room earlier and earlier. We had to be quiet in the evenings, and not too long in the mornings so Farid did not have to explain his tardiness to his brother.

Each day I would do my chores, and each evening I would watch the front door in anticipation. I could not believe Fereshteh had not told me just how wonderful sex was. I felt disappointed that we had lost a whole month of this form of fun. Some nights, Farid would come home with a gift for me. One night it was a sheer white negligee with lavender fur circling the collar, wrists, and the bottom. We had fun with that gift. Another time, he brought home an orange taffeta dress, saying it was our three-month anniversary. I was impressed that he remembered our wedding date. I was even more impressed at the reason why he picked orange. He said he thought I must like orange since that had been the colour of my lipstick on our wedding day. He remembered.

"You remembered!" I told him.

"Of course I did. You looked incredible."

"Then why were you looking away from me all night?"

"Not all night," he said, looking shy again. "I would glance at you when you were not looking."

The taffeta dress was a twisted, woven silk. It was fitted at the top and had a narrow skirt. The collar was wide, and I imagined wearing my mother's pearls with it.

"You looked great in the yellow dress too, but that was under unfavourable conditions, yes?"

I nodded, surprised he knew. I remembered how Nasim had bullied me into wearing Shole's yellow dress so she could anger her sister.

Months passed, and I noticed I had stopped bleeding. I was glad, since it allowed Farid and me to be intimate without the week of abstinence. I did not experience morning sickness or bloating, so I had none of the usual clues. By the eighth month of my pregnancy, my stomach began to protrude into a round ball. My appetite had gone crazy, and I could not get enough food in me. I thought I was getting fat from eating more than I normally did.

Khanum Piruz was the first to notice.

"You – impertinent child!" she yelled from behind me.

I was startled into dropping the knife I was using to cut up the parsley and leeks for ghorme sabzi.

"Why the secrecy?"

"I … I do not know what you mean, Khanum," I said, bending down to pick up the knife from the floor.

It was getting harder to bend over. Curiously, everything took more effort these days.

"You are going to have my grandchild, and you do not have the decency to tell me," she said angrily.

I was puzzled. I could only have a grandchild of hers if I were pregnant, which I was not.

"I am not pregnant," I assured her.

Suddenly a pot came flying at me, hitting me on the side of my head. I fell to the floor and must have stayed there until I felt myself being lifted and then lowered onto a bed. When I opened my eyes, I saw Farid's face over mine. He looked like an angel. The pained expression on his face worried me. There was a physical pain throbbing on the side of my head.

"How do you feel?" Farid asked, leaning so close to my face we could almost kiss.

"My head hurts," I said, lifting a hand to touch my temple, but it fell heavily to my side.

A new pain shot through my head.

"Stay still," Farid said softly as he tucked my hand by my side. "The doctor is on his way."

I felt a damp cloth on my forehead. Farid rose from sitting beside me on the bed and promised to return soon. He left the room and closed the door quietly behind him, but I could still hear him whisper to Khanum Piruz, who yelled her responses.

"She did not know, Maman. Nobody had told her."

"She is a deceiving, conniving little brat."

"She was not a little brat when you decided to make her my wife and have her do the housework."

"She wanted to keep this from me," Khanum Piruz accused. "She hates me."

"She does not hate you," Farid said, his voice softening. "She does not know how to hate. She is a very gentle soul."

"*Khodaya*! You are dough in her hand," Khanum Piruz said, recovering from her moment of vulnerability.

"I am curious why," Farid asked, "after all she has done for you, you did not put a pillow under her head or wipe the blood from her wound?"

I heard Malize and Soghra cry and run away from our bedroom door. I did not know they had been there.

"Now she has turned you against your sisters," Khanum Piruz wailed. "See what I mean. She is pure evil – she and her lying sister-in-law Shole. They are all liars."

I wondered what role Shole had played in this in order to be accused of lying.

I heard our door open and close. Farid's sigh told me he had found refuge in our little sanctuary. He walked to our cot and sat on the edge. His eyes were on his hands, which were clenched together in his lap. His mind must have been a tornado of thoughts. We had not yet had a chance to digest the idea of having a baby. Then he looked at me, took my hands in his, and smiled his crooked smile. Farid was back with me.

"That is great news," he said in a tired voice. "We are going to have a baby."

I was pregnant.

"I thought I was getting fat because I was eating so much," I confessed, hearing my words come out of my mouth unusually slowly. "I could not understand why I was always so hungry."

"I called the doctor, and he will be here soon. He will make sure you and the baby are fine," Farid promised.

I nodded and felt my eyes close without my permission. Sleep came easily with Farid by my side.

I was awakened when the doctor arrived. As he was getting his instruments ready, I became nervous and asked for Farid.

"I am right here," he said, taking my hand and sitting on the edge of our cot.

"The biology textbook is the next one I steal," I said in a groggy voice.

I saw Farid's confused expression and said no more.

The doctor said that everything was progressing as it should and I would deliver in a few weeks. Usually there were months to get used to the idea of having a baby and to plan for its arrival. We got a few weeks.

To Khanum Piruz's disgust, Farid grew increasingly excited as the day drew closer. Every evening, he would come home with something else for the baby. Saam was a doting brother-in-law; he would bring me glasses of water and place extra pillows behind me at dinner. The children loved to touch my belly or put their ear to it. The baby was very accommodating by being active so the children were always entertained. When Malize was not around, Soghra and Shakiba joined in the fun.

"All this fuss over a little brat," Malize said. "You would think they had never seen Maman have a baby before."

Nothing Malize or Khanum Piruz said could dampen the excitement that everyone felt over the new baby coming into the family.

"Little Akbar is going to be an uncle at the age of one," Sana pointed out.

Everyone cheered for Akbar, the uncle. Some came to pinch his cheeks, while others came to tickle him. Akbar giggled and enjoyed the attention.

Let the beauty of what you love be what you do.

—Rumi

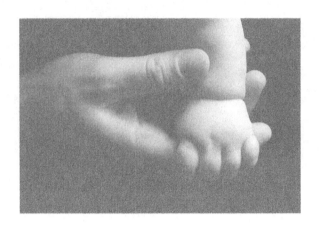

Chapter 11

Pantea (1311 SH)

The day arrived when the doctor came to the house and delivered a healthy baby girl for us. He handed her to me swaddled in a blanket. Farid and I spent hours lying beside each other in our cot, holding our daughter in our lap. We would stare at her little hands and her little feet. We would watch her tiny mouth move as if she had something to say. She would have our full attention. Farid would point out to me how amazing her ears were, and I would point out to him how cute her nose was. We agreed with each other on every point. We were filled with awe, watching her when she cried, when she nursed on my breasts, and when she was awake and alert for short periods of time. We decided that she was the brightest, strongest, and most beautiful baby in the world. That is why we named her Pantea, meaning "strong and immortal."

I read about Pantea in Soghra's history book. In the time of Cyrus the Great, the commander of the Persian army was a woman named Pantea. The army was maintained at ten thousand men who had been selected and trained from when they were seven years old. The army was called "immortal" because as one warrior was killed or wounded, another immediately replaced him, so the number of the army remained ten thousand men.

Our Pantea grew into a tenacious one-year-old with curly brown hair, emerald eyes, and a porcelain doll face. The boys, Akbar and Darius, were fascinated by her. They stayed close to me, observing everything I did for her.

"Did Pantea get an owie there?" asked Darius, pointing to her exposed nipple as I dressed her.

"No, azizam. That is normal."

Darius lifted his shirt, and Akbar did the same, imitating his older brother's every move.

"Look, I have two normals," Darius announced cheerfully.

Then, pointing to his little brother, he said, "So does Akbar."

Akbar grinned, happy to be included in something worth his brother's excitement.

"*Ayee, Ayee!*" Pantea said.

I quickly picked her up and headed for the potty in the corner. The boys ran ahead of me, making the sound of sirens. I sat her on the potty; the boys and I sat on the floor, waiting. There was a thump, and we all cheered. Pantea got up, and the boys peered into the potty in awe.

"It is cute," said Darius.

"It is cute," said Akbar, in imitation.

"It is dirty, and we cannot touch it, but it is cute," Darius concluded thoughtfully.

Pantea reached two years old with an intense curiosity. My time was consumed physically with the household chores and mentally with answering her unending questions. I always thought her questions were clever and worth asking, so answering them was my pleasure. I had begun reading Soghra's textbooks again, wanting to be ready for Pantea's curiosity.

"Can you count to five?" Saam asked Pantea at dinner.

Everyone stopped eating and looked at Pantea. My little girl stood up from the sofreh and, with her chin in the air, recited her numbers.

"One, two, three, four … six, seven, eight, nine …"

"All right, all right," Saam said, cutting her off while everyone laughed. "So I underestimated you."

Pantea was articulate and taller than her three-year-old Uncle Akbar, so people guessed her age incorrectly. She would proudly hold two fingers up, beaming at them. The person would apologize and quickly say, *"Musha Allah!"* which means "God willed it." For some, the phrase served to ward off the evil eye.

A woman commented on Pantea's eyes.

"Musha Allah, you have the most dazzling green eyes, little one!"

"I know," Pantea sighed exasperatedly.

Embarrassed, I quickly excused us from the woman, whose stare was lecturing me on how to teach my child humility.

"Pantea, jigar tala, it is rude to say 'I know'," I told her gently. "Just say thank you next time."

"But Maman," she whined with a shrug, "I have heard it sooooo many times."

"Even if you hear it a thousand times, the thousand-and-first time you still need to say thank you."

"All right," Pantea drawled.

Pantea began sleeping on the third floor on a cot of her own with Mina, Sana, and Saba. She felt comfortable with them and ready to leave her parents. She used my mattress with the pink rosebud bedding. Farid and I were excited to regain our privacy and return to our neglected game. We were wiser now and exercised more caution.

On my weekly trips to the market, I took Pantea with me in hopes of visiting Fereshteh. She had a son, Nima, who was the same age as Pantea, and another on the way. The two children played together and allowed their mothers to have a pleasant visit.

There was a shady pond behind the shops near Fereshteh's home. I had shown it to her before either of us had children. We visited it before and after we became mothers.

There were two graceful white swans living in the pond. They would swim close to each other, nuzzle, and intertwine their long necks in an endearing manner.

The local boys wondered at the swans' behaviour and reaction, so they threw sticks and stones at them, hoping to find answers to their curiosity.

Two younger boys did equal damage with their naive misunderstanding. They interpreted the swans' mating as aggression and decided to help the female swan.

"Look, Ebi! That one is beating up the other one."

"Oh, no! We need to rescue him."

The two boys threw sticks and stones at the male swan until he dismounted. Neither Fereshteh nor I felt it was our place to enlighten the young boys. We decided to leave it to their parents to attend to that business. Besides, we were savouring the dramatic irony of the situation as we observed the boys showing such conviction.

"I would buy front-row seat tickets to Ebi's wedding night to see the moment of realization as he recalls this encounter with the swans," I said to Fereshteh with a chuckle.

"Yes, the wife will wonder why he suddenly stopped, looked perplexed, and then sighed with his newfound understanding."

We laughed at the absurdity of the picture we were painting.

A change in attitude of the neighbourhood boys did not come soon enough. Eventually the swans disappeared from the pond.

One day, when I called on Fereshteh, an old man came to the wooden gate. He told me that the teacher and his wife had moved to Karaj. Although Karaj was only a forty-five-minute car ride from Tehran, it may as well have been forty-five hours. There was no chance of me visiting her now. The old man told me a promotion had made Agha Nemat move. I was happy for their good fortune but heartbroken at having lost my friend.

"You are the *aroos* of the Piruz woman," the man said, catching me off guard.

I looked at him in confusion. Who was this man? He stepped closer and glared at me as if I had sold him some wet timber. He glanced at Pantea momentarily but turned back on me. His mouth held no teeth, and his skin was like the dessert after a drought – brown and cracked. He was hunched over, and his head rested inches ahead of his neck. He began to shake a finger at me, making me uncomfortable. My upbringing dictated politeness in all situations, so my feet remained glued to the floor.

"That woman had six daughters", he yelled, "and did not name one after my dear wife, God rest her soul."

Pantea pulled at my dress.

"Why is he angry, Maman?"

"He wanted one of your cousins to have the name of his wife, azizam."

Khanum Piruz never made a secret of her distaste for people of this class. She openly criticized them and would never socialize with them. Yet this man felt that she should have named one of her daughters after his wife.

"How do you know Khanum Piruz?" I asked with curiosity.

He looked ashamed suddenly and dropped his finger and his stare. He turned to walk back in through the curtain door.

"You call her Khanum," I heard him mutter.

I remembered that anyone who raised his voice and then talked softly was not trustworthy.

"She killed my boy," said the old man with his back to me and his head hung low. "She killed him the same as if she drove that truck into his motorcycle. If she had not forced my son to fire his friend, the business would not have been cursed. Her greed left those children fatherless."

I was astonished. This man was Agha Piruz – Farid's grandfather. Why had no one mentioned him to me? Well, I suppose I knew why now that I had met him.

"Please, Agha Piruz, I have not introduced myself properly."

He turned to me with a pained expression.

"No need," he said. "I know who you are, and I know what you are up against. That woman will end you, too."

"She means well," I heard myself say, not sure why I was defending her.

The old man bent low and smiled toothlessly at Pantea.

"Farid makes a fine child," he said softly.

"What was your wife's name?" Pantea asked him.

Agha Piruz looked up at me, startled. I shrugged and smiled at him.

"Layla," he answered Pantea.

"You can call me Layla if you want to. I do not mind," said Pantea.

Agha Piruz gasped with delight and hugged his great-granddaughter.

"What is your name, azizam?"

"Pantea, like the soldiers' leader."

"Wow, that is a fine name for a young lady. You keep

your name. I will be happy to call you Pantea. My Layla will be happy too, God rest her soul."

"This is your great-grandfather, Pantea," I said.

He bowed his head towards me, winked at Pantea, and made his way back inside.

"We can visit you next time we come to shop," I said to his back. "I will bring the shirini if you provide the tea."

I saw him nod and raise a hand in acknowledgement before the curtain unfolded behind him.

I took Pantea's hand, and we walked home.

I went into the kitchen to unload the groceries, and Pantea went to the family room, and lay down among the already napping children. I had placed the pot of *kaleh pacheh* to simmer when I heard someone shuffle into the kitchen. I turned around, expecting one of the children had awakened early from their nap.

It was Khanum Piruz, standing on her two feet. My hands flew to my cheeks in surprise, and then I clapped in delight.

"Oh, Khanum," I exclaimed, "it is a miracle. You have gotten your strength back."

"Do not pretend that you are happy for me," Khanum Piruz snapped. "You are glad you will not have to do all the housework yourself."

"Oh no, Khanum," I tried to explain. "I am happy for you that you have your independence back. I know how you missed it."

There was a pause, during which Khanum Piruz actually looked surprised.

"Keep your thoughts to yourself," she said, remembering to be annoyed. "I do not need to hear them."

I had noticed recently that she was holding her own weight more and that I needed to do less. It had only been a matter of time before she was back on her feet. She turned gingerly to go back to her room and then looked as if she remembered something.

"You were back more quickly from the market today," she said accusingly.

Nothing was ever innocent in Khanum Piruz's eyes, but I told the truth anyway.

"I went to visit a friend."

"Female or male?"

"Female, of course," I said defensively, although I knew she trusted me and was being cruel intentionally.

"That Fereshteh girl, married to that poor schoolteacher?"

I was bewildered that she knew despite being bedridden. Khanum Piruz understood my expression.

"Yes, I have my ways of finding out things that affect my family," she said. "I do not want you taking our Pantea to that hovel. Your friend may be your kind, but she certainly is not one of us. I will not have Pantea playing in the dirt with some beggar's brat."

"Please do not judge my friends. They earn their living the same as your sons. Besides, my friend and her family have moved to Karaj, so I will not be seeing them any more."

I eased her mind at the cost of admitting my loss.

"Good. One less *besavad* in our midst."

"She is not illiterate," I said in her defence. "She studied with the help of her husband and got her diploma despite having one child and another on the way."

I was ready to go to battle with this woman for Fereshteh, but at the same time, I felt pity for her ignorance. She did not have more than an eighth-grade education, and neither did her late husband nor the twins. She revered education as the uneducated sometimes do. As frugal as she was, she spent extra money on private school believing that it offered her children the best education.

I heard shuffling in the next room. The children were rising from their naps early, no doubt because of our loud voices. Pantea walked into the kitchen, rubbing her eyes.

"We met my great-grandfather," she said to Khanum Piruz.

Khanum Piruz stared at me in disbelief. I had no rebuttal.

"Things will have to change around here," she muttered.

"What things?" I asked.

"I need to fix this," she said to herself as she shuffled to her room.

"Fix what?" I asked nervously.

"Send Farid to my room when he gets home," she called to me from down the hall.

Poor Farid. When Khanum Piruz asked to see him, it was usually to complain about me. I tried not to give her any reasons, but today I had failed.

Akbar and Darius were next after Pantea to come into the kitchen looking for cuddles and a snack. The rest of the children, from Mina to Soghra, were at Pishraft School. They all arrived home on the bus. Malize was attending the newly opened University of Tehran. I had heard at the market that this was one of Reza Shah's triumphs. She stayed at the university library until late most nights and bussed home or called one of the twins to pick her up.

I no longer envied any of them. My reading the textbooks was enough for me. I was happy in my role as

Pantea's mother. I considered it the most important role that I could have. I was thankful that Pantea had both parents to watch over her.

The front door opened, and I heard Saam call, "Mmmmm! Kaleh pacheh! My favourite."

"Yesterday you said the *lubia polo* on the stove was your favourite," I reminded him.

"Can I help it if every dish you cook is so good that it instantly becomes my favourite?"

He walked straight to the pot and stuck a spoon in for a taste. Farid walked in behind him and took me in his arms for a hello kiss.

"Must you do that in front of me?" Saam said, barely audible with a full mouth. "I am eating here."

Farid and I laughed.

The two brothers went to clean up for the meal as I remembered Khanum Piruz's order.

"Farid joon, your mother wants to see you," I called to him regretfully.

He raised one arm, nodded, and continued down the hall. I remembered, earlier today, Agha Piruz making the same gesture when I suggested another visit. The similarity was endearing.

When the table was set, I called everyone to the sofreh to eat. Everyone except Farid and his mother showed up, waiting eagerly. I told them to start and went to fetch the missing two. As I got closer to her room, I could hear Khanum Piruz's disgruntled voice through the slightly open door.

"Pari is nothing but a nuisance around here," she said. "I am well now, and that girl must go."

My knees softened, and I felt I was about to fall. I braced myself with a hand on the wall. This complaint was serious. She wanted to get rid of me. Outside her door, I froze.

"I am glad you are feeling stronger, Maman, but why not be patient and let all your strength return? Today is the first time you have stood on your own. You do not want to rush things."

Why was Farid commenting on his mother's health instead of how he would never stand for losing me? Where was that statement?

"You are twenty-one years old and so handsome," said Khanum Piruz. "You could have any girl in Tehran that you wanted."

"I have a wife," Farid reminded his mother.

There, he said it. I felt better hearing it from him, ignoring the lack of conviction in his voice.

"She is an orphan, a rag, with no education," Khanum Piruz insisted.

"Whose fault is her lack of education?" Farid said in my defence, though with a weakness that made me shiver. "She is intelligent and sweet and the mother of my child – your grandchild."

The words were perfect.

Khanum Piruz attacked her son mercilessly. "You have done enough harm by causing this family to become fatherless! You need to listen to me, pesaram."

I heard nothing from Farid. She had silenced him. I was starting to feel the floor beneath me dissolve and my body fall through it.

Khanum Piruz's voice softened.

"The child is not the issue. You can keep Pantea. Pari must go."

I could not stand it any longer. I pushed the door open and walked in without permission.

"I do not want to go," I blurted out. "Please, Khanum ..."

Khanum Piruz was sitting on the edge of her bed.

"See what I mean?" she yelled, without missing a beat. "She has no upbringing. She bursts into a room like a child even though she is married and a mother."

"You are talking about sending her away and keeping her child, Maman," Farid said meekly.

"She is not one of us, Farid jaan," Khanum Piruz went on. "She has had our Pantea consorting with beggars."

"No, no, they are not ... I will not ..." I said, desperately, trying to figure out what she wanted to hear.

"She will probably want to send our Pantea to public school."

"No, no," I cried. "You are wrong. I do not care where she goes to school. I mean ... I know she will succeed anywhere she goes because she is so hungry to learn."

"That is what you say now, but when the time comes, I know I will have problems with you."

The more distressed my voice sounded, the calmer hers became in response. I tried to regain some composure and remember what was most important to me.

"Listen, Khanum, get another wife for Farid if you want; I do not mind," I said, ignoring Farid's shocked protest.

He grabbed my arm. I shook it free so Khanum Piruz would see that I was not going to cling to him.

"All I need is a corner where I can live peacefully with my daughter."

"*Our* daughter!" Farid corrected.

I ignored him again. Khanum Piruz was the one to negotiate with. Farid was powerless where she was concerned. One reminder about his father, and he had become mute. I had just now realized this fact as I faced my executioner, alone.

"Please do not disgrace me with a divorce," I begged. "If you kick me out of your house, I have nowhere to go."

"You are going back to your brothers," she said, unmoved. "I already spoke to them before Farid got home, and they consented."

My knees became liquid under me, and the bedpost was too far away. I crumpled to the floor, and Farid was at my side.

"Are you all right?" he asked with concern in his beautiful eyes.

Poor Farid. He could not help me any more than he could help himself. His grandfather had known what I was up against. This woman had the power to bring Farid and me together – or to tear us apart by having one conversation with my brothers.

We held each other's gaze, wishing the world would lock in place and not let anyone come in to ruin it for us. But someone did.

"Get on your feet, girl," Khanum Piruz said, in her usual gruff manner.

I stood up, refusing Farid's hand – his last poor attempt at chivalry. With as much dignity as I could muster, I walked out of Khanum Piruz's room for the final time.

Part 2

You were born with wings, why prefer to crawl through life?

—Rumi

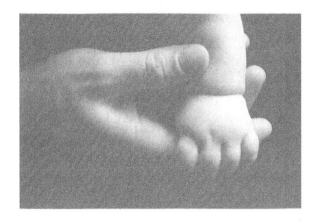

Chapter 12

Divergence (1313 SH)

Just as easily as I had left Baba's home, I returned with my carpet bag in hand. The girls were out, and my brothers were at work. I was grateful to come back when they were not around. Their presence would have only hurt.

I went straight to my room and unpacked my bag. I had not visited this house in the last three years while I lived next door. I walked around my room picking things up, remembering them, and then placing them back.

A sound at the door made me turn. There stood a large white cat as big as a raccoon. It was Kuchulu, but he was not very *kuchulu* any more. He was huge and meowing in a strong voice. I must have left the front door open and he found me. I knelt, and he trotted over to me. I petted him, and he purred. It felt as if no time had passed and as if my past had never existed. Still, it was a comfort to see him. It seemed Kuchulu knew to show up without being asked in my times of grief.

I stood and walked downstairs with Kuchulu at my ankle. I found myself in Baba's room. I did not feel his presence as I had when I was eleven. I picked my favourite poet, Molana, from the shelf, and held it in my hand. Even though I had dreamt of this moment while I was next door, holding the book now did not thrill me as I thought it would.

I felt cheated. When I longed to stay here and read these books, I was torn away from them and made a wife and mother. Now that I longed for nothing more than to be a mother, I was sent back to these books.

I did not want the books any more. I wanted my little girl.

September turned into October, but time did not ease my pain, as was the popular belief. In fact, with time I missed Pantea more until sometimes I thought I was going to burst with grief.

I kept myself busy during the days with housework and during the evenings with reading Baba's books. I had trouble focusing. I would read pages and realize I had not understood any of the passage because my mind had wandered. I missed Pantea the most when the house grew dark and quiet. I would wonder what she did that day, what she ate, what answers they were giving her, or whether they were ignoring her. I was told not to visit, but I wondered if she missed me or asked about me.

The girls did their part to put demands on me, which kept me sufficiently busy. Neither of them spoke of Pantea, which was a relief, but this was perhaps because they knew nothing about her. Neither of them had come to see her when she was born. I had not visited either, even after babies were born in Baba's house.

Shole had twins the same year as I had Pantea – a boy named Saeed and a girl named Shabnam. The following year, she produced a little brother for the twins and named him Reza. The three children were complete replicas of their mother – stout, with dark, straight hair and dark skin.

Nasim remained childless and was not allowed the liberties of a *khale*.

"Just because you cannot have a child of your own does not mean you can yell at mine," Shole said, berating her sister. "They have a mother, you know."

"Then keep control of them," Nasim said through gritted teeth.

Nasim had scolded Shole's toddler, Shabnam, for getting into her purse. Shabnam had spilled its contents all around herself on the kitchen floor. Red lipstick coloured the floor and Shabnam's face, arms, and clothes. She sat in the middle of her creation with a face that beamed with pride as if to say, "Do you like it?"

I walked past the drama and into the front yard. I had never seen lipstick on Nasim, so her owning a red shade of lipstick was very curious. I took the hose and began watering Baba's garden. It was a sunny Friday evening, and the water was bringing out the scent of the plants. I could smell jasmine and pansies right away. Even in October these flowers bloomed in Baba's garden.

Pari

As I walked around, hose in hand, the brick pond caught my attention. We had no use for it, since my brothers had indoor plumbing installed once the twins were born. I now washed the clothes in a deep concrete sink in the bathroom, and the dishes in a similar sink in the kitchen.

The girls had removed Baba's stone pedestal fountain, and stored it behind the fruit trees. It leaned there against the property wall, and I could see it whenever I walked through the trees. The pond was three feet deep and now housed several exotic fish. Apparently the girls liked fish.

Kuchulu, front paws on the edge of the pond, began to meow and slap the water surface.

"Ah, now that you are not frail, you forgot your loyalty and want a fish from the pond?" I accused playfully.

To my surprise, Kuchulu continued in a frenzy, now smacking the water surface and meowing even louder. I dropped the hose and marched over to the pond to shoo him away. As I got closer, Kuchulu meowed softly, leaning into the pond. My attention was drawn to the pond. The fish were swimming near the bottom. Something else was at the bottom – a small child. It was Reza. I leaned over the side and pulled him out. My head had to go into the water so my arms could reach him. I held him to my chest, and right away he coughed up water and began to cry. The water was chilly. I hurried into the house, tore off his wet clothes, and wrapped him in a blanket. The twins came running into the family room when they heard their little brother crying.

Shabnam, remnants of red lipstick on her neck and nose, became instantly attentive. She was willing to fetch whatever I named, including a towel, dry clothes, and hot tea from the samovar.

With enough cuddling, Reza's nerves calmed, and he relaxed in my arms. Soon he became bored of sitting, pushed out of my arms, and was ready to play. His siblings were more than happy to accommodate him.

"Here, Reza, you can play with my dumper truck," Saeed said, handing his prized possession to his little brother.

"You want to colour with me," Shabnam suggested, willing to let him touch her precious colouring pencils.

Escaped tragedy seemed to encourage generosity.

"What happened?" Shole asked, walking into the family room after the storm had passed. "What was the tea for?"

"Reza fell into the pond and almost drowned," Saeed blurted with alarm.

"What?!" Shole screamed, picking up Reza and examining him from top to bottom.

"He is fine, Shole," I said, trying to reassure her.

"I suppose you had something to do with this!" Shole accused correctly. But since Reza and I were the only two with wet hair, it must have been an easy guess.

"If you mean I was the one who pulled him out, yes, but it was Kuchulu who alerted me."

"Why did you not say anything, Shabnam?"

Shabnam shrugged innocently.

"When you got the tea," Shole said, raising her voice, "why did you not tell me?"

"You were busy yelling at Khale, and you told me to never interrupt you."

Shole glared at her. "You pick now to be obedient?" she snapped, storming out of the room with Reza.

Reza was happily holding the dump truck in one hand and a yellow colouring pencil in the other. He grinned at us over his mother's shoulder, head bopping up and down, as he disappeared from the room.

At the dinner table that night, the conversation was about Reza falling into the pond, and Kuchulu saving him. I was fine with Kuchulu getting all the credit.

Coincidentally, Kuchulu was allowed inside after the rescue.

Khale Sara phoned to say she was coming for dinner. That was good news. In the last three years, I saw Khale Sara three times: after Pantea was born, and at her first two birthdays.

Khale Sara seemed to attract disapproving glares and raised eyebrows wherever she went. People were not accustomed to seeing a woman be a successful lawyer and own an elegant home without the help of a husband.

I heard Shole telling Nasim that Khale Sara must have given sexual favours to male lawyers in order to rise to her position. Rahim Agha, although a spiritual man, did everything but pat Khale Sara on the head when speaking about her work. Khale Sara must have been fearless to have lived her life as she wanted to, despite the social reactions.

* * *

"We do not live in a time completely void of successful female lawyers," Khale Sara said in defence of her career choice.

Baba was cleaning the pond and refilling it with water. I had climbed inside and was scrubbing where he could not reach.

"Of course, women can do whatever and be whoever they want to be," Baba answered her, fetching a bucket of water from the ditch outside our gate.

"Women have been practicing law all over the world for the last sixty-six years: Arabella Mansfield of the United States, Eliza Orme of Britain, and Lydia Poet of Italy, to name a few."

"I am convinced. Why do you feel you need to give me so many facts?"

"Not a single man – other than you – respects what I do. The women are worse. You would think they would support their own gender."

"The women are jealous, and the men are afraid of you," Baba said pragmatically. "Why do you care what they think?"

"I do not care, I suppose." Khale Sara said thoughtfully. "I just want them to be wiser."

"I know. Me too."

* * *

I finished making apple stew for dinner and waited impatiently for Khale Sara. I placed a bowl of leftover rice and stew for Kuchulu. The children, draped over the carpet cushions like honey over baklava, woke up from their nap one at a time. I turned the volume up on the radio, which was playing an upbeat folk song.

"Ye gole saye chaman, saye chaman ..." sang the radio.

I washed the children's faces and swayed to the music with each one before setting them down at the table to have their snack. Reza and Saeed giggled as I swung them around, but Shabnam wore a scowl, as it took her longer to fully awaken.

Under my care, the three children sat at the table when they ate, but with their mother, they ate and ran around the house recklessly while making a mess. I had learned to say nothing to Shole. Her generic response to all comments regarding her children was "They are my children, not yours."

Oddly, Nasim and I had something in common. We both longed to have a child of our own. I had tasted the thrill of motherhood, so I knew what I longed for. Nasim could only imagine what it would be like. I could not decide which was more difficult to bear. I was reminded of a poem Baba once read to me: "Happy is the bird who never saw a cage. Happier is the bird that saw it, and escaped."

The apple stew was on the wood stove, keeping warm for dinner. My brothers arrived home, had tea, and disappeared into their rooms until they were called for dinner. The girls had made a habit of being where their husbands were, so they were out of sight as well. That left the three children and me on the carpet cushions, having a tickle fight in between my reading to them.

The doorbell rang, and I jumped up. The children fell away from me like the hold-down posts of a rocket accelerating into the air. I opened the door and saw Khale Sara standing there like a beauty queen with a sweet smile, a bouquet of flowers in one hand and a box of chocolates in the other.

"Salaam, azizam," she said in a sweet voice.

I jumped into her arms, almost making her drop everything.

"Take it easy, Pari joon."

I took the flowers from her and put them in a vase. When I returned with the vase and flowers, she had made herself comfortable on the cushions, allowing the children to climb all over her as if she were a climbing frame. I placed the vase on the low table with the large bowl of fruit, small dishes, and knives. I went back for the tea tray. By the time I served a glass of tea with dates, the boys had lost interest and left the room. Shabnam climbed onto my lap and curled up quietly as I answered Khale Sara's questions.

"Have you seen Pantea?"

"Not since I returned. They said it is best for her if I have no contact."

I did not tell her that I had been begging at their door with no success.

"Are the papers signed yet?"

"Yes. They seemed in a hurry about that."

"Has Farid married that girl?"

"I think so," I said, feeling something tighten around my heart.

"How are you doing?"

"Fine. I keep busy."

With that, a flood of tears ran down my face.

Khale Sara picked up Shabnam from my lap and whispered to her to go play with her brothers. I noticed Shabnam's anxious eyes on me as she left the room. My aunt came and sat close to me on the cushions, placing one arm around me. I felt better but could not stop the tears.

"Pantea will be fine. You have to stop thinking about her."

"Yes, yes, I know," I said between sobs. "Shabnam is a help. Every time I hold her, I feel better."

"Listen to me, Pari joon," Khale Sara said in a serious voice. "You cannot be thinking of your child. You are a child yourself. You need to be in school. How old are you now?"

"Fifteen."

I sniffled, and Khale Sara gave me a handkerchief.

"You used to love school. Do you not miss it?"

I nodded as I blew my nose.

"I will speak to the principal at Movafagh Secondary School and arrange for you to write the placement exam. How would you like that?"

"That would be out of the question," Shole said as she walked in, carrying baby Reza on one hip.

"Why not? She is still school aged," Khale Sara argued.

"That is not the point, Sara joon. We need her at home to help us."

"I can do both," I said, suddenly feeling the old excitement for school.

"Pari joon," Khale Sara said to me, though holding her eyes on Shole, "Shole is a grown woman, and she does not work outside of the home. Certainly she can handle her own chores without you. What has she been doing for the last three years when you were away?"

"Honestly, Sara," Shole said with a sigh, "we did not invite you here to interfere."

"You did not invite me at all. I came to advocate for my sister's child. Farid was a good man, and I knew he would make my niece happy, but his mother ended that. Now she needs to return to school. As you may or may not know, Pari is smart and can excel at anything she puts her mind to."

Khale thinks I am smart! Capable of becoming anything I want!

I expected Shole to speak next, but after an awkward silence, she left the room.

"Now, Pari joon," Khale Sara said to me, "You have the placement exam to prepare for."

At the dinner table, everyone was quiet except the children. Khale Sara praised the apple stew and then fell into silence along with the other adults. My brothers never looked up from their plates until the end of the meal. They retired to the family room to receive their tea. Saeed finished his meal, and played with Kuchulu near the table.

"What is a Yezid?" Shabnam asked.

"*Who* is Yezid," Shole corrected.

I waited for Shole to answer, but she took another mouthful from her plate. The others remained focused on their plates too.

"Yezid was the Umayyad caliph who hurt Prophet Muhammad's family," I told Shabnam. "Hussein, grandson of the Prophet, refused to declare allegiance to him, to be his friend."

"Were you listening to your grandfather's radio, Shabnam joon?" Khale Sara asked.

"Yes. There was a fight in Mashhad, and everyone was yelling, 'The Shah is a new Yezid!'"

Shole giggled.

"Shabnam joon, the fight was a rebellion at the Imam Reza shrine," Khale Sara confirmed, looking sternly at Shole. "They have been repeating the story for days on the radio. The local police would not enter the mosque, but after four days, the Shah sent an army."

Hundreds and thousands were killed, injured, and imprisoned in the uprising, both protesters and villagers. Many soldiers felt guilty for entering the mosque. Two were executed for not following orders, and one killed himself.

"Sara joon," Shole said with a whine, "let us not talk about morbid things at the dinner table, all right?"

Her voice became very high on the last word.

"When I am grown up, I am going to go to a revelliom," said Reza.

"*Rebellion*," Shole corrected.

"I hope not," I said to Reza. "I will be very sad if you do."

"Do not worry, *Ameh* joon. I will not get killed. Saeed will be there with me."

Saeed looked up when he heard his name, but he returned to petting Kuchulu.

Khale Sara arranged for me to write the placement exam. She picked me up and drove me to Movafagh Secondary School. She waited until I came out of the examination room before handing me something wrapped in brown paper.

"It is for your first day of school, Pari joon."

I unwrapped the paper, and there was a new, neatly folded school uniform.

"Your old one is probably too small for you. You seem to get taller every time I see you. I think you will be as tall as Nargis."

Comments like that were always welcome. I relished hearing that I was becoming more and more like my mother.

"Mamnoon, Khale," I said, giving her a hug.

Three years out of school, and I was placed in grade eleven – one year ahead for my age. I owed it to reading all those "borrowed" textbooks in secret.

Khanum Felfeli, the secretary of Movafagh School, phoned with the news.

"Could you tell me if Kobra Sultani is in my class?" I asked.

"Yes, azizam, I see her name on the list."

"It is October," I said timidly. "The students are a month ahead of me in their lessons. What if I cannot catch up?"

"You are Pari Pushtekar, correct?"

"Yes, Khanum."

"You are the student who was advanced two grades. I think you can catch up a month."

"You remember me?"

"Of course, azizam. Usually I remember the students who stand out in a good way … or in a bad way," she said with a chuckle.

On my first day, I came early and took a seat in the back to be less visible. As the others walked in, I recognized each student. I remembered them from when we were classmates and from when they teased me about being married. We were once friends, but now they looked at me as if I did not belong there. I wished Agha Nemat were still at this school. I busied myself by slowly taking a notebook and pencil out of my school bag.

Kobra entered the classroom; I relaxed. Her walk demanded that the path be cleared for her. I watched students step aside as she walked a straight line through them. She spotted me but was composed. I supposed she had asked Khanum Felfeli about me – the same as I had asked about her. Kobra may have heard that I had been turned out of my neighbour's house and sent home. She sat beside me with that familiar sympathetic look in her eyes. It was like old times again. We did not talk about the past three years. Once again we were friends and school was the highlight of my days.

As time went on, the routine of doing assignments and reading poetry with Kobra filled me with an old, familiar contentment. The better I did in school, the more encouragement I received from my teachers. Khanum Sadaf, my new math teacher, was especially generous. She was willing to give me extra help before and after school when I needed it.

One day as I was leaving her classroom, I thanked her for the extra explanations and apologized for taking up her time.

"I am available to all of my students outside of class," Khanum Sadaf said. "Not every student uses that opportunity. I am glad you do."

"Perhaps because I was away for so long, I need the extra help and they do not," I said.

"I mark all the papers, remember," Khanum Sadaf said with a knowing smile. "You are wise to seek help."

The occasional taunting from the other girls, mostly Homa and Sekine, became bearable. I decided that they did not know much beyond their books. My education had taken a detour to teach me the pain of childbirth, the rewards of motherhood, and the horror of losing my baby.

These experiences were mine alone.

They could not see, inside my head, the memories that I kept hidden for my own survival. All they could see was a classmate that had left and now was sitting among them.

Courses were finished, exams were written, and I received my diploma at the end of two years. Khale Sara was hopeful that I would go to university. I was in the process of deciding on a profession when a suitor came to call on me.

Gamble everything for love, if you are a
true human being. Half-heartedness does not
reach into majesty.

—Rumi

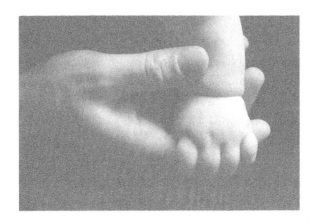

Chapter 13

Mahmood (1315 SH)

Mahmood was over forty years old and a mechanical engineer. He owned a mansion in Sa'adat Abad, up the hill from us. That fascinated the girls. He had made it very clear that he wanted to start a family. He had heard that I had already had a baby, and he wanted me to bear a child for him. I wanted another baby too.

When I opened the door for Mahmood, I spotted Kuchulu hiding under the honeysuckle bush. He usually came to the door as soon as I opened it, so it was strange for him to keep his distance.

Mahmood had thick, black, curly hair, and he was short

enough that I could see the top of his head had no hair. His face looked as if everything was too big for it. His fingers were short, thick sausages, and despite his height, he had very long feet. I decided that my suitor was a replica of a circus clown. I left the room hoping this was a bad dream.

I was wrong. This was my new reality. After a long goodbye with Kuchulu, I moved to the house on the hill, carpet bag in hand.

The house had marble tiles on the floors and on the walls. The ceilings were very high in every room. There were immense carved pillars from floor to ceiling like those in Persepolis. Silk carpets were everywhere – on floors, on walls, and on furniture. There was a waterfall from the second floor to the main entrance. At the bottom were exotic fish, oblivious to their surroundings.

Mahmood planned a magnificent wedding and invited many people who were strangers to me. Everything was elaborate, but the only people who were impressed were the girls. The other guests seemed accustomed to this level of extravagance.

No one spoke to me about a wedding dress, so I wore my white dress, which got no comments either way. When Khale Sara arrived, she took one look at me and tried very hard to hide her disappointment. I was not sure which one of the numerous failures she had noted: the white dress, the plain hairdo, or how utterly out of place I looked in this ceremony.

My own regret was that the day of my graduation from Movafagh Secondary School became the day of my second wedding. I thought it curious when Shole asked me the date of my graduation ceremony. She had never shown any interest in things that concerned me. She must have forgotten the date, though, since she planned the wedding for the same day.

Before the guests arrived, Mahmood asked me for my wedding band. I retrieved it from my red pouch and handed it to him. I thought of all the possible reasons why he may have wanted the golden band. I decided to believe my favourite – that he did not want the past to interfere with our future. I was consoled with that idea until he placed my golden band back on my finger during our wedding ceremony. I was confused at first, but then I decided that the band was useless in the velvet pouch. Now it served as a symbol that I was married again.

The wedding night consisted of Mahmood lying on top of me and panting until he was done. He rolled to his side of the bed and fell asleep with his back to me. I was still in my wedding dress. He had not seemed to have any use for my lips or my breasts.

As I lay there considering this man, I concluded that Mahmood had spent half of his life in school and the other half working as a mechanical engineer. It made sense that his approach to me would be mechanical.

There were many specialized servants in the house: Samad Agha, the chauffeur; Jafar Agha, the gardener; Khanum Parvin, the cook; and Khanum Sophia, the housekeeper. Mahmood had promised me a nanny once we had children.

Since I did not need to do any chores, my days were spent alone with what seemed to be a sea of books on endless shelves. They were housed in a grand library with overheight ceilings. The heavy, solid maple doors opened gracefully into the library, and on the opposite wall, French doors opened to a lush, fragrant garden. Reading the multitude of books and strolling through the massive garden became my pastime.

As I read and learned, I thought about my teacher, Khanum Sadaf. I wondered whom she was teaching now. I wondered what it would be like to be a teacher and have a new group of students each year. I imagined helping them learn and get excited about the future.

* * *

I had gone to Khanum Sadaf's classroom after my last exam to say goodbye.

"You will be teaching this same material all over again next year and the next. Do you not get tired of repeating it?"

Khanum Sadaf gave me that knowing smile. I knew she loved her job. I wanted to hear from her why this was so.

"Sure, it is the same material, but I will be teaching it to new students. Those students have not learned this material yet, and it is my privilege to be the one to present it to them."

Khanum Sadaf's answer satisfied me.

* * *

I appreciated my isolation. It was the first time that I had only myself for company, and I savoured it. It allowed me to reflect and get to know myself. Any topic that I was interested in, I could find a book on it somewhere in that library. My education continued in a self-directed way.

Somehow, the four adults that worked on the property, inside and out, efficiently managed to stay out of my sight. The house would have been completely silent, except there was a radio in almost every room. I turned them all on so I would have company when I walked from room to room.

I knew a child would cheer up this big, empty house.

It was the beginning of summer, and I was in the library, lounging on the sofa with a book. I opened the tall French doors to the garden and welcomed the fresh air that rolled in. With it, the scent of jasmine and honeysuckle drifted in.

I got up to change books from the shelves when my attention went to the radio.

"A war broke out yesterday, July 7, between Communist China and the Empire of Japan," the announcer said.

I ran to the radio and turned up the volume.

"The battle began near the city of Beijing," the announcer continued. "It is an open-warfare battle, and China appears to be at a disadvantage."

People were dying in battle. My problems seemed small in comparison.

Most evenings, I was told Mahmood had called to say he was working late. Dinner was served to me at the grand dining table that seated twelve. I ate there alone.

Despite Mahmood's absence during the day, he would still show up late in the evening, pump me full of his sperm, and prove he was dedicated to his goal. Although I did not appreciate his manner, I was looking forward to having a baby.

Every month that I bled, I became disappointed. When

we had to abstain from sex, Mahmood knew another month had failed. I tried to help by keeping my activity level down, and even taking a nap during the day. I refrained from reading exciting books to stay calm and reduce stress. Nothing helped.

I began yearning for the company of others. One night when Khanum Parvin brought my plate, I asked her to join me, but she looked startled.

"That would not be appropriate, Khanum," she said firmly.

"Then may I eat with you in the kitchen?" I asked.

She looked horrified at that suggestion.

"That is simply not done!" she said with a frown.

Her behaviour and words seemed to be that of a servant's, but somehow I felt the power was in her hands.

A year passed, and no baby arrived. Mahmood was no longer gentle. Sex became his chance to release his frustration, leaving me in pain when he was done. I came to hate when he entered the room, and I felt helpless to escape his violence. Talking to him only made him more aggressive.

One evening he came home and just went to sleep. I was relieved.

In the morning, he announced he was going to divorce me. We were seated, as usual, at either end of the long breakfast table, so I could barely see his expression. Mahmood had insisted on this seating arrangement from the start. I noticed he had timed the dropping of this bomb for the end of breakfast so there would be no opportunity for discussion. But I had things to say.

"It will be humiliating for me to return to my father's home after a second divorce," I said, trying to appeal to his sense of decency.

"I was clear from the start. I was marrying to have a child, and you have not held up your end of the bargain."

"What makes you think I am responsible?" I asked, immediately regretting it.

"How dare you?" he growled, standing up with his ten sausages planted firmly on the table. "You are insinuating that I cannot impregnate you?"

"W ... well, it seems to me that if I have become pregnant before and you have never ... made a woman pregnant, then perhaps the reason is ... with you and not with me."

Mahmood intentionally walked the ten steps to my end of the table, slowly. I began to wonder if the reason why we saw each other only in bed and at the breakfast table was so he could look down on me.

"I picked you out of rubble," he declared. "I can return you to that same rubble. Do not act proud. You had nothing when you came to me."

I noticed one of his hands had made a fist, but I was on fire.

"Everyone comes to this world with nothing," I said, ironically referring to one of his books on philosophy. "We turn and turn around ourselves like a silkworm. We make our own cocoon until we have our precious silk, whatever that may be to each of us."

Mahmood stood in silent anger. It was not clear whether he understood what I had said. Regardless, he turned on his heels, picked up his briefcase, and marched out the door. That was the last time I saw Mahmood.

To love is human. To feel pain is human. Yet to still love despite the pain is pure angel.

—Rumi

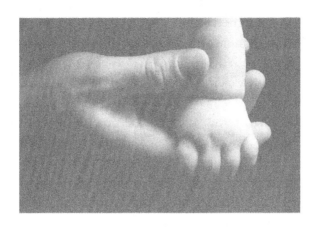

Chapter 14

Abaas (1316 SH)

I arrived at Baba's gate that evening. I got out of the black Benz, thanked Samad Agha for the ride, and walked back into Baba's house, carpet bag in hand. Kuchulu happily greeted me in the front yard and received a generous helping of affection. When I stood up, I noticed many changes. There was a new Cabriolet in the garage. There was a new garage. Inside, silk and wool Persian carpets lay on tiled floors instead of dirt floors covered with wicker. I peeked into the kitchen to ensure that dinner was made, and it was – on a gas stove. Gone was the wood stove. An icebox stood proudly next to the sink. Our candlestick phone had been replaced by a shiny black desk-set telephone. In the hall off the kitchen, there stood a magnificent grandfather clock. The details in the dark wood were impressive. It stood taller and wider than me. In the living room were new furniture and new tapestry. My brothers' business must have done exceptionally well that year.

I continued to my room, unpacked, and laid on my bed. The familiarity was soothing. Getting reacquainted with my room was becoming second nature to me now. Just as I sank into my solitude, the girls materialized at my door. Shole leaned on one side, arms crossed and an impish look on her face. Nasim stood beside her, arms hung heavy and a bland expression on her face.

"Oh look, Nasim. Crazy Pari is back," Shole said.

Nasim, of course, remained silent, but her eyes were fixed on me.

"Salaam," I greeted them with a bow of my head.

I remained hopeful that if I continued to treat them with respect, eventually they would reciprocate.

"Nasim, how long do you think Crazy Pari will be with us this time?" Shole asked.

I heard the front door open, and the girls flew to greet their husbands.

When I went down for dinner, Shole was wearing new clothes and jewels. At dinner, I congratulated my brothers on their good fortune, but they looked uncomfortable. Shole changed the subject.

"Why did you leave Mahmood, Pari joon?" she asked.

She knew better than to call me Crazy Pari in front of my brothers. Apparently Shole did not know that the divorce had been Mahmood's choice. My pride kept me from correcting her.

"Nasim joon," Shole said in a high voice, "do you not think a person giving up that kind of lifestyle would have to be crazy?"

Amir slapped the table with an open hand, which startled me. He picked up his spoon and fork, and continued to eat with his head down.

"He seemed like a generous man, right Ali?" Shole deliberately continued.

"Pass the sabzi," Ali said – code for "stop talking", which she did.

Ali hated sabzi.

Back in my room that night, before my eyes closed, I lay in my bed, staring at the ceiling. I recounted this second marriage: a life of leisure for a year, boundless reading material, a chance to see how the extravagantly rich live, and the realization that it does not necessarily bring happiness.

The girls thought I was crazy to give it up, and I let them. I was glad to be home. There were still books I wanted to read and reread from Baba's collection. It seemed that I was never home long enough to get through all of them. This time was no exception.

Khale Sara came for a visit one morning. I was thrilled to see her. The girls stayed out of the family room and minded the children while we visited. It was out of character, but I appreciated it. I immediately brought in the tea tray and sat beside her on the cushions. After the traditional inquiry into everyone's health, Khale Sara began the real conversation.

Pari

"So how did he treat you?" she asked, looking intensely into my eyes.

"It was not so bad, Khale," I said with a laugh to convince her.

She did not believe me. Khale Sara was too smart to accept a lie.

"Did he beat you?" she asked, apprehensive about hearing what she feared the most.

"No," I said firmly to dispel unnecessary anxiety.

"Well, what was the problem?"

"He did not make me pregnant, and that was the only thing he had wanted from me."

Saying it out loud hurt.

"That was it?"

"Unfortunately, yes."

"Panah bar Khoda!" she sighed, looking to the ceiling. "He was shooting blanks."

"Yes. Yes, he was," I agreed quietly.

Khale Sara's head spun towards me. After staring at me in shock, she burst out laughing. I, in my misery, joined her. It made me feel better. It seemed she did not expect me to understand her comment.

"You have grown up, my little Pari joon."

"Some of the books in his library do contain useful information."

"Apparently they do," she said with a wide grin.

"Too bad he did not read any of them."

"How do you know?"

"The bindings were tight; the pages unwrinkled. The intention of the books must have been to impress – like everything else in that house."

I told Khale the exchange between Mahmood and me over our last breakfast together. She let me finish before telling me what she had found out about Mahmood.

"The story is", Khale Sara whispered, although we were alone in the room, "that he was married before, and is now asking around to marry again. He will not accept that the fault is with him. He believes that if he looks long enough, eventually he will find a woman he can impregnate."

"Too bad Shole did not know this before she and Ali accepted Mahmood."

"Who could resist such a life-changing mahr?" Khale Sara said, but then looked regretful.

"What mahr?" I asked. "I did not see any mahr."

"Yes, you did, Pari joon. You just did not know you were looking at it."

We finished sipping our tea. I poured us another glass.

"Have you given any thought to continuing your education?" Khale Sara asked.

"No," I lied.

* * *

I talked to Kobra after I returned home, and she told me that she was studying to be a nurse. Sekine had taken some business courses and was working in her parents' shop.

"How about Homa?" I asked Kobra.

"She was married the same time you were, and she has a little baby."

"Mobarak!" I cried.

I was happy for Homa, but there was an ache inside

of me that would not go away. I had waited month after month for a year to become a mother again. I had prepared myself for holding my baby and filling my days with the tasks of motherhood. Mahmood may have been angry, but my own disappointment was great. I found myself longing for what Homa had – not what the other girls had.

*　*　*

"I want to be a mother more than anything," I admitted to Khale Sara.

"In that case, do you want to try again? With a nice man."

"Khale!"

"This man is a tailor. He is humble and gentle and will not hurt you."

"I just got settled in my room. I want some peace," I said, stalling.

"You will have peace with him."

"Did the girls set you up to this?"

Khale Sara looked hurt.

"No," she said soberly. "They have nothing to gain this time. Not from this man."

"What do you mean?"

"Never mind. You will not have peace here – not with those two. Abaas Tabriz is not well off, but he makes a living. He will take care of you."

"Why are you encouraging me to get married – for the third time – when you have not wanted to be married at all?"

Khale looked down at her tea glass. I was thinking of an appropriate apology, but she was quicker.

"I did want to marry. I loved a man once – and still do, even though he is gone. Now I understand him. He was wonderful, and I knew I would be happy with him."

"Why did you not marry him?"

"He was already married."

"Oh," I said, disappointed at the way life treats people.

"I want happiness for you, Pari joon," Khale said, returning to the present.

"What is so special about this man that you are selling him to me?"

"Oh, I am not selling him," Khale Sara said, adopting a noble tone. "I am presenting him. Abaas Tabriz happens to be a sayyid."

I was impressed, but I tried to appear aloof.

"I know the family," Khale continued. "Khanum Tabriz, Abaas' mother, is well known, and respected in the community."

"Does Abaas want to get married?" I asked. "Have you told him about me? Does he accept that this will be my third marriage?"

"Yes, yes, and yes."

"Then there is something wrong with him," I concluded, setting my tea glass in the tray and leaning back against the cushions.

"Nothing is wrong with him," Khale Sara said softly. "He has an open mind."

We sat in silence for a while. It seemed quiet despite there being four adults and three children elsewhere in the house. Kuchulu had been lying beside my cushion but was disturbed when I leaned back. He got up, slowly stretched his long body, and climbed onto my lap in his usual carefree manner.

"I do not care if he is poor," I began calmly, building to a crescendo. "I do not even care if he is not handsome. I want someone who has a mind of his own. I do not want someone who only has his own mind. I want a baby. I want a family of my …" I stopped before the tears came.

"My poor Pari joon!" Khale Sara put an arm around me and rocked me gently.

It was comforting to be cuddled by Khale. I imagined this was how it would have felt with my mother. Khale Sara was not usually physically affectionate, so I appreciated her effort.

There in the comfort of her embrace, I considered my options.

"Does 'presenting' mean I can say no?" I asked.

"That is right. It also means you can say yes. You do not want to live in this household. You want a home of your own."

I trusted Khale Sara and felt empowered that I had a choice. I decided to try again.

"I am willing to meet him," I said.

Khale Sara told me she would arrange it. First he would come for a visit, and we could chat. We could meet as many times as I wanted, to be sure. If both of us were in favour of proceeding, then plans would be made for a wedding. I imagined wearing my white dress for a third time and found the idea comical.

Khale Sara told the girls about another suitor coming

to see me, and left. Shole remained civil until Khale Sara was gone.

In the kitchen, the children ate their lunch and lay down in the family room for their nap. When they were settled down, they called me to read to them, which I relished. When I returned, the girls had already filled their plates and were eating at the kitchen table. I poured myself some rice and stew, and sat at the table.

"Why do you want to put yourself through that again, Crazy Pari?" Shole said bluntly.

"Every girl dreams of having her own home and family," I said. "I am still hopeful that I can have that."

"You do not know what you are doing," Shole yelled, escalating without warning. "Nasim, do you think Crazy Pari is making a mistake?"

Nasim nodded without looking up from her plate. I felt her pain. For a woman, life needed to be filled either with a career, like Khale Sara, or with children, like Shole. Nasim and I yearned for a purpose in our lives.

"Your brothers should have been consulted," Shole said as if she were hurt. "Sara does not have the right to make arrangements behind their back."

"That never stopped you," Nasim whispered.

"What did you say?" Shole demanded, turning to her sister.

"What is upsetting you?" asked Nasim, watching her fork push the food around her plate. "That Sara planned this or that you did not?"

Shole's fury turned to Nasim, so I quietly slipped out of the kitchen. With the girls, it was difficult to tell who was winning the argument.

I entered my room and found Shabnam jumping on my bed.

"Shabnam joon, do not jump on the bed. The feather mattress might tear. There would be feathers everywhere, and I would have to buy another mattress. Besides, you may fall off the bed and bump your head."

Shabnam quickly sat on the bed and apologized. I sat beside her and put one arm around her shoulder.

"Ameh joon?"

"Yes, azizam," I said, loving being called Ameh.

"There is a girl at school who teases me and makes the other girls laugh at me."

"If she is trying to upset you, she is only rewarded if you get upset."

"I hate her."

"You do not hate her."

"Yes I do," Shabnam said, facing me so I saw how serious she was.

"Tell me, if you saw her lying on the street, bleeding from the head, would you run to help her?"

"Of course," Shabnam said with conviction.

"Well, then you do not hate her."

We sat there for a while as Shabnam considered this new point of view. She stood on her knees, gave me a hug, and left to get ready for bed.

* * *

The day of the suitor's visit arrived, and I made myself presentable. My darling Pantea had not made any effect on me physically. I felt confident in my black slacks and button-down orange blouse, courtesy of the Piruz family. I brushed my long, curly brown hair and tied it with the yellow ribbon. I felt pretty. I decided to refrain from makeup and just put on a little raspberry-scented lip gloss.

Farid and Mahmood came into my mind, but I chased them away. What was past was past, and today was a new beginning. I was keeping my head clear for new possibilities.

"If you fail," Baba had said, "and only the failure comes into your head when you try again, then you are sure to fail again."

When I remembered those words, I realized it was the first time in six years that I had felt Baba's presence. I was sure that the decision I made about this suitor would have Baba's blessing.

The doorbell rang, and I opened it to find a tall, slim man whose face was pleasant despite a long, thin nose and thin lips. His dark eyes looked kind, and he bowed his head when he said hello. My eyes fell on Kuchulu, who was affectionately leaning against and caressing his leg.

Abaas held his hat in one hand and a bouquet of red roses in the other. I had read that white roses symbolize purity, yellow roses represent friendship, and red roses mean love. I thought it was presumptuous of him to bring red roses to a first meeting, but I dismissed it as optimism.

I invited him in, and led him to the living room. I went to the kitchen and put the flowers in a vase. I placed the vase on the tea tray and brought the ensemble into the living room. Abaas stood up from the sofa as I entered the room. I set the tray on the low table and sat in a chair across from him.

I, too, had acted with optimism by putting a bowl of noghl on the tea tray. Although noghl is a popular sweet for a tea tray, it is also a white wedding confectionery that the bride and groom are showered with to symbolize a sweet future together. I had missed it the first two times, but I hoped that this time it would bring us luck.

We spoke about his job and what he sewed. We talked about my previous two marriages, but he did not bolt. He was gentle, as Khale Sara had claimed. His voice was calm but strong. He knew what he wanted, and he spoke about the future with determination. I liked that he had dreams.

"There is not much that I can offer right now," he said, looking down at his hands.

Then he looked up with his dark eyes full of hope.

"I have started my own business. I did not like working for someone else, having them take the profit, and leaving me with a beggar's share. I know my business will do well. Soon we could build our own home. I am renting a little shack in Karaj now, but the future looks bright for us."

He was already referring to himself and me as "us". It made him look positive and in control. I felt safe.

"Karaj," I said, remembering Fereshteh Nemat had moved there. "I would like living there."

"Great!" he said excitedly.

"Do you want children?" I asked, really wanting to know if he could make me pregnant.

"Yes, I love children."

His nervous downward glance must have been from the thought of us having sex. I liked a man with humility.

Abaas was respectful and wanted children. Now that the choice was mine, I realized I did not have a very long list of criteria for choosing a husband. Khale Sara approved of him. I felt Baba in the room – saw his smiling eyes looking at me. I felt at peace with Abaas.

I said yes.

In your light I learn how to love. In your beauty, how to make poems. You dance inside my chest where no-one sees you, but sometimes I do, and that sight becomes this art.

—Rumi

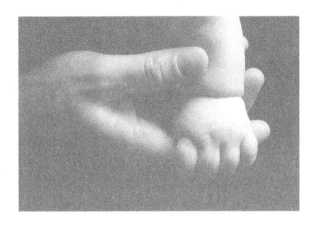

Chapter 15

Benevolent (1316 SH)

Khale Sara took over the preparations for the wedding ceremony with great enthusiasm. She held it in her garden, even though it was smaller than Baba's, and decorated it magnificently. She hung many cheerful lanterns from the trees, pillars, and porch. There were several tables with white tablecloths, and chairs tied with bows. The guests were close relatives, but my brothers and their wives did not show up. I knew the girls were not happy about this arrangement but felt hurt that my brothers were not there.

In all the commotion, I had forgotten to say goodbye to Kuchulu. This would be the third time I left him, but secretly I hoped I would not return. I trusted that he would be cared for in Baba's home.

Abass' mother, Khanum Tabriz, the only family he had, was present but quiet. I was not sure if she was shy, reserved, or discontented. She was the female version of her son: tall and slim, with thin facial features. My attention was drawn to her exceptionally large hands. They looked like a man's hands. My hands were large as well. I was glad that I had this in common with my mother-in-law.

"Do you play the piano, Khanum Tabriz?" I asked her.

She looked at me with a frown and shook her head. I decided it was not as exciting as I thought, having large hands in common.

The meal was catered and delicious. Khale Sara was an animated hostess, moving from one table to another, keeping the mood cheerful. The guests were drawn to her and began mirroring her enthusiasm.

An instrumental trio composed of a santur, dombak, and sitar played in a corner of the garden. Persian melodies filled the air with sweet nostalgia. The repertoire ranged from folk songs to current artists like Mahvash – a performer of risqué songs in cabarets, radio, and movies. Her lyrics were popular because they spoke of the problems of the common people. When the older generation recognized her music, Khale got some disapproving glances. As usual, she accepted the objections and sustained her support of risk-takers.

The trio played a rendition of "Gole Gandom" that made me gasp in delight. When my eyes found Khale Sara, she was looking at me with that sweet smile. I know we were both remembering Baba at that moment. The trio did a fine job of producing the spirit of the music. I recalled my own performance of it on the piano and Baba's awestruck expression.

"What are you thinking?"

It was Abaas sitting beside me in a white jacket and dark pants. He looked handsome.

"You were smiling, looking as though you were a thousand miles away," he said calmly.

"I was remembering my father. He would have liked you."

"I would have been honoured to meet him."

"He is with us tonight. He can see how wonderful you are. He told me to tell you how handsome you look in your suit."

I made him blush.

"I chose a white jacket to match you," he told me.

"Good choice."

We exchanged glances, and we exchanged words. We were aware of one another and enjoyed each other's company. I had learned not to take any of these for granted.

Of all my weddings, this one was my favourite.

*   *   *

My wedding dress for the evening was a surprise. Khale Sara pulled me into her room before the guests arrived and stood me in front of her full-length mirror. From her closet she pulled out the prettiest wedding dress I had ever seen. It looked like a long satin hourglass, with sheer fabric and lace weaving in and around the sleeves and the bottom.

"Khale, this is too much," I whispered.

"Nothing is too much for you, Pari joon."

"You have already made so much effort on this wedding. You should not have bought me a dress, too."

"I did not buy it."

I was puzzled. She held the dress up to me and nodded her approval. She helped me pull it over my head and let it fall down. It fit perfectly. I felt exquisite in it. Khale Sara was standing behind me as we both stared at my reflection in her mirror.

"How did you know my size?" I asked in disbelief. "A tailor could not have done better, I am sure."

"This dress belonged to your mother," Khale Sara confessed.

My hands flew to my cheeks. I spun around to face her. I could not form any words. I whirled back to gape at my reflection. My hands slowly moved over the pearls, the lace, and the satin. I imagined my mother wearing this dress and standing next to Baba. I looked past my reflection and saw that Khale Sara was crying.

"You look like her, Pari joon," Khale Sara sobbed.

I turned and embraced her. I realized I was missing someone I only dreamed about, but she was missing someone she knew. I had many questions as teardrops rolled down my cheeks. Khale Sara grabbed a handkerchief for herself and handed one to me.

"Your mother gave this dress to me after her wedding and said it was her wish that I wear it at mine. It was the only thing I owned of hers, and after her death, it became even more precious to me. As time went on, I realized that I had resigned to remain unwed. When they married you to Farid, it was almost a joke – a child of twelve given to a household with almost a dozen children to be their ..."

Khale cursed and then looked sorry that she had.

"I already know the reason I was married to Farid. On my last day in the Piruz home, Shakiba told me the end of the conversation between her mother and the girls. I had missed hearing it because Khanum Piruz was irritated and Nasim whispered to me to go home."

We both shrugged as if on cue.

"For the second wedding, I was sure that rich donkey would buy you an extravagant gown. I was sorry when I saw you in your plain white dress. I picked Abaas for you because he is a good man. I know now that I will never wear this gown, but until today it was difficult for me to let it go. Seeing you shine in it now, I know I am doing the right thing. It is what Nargis would have wanted."

We hugged again and shed more tears. We cleaned our faces and put on our makeup.

* * *

At the end of the party, we thanked everyone in turn for coming to celebrate with us. I gave an extra-long hug to Khale Sara and walked with my new husband to our taxicab. The guests threw noghl at us until we reached the cab. It both startled and thrilled me. We ducked into the cab, giggling and feeding each other noghl that had landed on our laps, in my veil, and in Abass' thick hair.

The forty-five-minute drive went by slowly. The conversation between us had decreased to me asking closed-ended questions, and Abaas terminating them with a yes or a no. I could not stop wondering how this man handled a woman in bed.

As it turned out, I had nothing to worry about. Although he was not passionate like Farid, he was not mechanical like Mahmood. He was sweet and gentle, and he let me lead to avoid disappointing me.

I can live with that, I thought, lying beside him and listening to his even breathing in the dark.

Your task is not to seek for love, but merely to seek and find all the barriers within yourself that you have built against it.

—Rumi

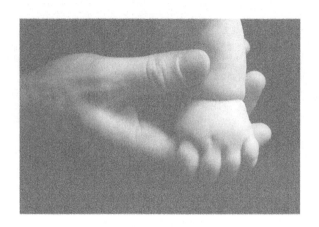

Chapter 16

Connected (1316 SH)

I was in charge of my own home for the first time – a kagel home with a wooden fence. I would make breakfast for the two of us. Abaas would pick up bread from the local baker, Aref Agha. We ate together, making sexual jokes in anticipation of our next interlude. Each morning, Abaas took his leather sewing bag and left for work, while I stayed home to do the usual chores. He had some regular customers who called on him to do sewing jobs in their homes, and he got more projects through referrals.

The curtain entrance allowed a cool breeze to enter and refresh our one-room retreat. There was a cot, a kerosene lamp, a wood stove, and a table with two chairs. It was enough for us. I did not entertain, and we did not have children yet, so it was our little corner of heaven. Abaas had suggested we wait until his business became more stable before entering the world of parenthood, and I warily agreed.

Here in Karaj, I wore a chadore when I went out. In Tehran, the elderly women who were *momen* wore hijab. I had noticed that in this small village, women were free to choose hijab, so most of them wore a chadore. I followed in step. I used the same chadore I prayed with, and I tried not to get it dirty.

I busied myself with small errands that I created. There was a metalworker near us where I had taken our few copper dishes for him to polish. I went to pick them up from his store, and he quoted the price as seventy toman. His son had placed the dishes on the counter and was waiting for me to pay. I knew the price should have been less than one tenth of his quote.

"That is too much money for *sefid kardan*," I protested. "Would a copper dealer buy these dishes from you for that amount?"

"That is the price, Khanum," the ironworker said, unmoved.

I looked at this thin, darkly tanned man who was seated on a wooden crate just inside his doorway. He was polishing another piece of copper with a rag, seemingly oblivious to me.

"Keep them," I said, turning to walk out of his store.

"Khanum!" the metalworker exclaimed, suddenly on his feet. "You need to pay for these. I have done the job."

"I do not want them. Sell them to someone, and keep the money."

I walked into the fresh air and wondered what we would eat off of that night. A short walk down the street, I found a shop which had kitchenware piled high on either side of the entrance. I walked in and immediately picked out a set of china plates for ten toman. I knew they were not practical, especially with children in our future, but I felt confident that our children could learn to be careful. Then I saw a Pyrex pot for cooking rice. It was priced at thirty toman. I could see the *tadeeg* forming at the bottom through the glass and take it off the heat when it was golden. I would never burn the tadeeg with this pot. I paid and came out.

As I headed home, I saw a stonecutter on the opposite side of the dirt road. He was seated on a stool outside of his store, cutting a pot. The street was empty except for a few boys playing with a football. Their school was after lunch. I crossed the street and asked the stonecutter to show me a medium-sized pot for *khoresht*.

"I want it hand cut so it is thicker. Do not give me a machine-cut pot. They are too thin, so they break easily."

"Eh? You seem to know your pots, Khanum," said the stonecutter, smiling and showing very few teeth.

I had worked with many stone pots in different kitchens, it was true. He got up from his stool – a skinny little man with white hair only around his ears. There were pots on the floor, on hooks, on shelves, and all around the shop. He picked one and handed it to me. It was conical, with a small, flat top for a lid, and a wide, flat bottom where it sat. The substantial weight immediately told me that it was hand cut. I lifted the lid, and, sure enough, the walls were thick with the subtle texture of hammer-and-chisel cuts.

"I will take this," I said triumphantly.

"Seezdah toman, lotfan," said the stonecutter with a mouth that stuck out like a fish's.

"Seezdah toman?" I repeated his quote of thirteen toman, hoping he would hear the alarm in my voice and come down in price.

"Bale, Khanum, seezdah toman!"

He looked as if he were about to kiss a girl. I felt sorry for the girl. Thirteen toman seemed reasonable, and I had never picked up the art of bargaining from Baba, who always paid the asking price. Then an idea came to me.

"Thirteen is an unlucky number, agha," I said, feeling clever.

"Then you pay fourteen," said his lips, as he wrapped the pot presumptuously in newspaper and placed it on his counter.

He was good.

I walked home with my hands filled with a whole new kitchen for the total price of forty-three toman – a savings of twenty-seven toman from what the ironworker wanted to charge me for a few copper dishes. I felt victorious despite the difficulty of balancing my parcels. The Pyrex pot did not fit into the narrow opening of the stone pot. The stone pot's bottom was too large to fit into the Pyrex pot. The china dishes were in a taped box. With great difficulty, I managed to get all the way home, using both arms for the three parcels and my teeth for holding my chador on my head.

"I saved almost thirty toman today," I announced to Abaas as I served our dinner from our new pots onto our china plates. He was seated at the wooden table, sipping his tea – a ritual he looked forward to after work.

"The more you save, azizam, the more nervous I become," he said playfully.

In the evenings, Abaas and I would take our chairs, and sit outside, where the air was cool and the night was drenched in moonlight. After dinner, we would sip our tea and talk about the future. Abaas would talk about his business and how he dreamed of it growing into a huge success. He would tell me that one day his reputation would get him more contracts. Large stores would hire him to sew their window coverings and design their spaces with exquisite tapestry.

"I would no longer be just a poor tailor, but an interior decorator."

I loved hearing him talk about the future. It turned his eyes ablaze, his hands alive with vivid gestures, and his voice into a song of passion. Talk like this always sealed the deal on him being his most confident in bed that night.

Most days, I would finish my chores an hour or two before Abaas returned home from work. I would relax on our cot, reading one of the many books that I had taken from Baba's shelf without permission. This time when I left Baba's home, I took very few items of clothing and filled most of my carpet bag with my favourite books. At the age of eighteen, I had learned not to ask permission from those who had no say in the matter.

* * *

"Khodaya! What is in here?" Abaas asked, pulling my bag from the taxicab once we had arrived at our new home in Karaj.

"Just a few things I cannot live without," I replied innocently.

"I did not realize that you could not live without solid bricks," Abaas joked as he grunted through the task. Still, once he closed the trunk, he rushed over to my side of the cab to open the door for me. I had married a gentleman – one with a good sense of humour.

* * *

Our budget was limited, so I had to conserve, which had been the way of life growing up in Baba's house. Although money had not been an issue with Baba, on principle, he never tolerated waste. I learned to stick thin pieces of soap together to make one large ball of soap and use them up. He insisted on placing partially used matchsticks on a plate by the wood stove to reuse them until the entire length was gone.

In Karaj, I fetched water from the well down the street. None was thrown away until it had been used for at least two jobs. Water used to wash produce was reused to wash clothing. I would let the sand and dirt settle after washing produce, and then use the clear water for dirty clothes. Water used for tea would then water our few houseplants. The planters of mint, parsley, and basil thrived on the tea water and made our home fragrant. Once I had accumulated a sizable garden, I understood the love Baba had for his own garden. It was a thrill to watch what we planted grow and to then harvest it.

Abaas took an interest in cooking. He would stay by my side in the kitchen and observe me with interest. He would offer to do little things that he had previously observed and now was anticipating. I took Baba's role with Abaas, guiding him and giving him freedom to learn how to cook.

We had finished eating dinner on a Thursday evening, and I was washing the dishes. Abaas was drying them before placing them back in the cupboard.

"You do whatever you want tomorrow," he told me. "I am preparing the meals."

"What are you talking about?"

"I have been watching you, and I think I can prepare the meals for a day."

"It is your day off, too," I protested. "You need a break."

"That would be a break for me. I would enjoy it."

"I always prepare Friday's meal on Thursday so we can have time for each other on Friday."

"Even better," he said with excitement. "Then you will not have to cook for Saturday either. You can read Molana, your favourite, or any book you choose from your father's collection. What a treat."

I adored him for knowing that was a treat for me.

I did not want to be an obstacle to him. He seemed eager and sure, so I stepped aside and let him have the kitchen Friday.

Abaas showed a little flexibility when he allowed me to pick up the morning bread while he arranged the rest of the breakfast. I liked the walk in the early morning. The streets were quiet, the air was fresh, and there were no young girls with hoses.

Often I would think of Baba.

There were two bakers on our street: Aref Agha made *naan barbari* and Derafsh Agha made *naan sangak*. Both breads were laid on a *naandle* – a paddle with a long handle that aided in placing the dough inside a tandoor to bake. I liked seeing the process of naan baking just as I had when I was a little girl.

Naan barbari was a fluffy flatbread topped with sesame seeds that melted in one's mouth. It was modestly sized, oval shaped, and easy to carry. Naan sangak was huge, thin, and chewy. It was baked over small rocks, hence its name, "sangak", meaning "little rocks". The surface of the bread took on the indentations of the rocks, so it looked like a leopard's skin. It was carried over a shoulder or draped across an arm. Naan sangak seemed like a vulgar bread to me, so I bought barbari from Aref Agha.

I sat in the kitchen, watching Abaas. I offered to help a few times, but he was determined to do it alone. Truly, he was loving the task.

We ate well that day. Breakfast was naan barbari, homemade goat cheese from the neighbour's goats, walnuts from Baba's tree, and fresh mint from our planter. Lunch was awash with naan barbari, and dinner was *ab goosht*. I enjoyed not cooking that day more than I enjoyed not cooking for a year in Mahmood's house. This time I did not have to cook, because someone cared enough to want to cook for both of us.

After we finished washing the dinner dishes, we retired to our usual seating outside. This time I brought a copy of Ferdowsi, another great Iranian poet.

"Since you called it a treat," I said with a grin, "I thought we could read together: one poem me and one poem you. What do you think?"

"No!" Abaas cried, and he immediately looked sorry for having startled me.

He must have become tired from the day's cooking.

"Cooking may have been fun for a day, but you do not have to do it again," I wanted to reassure him.

I admired him for trying.

"I – I do feel tired," he admitted.

"You worked very hard," I agreed, affectionately. "How about I read and you relax?"

"Yes, yes," he said, his face brightening again. "I love to listen."

He slid down to the edge of his seat, crossed his legs at the ankles, and rested his head on his knit fingers.

Abaas began cooking on Fridays routinely. Nothing I said seemed to dissuade him. I did not dare tell anyone about this weekly role reversal. I knew people would judge me as a bad wife. They would not understand. I could see that Abaas genuinely delighted in cooking. It was a pleasure to watch him revel in his self-appointed chore every Friday.

I found where Fereshteh lived. The communities in Karaj were widespread, so I considered myself lucky to be living close enough to walk to her. I visited her on my way back from the market every Wednesday. It was like old times. The difference was that I needed to go to the market more than once a week again, because we did not have a refrigeration system.

Fereshteh had two boys now: three-year-old Niku and five-year-old Nima. They were adventurous but had boundaries. On one of my visits, they dazzled me with an elaborate cushion fort they had built. The cushions were the walls, and sheets of all colours draped over as a roof and doorways. Their toys came in and out as they decorated the interior. These children were allowed to be creative without being reprimanded for it. They were so much more uninhibited than Darius and Akbar.

Khanum Piruz's children had seemed sedate. Their toys were minimal and needed to be kept out of her sight. She used to scream at them if they climbed onto the living room furniture. Furniture was for guests, although I saw none in the three years I lived there; not even the girls visited. If they were not allowed to sit on them, who knows what would have happened to them if they were to build forts with the cushions?

I worried about Pantea. How many times a day did my baby hear a scream that stopped her creativity? I felt sick to my stomach that I could not be there to comfort her and protect her against Khanum Piruz.

Sometimes I visited Fereshteh in the mornings, when the boys were home; and other times I came in the afternoon, when they were in school. I left my cloth grocery bags outside the front door but inside the front gate. I laid my chador folded on top of the bags and entered. Her new home was modest but stylish. I guessed that Agha Nemat's promotion had helped improve their lifestyle. Fereshteh brought in the tea tray, and we both sat in anticipation of our treasured chats. The conversation started prescriptively with everyone's health and contentment at work and home. Fereshteh was sensible enough to avoid the subject of Pantea.

There was something today that I wanted her opinion on, but I was still apprehensive about asking her.

"Fereshteh," I began hesitantly.

"Yes, Pari joon," she replied, sipping her tea as she leaned comfortably against the few remaining cushions.

"Would you accept Agha Nemat cooking the Friday meals?"

There, I said it. I braced myself, because I knew what a traditional Iranian housewife's opinion was. Before I let anyone find out about Abaas' cooking adventures, I had to test the waters with my dear friend, Fereshteh, whom I considered a good measuring stick.

Abaas' mother, Khanum Tabriz, seldom came to visit. When she did visit, I was always worried that Abaas would innocently tell her about his Friday pastime.

"I would be devastated!" she said, confirming my worst fears. "If Shahram ever stepped into the kitchen, then I may as well lie on the ground with my head towards the qiblah."

I thought a consequence of death was an overreaction, but I understood her point.

"All right," I said before the shade of red on her face darkened. "I was just asking."

Fereshteh had one marriage and two children. I knew they made a good team as parents. I admired her steadfast faith in the traditional ideas of marriage, although some may have thought them inflexible. She certainly had transformed from that young girl crying behind the curtain into a confident woman. I felt proud of her.

I continued to live with Abaas in our childless home. The days began to merge into one, and my loneliness grew. My longing for Pantea was still an unbearable ache. Wherever I turned, there was a mother with a child, and I was reminded of my own baby in Tehran. She was the same age as Nima.

The Piruz family did not answer any of my letters. I continued to write, perhaps for myself if not for Pantea. The first few weeks after I was sent out of their house, I had gone to their gate and begged to see her, but no one had answered. I stood outside on the street, hoping to get a glimpse of her in case she was taken on an outing, but that never happened. I went before dark to catch Farid and Saam leaving for work, but their Opel had tinted windows, and they drove away. I wanted to hear any news of Pantea. Was she happy? What funny little thing had she said or done? What had been her latest discovery? I ran along the driver's side, banging on the tinted window as it pulled onto the street, but no one had answered.

The last time I made this pathetic attempt, I heard Saam call to me from the passenger side as the Opel outran me. He rolled down his window to make sure I heard those three precious words that had the power to calm me.

"Pantea is fine, khahar joon."

The car drove away, leaving me standing there staring at it until it was out of view. Then I turned to look at the gate that held my baby away from me.

It made me sad that my little girl would grow up without her mother just as I had. I secretly hoped that once she was old enough, she would come looking for me. God be willing that I live that long, I would receive her with open arms.

Not living next door to the Piruz house made it easier to avoid humiliating myself.

Recently, every visit with Fereshteh ended the same way. She invited Abaas and me for dinner on Friday. I would tell Abaas, and he would refuse. I began feeling embarrassed to decline my friend's invitation repeatedly. I was running out of reasons, and she was feeling unappreciated.

On one occasion, I insisted to Abaas that we accept their invitation, telling him that my friend may become hurt if we continued to say no. Abaas reluctantly agreed, and on my following visit, I told Fereshteh that we accepted.

Friday evening arrived, and Farid put on the only suit he owned – a white jacket and black pants. I put on the only appropriate dress I owned – the orange taffeta that Farid had given to me. It was sleeveless, with a round neck and a fitted bodice. Just as I expected, my mother's pearls looked exquisite with the dress.

I had very few occasions to wear it, although I did wear it often around Mahmood's house. I was happy that I fit into it still. Mahmood had told me that he hated it. I reasoned that since he did not buy me a new dress, he had to see me in this one.

Abaas and I walked to the Nemat home. On the way, Abaas fidgeted with his sleeves and talked like a crazy person.

"These people are too rich for us," he stammered.

"What do you mean?" I asked. "She is my friend, and he used to be my teacher."

"Does not matter. They will look down on us."

He was getting anxious and beginning to affect me.

"Since when do you care what other people think?" I said, trying to stay calm for his benefit. "You are a sayyid!"

"Does not matter. If you are poor, everyone looks down on …"

I stopped at the gate, and Abaas fell silent. I rang the bell, and the gate was opened. Agha Nemat wore a bright smile and gestured with his whole arm for us to come in. He said the boys were playing in their rooms and Fereshteh was in the kitchen.

"You have a beautiful home, Agha Nemat," Abaas said.

I was grateful that the man of a few seconds prior had vanished and my gentle, soft-spoken Abaas was back.

"Thank you, Abass Agha," Agha Nemat replied. "My wife and I are honoured you accepted our humble invitation to our home."

This was the first time I was seeing my math teacher from six years ago. Fereshteh had spoken of him to me, and I am sure she had spoken of me to him. It felt awkward to be in his house with him in it. I told myself that I was not a little girl in the presence of my teacher, but an adult guest in his home.

"So how is my star math student?" Agha Nemat asked me.

That did not help.

I nodded and hurried into the kitchen to help Fereshteh.

We ate at the dinner table. The boys were surprisingly well behaved. As soon as dinner was over, they asked if they could be excused from the table. I wondered which planet Abaas and I had landed on. Nima whispered something in Niku's ear, and they bolted out of the room, squealing with delight.

"You will have to excuse them," Agha Nemat apologized.

"Yes, they are still learning their manners," Fereshteh

agreed with her husband as she and I stood to clear the table. Panic struck me when Abaas stood to bring his plate into the kitchen. Agha Nemat distracted him with an offer of a walk through their garden. I was grateful to my core.

Fereshteh and I had a pleasant chat while we washed and dried the dishes. I asked about her grandparents, who came for short visits every Friday afternoon. They always brought a small trinket for their great-grandsons. Fereshteh asked me about Khale Sara, whom I had not seen since our wedding in her garden. She had told me to keep the wedding dress and pass it on. She could not have known how sad it made me knowing that I may never see my Pantea wear it.

We assembled the tea tray with the tea glasses, dates, sugar cubes, and shirini. A fruit basket with a stack of small plates and fruit knives was already on the low table in the living room. Across the room were glass doors that opened to the garden, where the men were strolling. Fereshteh called to them, and the four of us sat on the carpet cushions, feeling the evening breeze drifting in through the open doorway.

"Agha Tabriz, did you know that your wife was my top student in math?"

To my dismay, Agha Nemat brought up the topic again. My face must have turned bright red, because Fereshteh mercifully changed the subject.

"How is your business developing, Agha Tabriz?"

Abaas always took great pleasure in discussing his future plans for his business, but tonight he kept it short and asked Agha Nemat about his school.

"I miss teaching," Agha Nemat began. "I loved being responsible for clarifying concepts for my students.

Administration has its rewards too. As principal, I set the tone in my school, and I strive to set a positive one."

"Of course you do, azizam," Fereshteh said in support of her husband.

The boys turned up one more time to pick a cookie from the tea tray and say goodnight. Abaas used this cue to say thank you and good evening. Fereshteh and Agha Nemat did their best to encourage us to stay longer, but Abaas brilliantly pointed out how important the children's bedtime routine was.

"Your children are the most important project in your life," Abaas began. "Tonight they will require supervision of their hygiene, then a bedtime story to develop their imagination, and then a kiss goodnight to let them know they are loved. Pari and I would not dream of intruding on this essential routine."

Agha Nemat and Fereshteh were impressed by Abaas' parenting philosophy, but I was astounded. I had no idea Abaas had such a noble outlook on child rearing. I gladly joined Abaas in saying thank you and goodbye to our friends.

On our walk home, I periodically glanced up at Abaas with adoration. This was the man I wanted to have children with. Now that I knew how he felt about parenting, I fell in love with him all over again. I was holding his hand but walking on a cloud.

"I do not know if I could ever give you a home like that," Abaas said sadly.

I stopped to face him. I was baffled. Where was I in this incredible sphere of existence, and where was he? The moonlight was on his face, so I could see he was in great pain.

"I do not care about a home like that," I said, choosing

my words carefully. "Those things do not matter to me. I had them, and it does not guarantee happiness."

"Rich people always say that, but they expect it nevertheless."

I took each of his hands in each of mine, and held them to my chest.

"All I can do is tell you what is in here," I said, in surrender. "It is up to you to believe me."

"You are too courteous to tell me how envious you are of Fereshteh."

"Well, I am not envious of her. I am happy for her. She used to live in a home with no more than what we have. They have been working at it for six years. We have only begun."

"See, see?" Abaas burst out, pointing his finger in my face. "You hope that in six years we will have what they have."

"They were happy before they acquired all of this. Sure, they strove for better, and they accomplished it, but they were happy anyway."

"Now we are not happy?"

"Panah bar Khoda!" I sighed in exasperation. "Do you not hear me? I love you! I love your gentleness, your dreams for our future, and even your enthusiasm for cooking. What you said back there about children being the most important project in life – it moved me. I do not want anyone but you."

He leaned forward and took me in his arms. The abruptness made my mouth fly open as he kissed me. Somehow our tongues met and caressed. It was magical. This was a new addition to our lovemaking repertoire. We hurried home to practise while it was fresh on our minds. Holding hands, giggling, skipping, and running, we forgot our argument like typical newlyweds.

Don't grieve. Anything you lose comes round in another form.

—Rumi

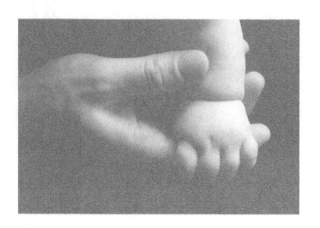

Chapter 17

Perception (1316 SH)

It was Wednesday morning, and I was off to the market. I was excited to see Fereshteh, but today I had an extra reason for my enthusiasm. This time it took only two missed periods for me to notice I was pregnant. My mind was racing through a list of all the ways in which our lives would change. They were all good.

I imagined my baby's first words, his first step, and how he would be curious and full of questions. I promised myself to answer every one of them with patience. I swore I would never lose my temper if he spilled his drink carelessly. He would accompany me to the market and play with Nima and Niku on the way back.

When I arrived at Fereshteh's home, Niku opened the gate. There was a ribbon tying his bangs above his head so the hair came down like a fountain of water. It was called a *Goje Farangi*, a tomato, and was reserved for girls. Nima appeared behind him, and then Fereshteh to complete the welcoming trio. As we entered the house, we said the customary hello, how are you, how is Abaas, how are your grandparents, and so on. I was ambushed in the family room by the boys, who told me all their latest news. Fereshteh continued into the kitchen with a smile that promised she would return with tea.

"I like your hair, Niku," I said when it was my turn to talk.

"He looks like a girl," said Nima, teasing his younger brother.

"I am a spouting whale," Niku corrected.

"I have not had a chance to take them for a haircut," Fereshteh explained as she brought in the tea tray. "I tied the ribbon to keep his hair out of his face. Nima would not let me do it to his hair."

Nima made a face.

We sat on the cushions, and Fereshteh allowed the boys to take one shirini each before disappearing to their room to play. We relaxed against the cushions, tea glasses in our hands, sipping slowly.

"I am pregnant!" I exclaimed.

Fereshteh spit her tea back into her glass. A shriek told me she was happy for me. She set her tea down carelessly, so it splashed and spilled into the saucer. She jumped off her cushion, gave me a hug, pulled back to grin at me, and then hugged me again.

"Well, you get right to your news without any preliminaries," she said, laughing.

We had to explain to the boys, who had run into the room, why their mother had screamed. They cheered supportively when we told them I had a baby in my belly. They asked to touch my belly, were disappointed that they did not feel anything, and went back to their play.

"Mobarak, mobarak," Fereshteh said, congratulating me.

"I have not told Abaas yet."

"What? He is supposed to be the first to find out."

"Today is seven days past my second missed period. I have not gone to the doctor yet."

I did not tell her that during my first pregnancy I did not visit a doctor until I was eight months pregnant, and then only after being knocked unconscious.

"I can give you my doctor's number in Tehran," Fereshteh offered. "He is gentle and conscientious."

"That would be helpful. Thank you."

That evening, waiting for Abaas seemed to last forever. I had the meal ready, the table set, and a tall tin holding five white tulips with long green leaves. The flowers were an extravagance, but this was a special occasion. It was fascinating how green and white made the room look elegant. I alternated between sitting on the wooden chair at the table and lying on our cot. I tried to pass the time by reading works of Khayyam, but I felt distracted. Usually his poems, mathematical calculations, and astronomical discoveries had me mesmerized. It was the end of the summer, and I wondered if we would be cold here in the winter. Fortunately, the baby was due in late spring, when it would be warm again.

I decided to build a cradle myself. Baba had said I handled tools well when I helped him build our wooden radio.

Abaas came through the curtain, placed his leather sewing bag inside the closet and graciously complimented me on the fragrant adas polo.

"With dates," I announced proudly.

"Even better," he said with a ceremonial deep bow.

We met in the middle of the floor, embraced, and practised our magical kiss.

He hung his hat and coat on a nail on the wall. He washed his hands and face in the washbasin and sat at the table patiently. I served him a cup of tea to help him relax. Then I poured two plates of lentil rice, offered the bowl of homemade yogurt and the basket of mint, basil, and goat cheese. We ate our fill, and he helped me clean up the kitchen.

I was very proud of myself for waiting until after dinner, when we sat outside comfortably, before sharing my life-changing news. I did not get the opportunity to announce my pregnancy the first time, so I wanted to do it right this time. Abaas was in his normal position – eyes closed, ankles crossed, and head rested against knit fingers behind his head.

"I have fantastic news," I began, aiming to pique his curiosity.

"How wonderful. What is it, azizam?"

I knew he was going to be ecstatic, but how was he

going to react? Would he lean over and give me one of his magical kisses; or would he jump to his feet, pick me up, and twirl me around the room; or would he put an extra pillow behind me and pamper me as if I were an empress? I decided to speak and let him choose.

"I am with child," I said, trying to sound dignified.

Abaas stopped smiling. His face began to distort. I began to worry.

"You mean you are *pregnant?*" he asked, saying the word "pregnant" as if it were profanity.

"Yes, we are going to be parents – that most important job in …" I said, starting to quote him.

"How did this happen?" he yelled.

I became scared. Abaas actually yelled at me. What did he mean, "how"? He must have known how babies are made. I decided this was a rhetorical question.

"We were being careful," he barked. "I do not understand."

"No contraceptive method is one hundred percent guaranteed," I said, trying to help.

"Abstinence is!" he whispered to himself.

"You must have faith," I said tenderly, wanting to calm him. "You are a sayyid."

"Would you stop throwing that word in my face? I could barely feed myself, and then I included you. Now you are including a baby. How do you expect me to manage?"

"We are not starving, and yes, we have a roof over our heads," I said, but I knew he was worried about the winter, and so was I. "We will need to get more firewood."

"Firewood? That is your answer?"

"You are displeased," I said softly.

"Displeased?" Abaas was screaming now. "Displeased is what I would be if there was no water in the washbasin or too much salt in the rice, or so many other little things. You are pregnant! That makes me devastated, desperate, destitute"

He got up from his chair and walked into the darkness. He had never left me in the night. I felt lost. I did not know whether to follow him or wait for him. I was not comfortable outside by myself, so I took the chairs inside, climbed into our cot, and cried myself to sleep.

When I opened my eyes, it was morning. I reached for Abaas beside me, but he was not there. I thought perhaps he had gone to pick up bread from Aref Agha. I knew we were not out of bread, but it was comforting to think he was doing something normal. I stubbornly ignored his coat and hat still hanging on the hook on the wall.

I put some water on to boil for tea and set the breakfast table. I sat at the table waiting for him, but he did not show up. I had no appetite, but I forced myself to eat something for our baby's sake. I put away the food and poured the cool tea into the planters of mint, parsley, and basil. I managed to make some food for dinner, but Abaas did not show up. I decided that in listing his devastation, desperation, and destitution, he had failed to mention his desertion.

Yesterday I was clever, so I wanted to change the world. Today I am wise, so I am changing myself.

—Rumi

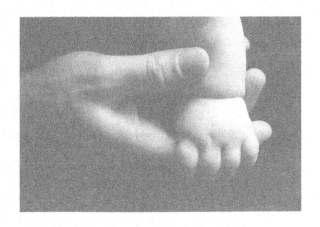

Chapter 18

Solo (1316 SH)

It is amazing how you can get by with hardly any money. Abaas should have seen me now. I would show up at the end of the day, and Aref Agha would give me the bread that had not sold that day. From the grocer, I got produce that had wilted or partially spoiled. Our farm neighbours, Khanum and Agha Faal, had goats that needed milking and eggs that needed gathering. For a few daily chores, I got free milk and eggs. I managed to turn the milk into butter, yogurt, and cheese, and still have enough to drink. It was already cold enough that I kept perishables outside under a crate with a heavy brick on it. In the cupboards, there was still a good supply of rice and legumes, so dinners were a variety of rice plates.

I tried to maintain some form of normalcy. I continued my visits with Fereshteh. Seeing her lifted my spirits and kept me sane. The visits became fewer as the months went by. I did not have the energy to walk that far or continue my lies. In the beginning, I felt no guilt in telling her that Abaas took the news well. It was frightening to think I was walking into a tunnel of wrongdoings with no conscience. Then one day, it all caught up to me.

"We are both so happy," I said, biting my lower lip to prevent tears.

It was like a gift. I felt my conscience had returned to me.

"It is normal to be extra emotional when you are expecting," she said, rubbing my back.

Fereshteh misinterpreted the situation. My secret was still mine to bear.

One day when I arrived with my bags of bread and produce, she saw I had a bunch of daisies that I had picked from the side of the road. She took them from me and placed them in a vase with gorgeous blue *Minakari* (enamelling). At the front door, when I was about to leave with my bags in hands and my chador tied under my chin, Fereshteh suddenly remembered the daisies. She ran back to the family room even though I called to her to keep them.

"I have never brought you anything, Fereshteh joon," I called after her. "Please accept the flowers as a small gift. Really, they are unworthy of you."

Fereshteh returned and handed me the daisies, which were still inside the vase.

"Please, it is I who owe you a kindness. Accept this from me, Pari joon. You helped me when I was young and isolated. Remember? Let me give this to you, my friend."

I hesitantly took the vase full of daisies and thanked her.

The rent collector, Jaleh Khanum, came three times after Abaas left – once at the end of the month and every two weeks after that. She stood impatiently at the curtain entrance while I gave the same excuse.

"My husband is away on business and will pay when he returns."

The third time she heard the same answer, she smirked and placed her hands on her round hips. I presumed the body language meant, "How gullible do you think I am?"

"Your husband is not coming back, is he?"

I shook my head. I was now four months pregnant, with a round belly to prove it. It had taken eight months to show with Pantea. I supposed my stomach muscles knew the routine and gave way sooner this time.

Jaleh Khanum was tapping her foot. She was not unattractive, but her businesslike attitude made her seem cold. I knew I was in trouble, but my biggest concern was the baby. Instinctively, I placed my hand over my belly as protection. Jaleh Khanum's stare dropped to my belly, and suddenly her expression softened.

"You poor child," she sighed. "You have a baby in there?"

I nodded, feeling both miserable and ecstatic. My pregnancies had a way of becoming a double-edged sword. Jaleh Khanum shook her head, turned, and walked out.

"I will not be coming around any more, *dokhtaram*," I heard her say as she passed our wooden gate.

I took more naps during the days and sat to read more. I stopped missing Abaas the day I felt the baby's first kick. My days and nights engulfed me with thoughts of the baby. I decided on the name: Audel for a boy, the girl's version being Audele; it meant "impartial, just, and fair".

I took Abaas' leather sewing bag out of the closet and put it to work. First I turned his white shirts into squares to be used as diapers and sheets. Then I used his pyjamas to sew undershirts and his wool pants to sew sweaters. I exchanged Abaas' closet for the baby's closet. His chocolate-brown coat that hung on the nail was useful to me on my walks.

I turned to my clothes. I made a pillow and blanket set from my taffeta dress. I made little socks for the baby's feet to keep him warm and for his hands so he would not scratch himself.

I even enlisted the help of my neighbours, Khanum and Agha Faal. I asked for the feathers of the chickens that Khanum Faal butchered. I helped her defeather and clean the chickens in return. It was exciting preparing the chickens for their icebox.

My job was to catch the chickens and put them upside down through a wooden funnel so its head stuck out the narrow end at the bottom. Khanum Faal calmly slit their throats while reciting a part of the Quran "bismillah al-rahman al-rahim [in the name of God, most gracious, most merciful]." I was told the meat would be the healthiest when the blood was allowed to drain out completely.

To defeather the chickens, we brought a large pot of water to a boil. We held the chickens by the feet and dunked them into the water. If they stayed too long in the water, the skin would come off with the feathers. If they were taken out too soon, the feathers would not come out easily.

Once all the chickens were defeathered, we proceeded to gut them. This part was my favourite. I cut an opening below the breastbone. I reached in and took out all the organs. Khanum Faal was happy to go through each part and name them with me. She told me what the purpose of each organ was. I had only seen pictures of organs in textbooks. What I was looking at took my breath away. There was a thin membrane that encased each organ. The liver seemed to spread out over the smaller organs like a chicken spreading its wings over its chicks. The organs underneath folded against each other in seamless harmony. My mind raced to my baby and how all these parts were growing inside of him.

I sterilized the feathers in boiling water, tore the down from the shaft, and stuffed the cradle mattress with it.

One evening as I was leaving the Faal home, I saw a pair of knitting needles stuck through a ball of yarn. It had been left on a pile of logs outside of the barn where we were cleaning the chicken. I told Khanum Faal that I needed some wool soakers for the baby. I asked her if she would be willing to teach me how to knit my own. As had been my experience in this little community, Khanum Faal was happy to help. She offered the needles, the expertise, and even the wool. I managed to pack away five hand-knit wool soakers in the next few weeks.

On my way home from what turned out to be my last visit with Fereshteh, I felt so tired with the bags in my hands that I decided to take a bus home. Walking to the bus stop,

I passed by a pastry shop. I had seen the shop before, but I was not accustomed to buying shirini. I had seen shirini at weddings and funerals but had never felt inclined to eat any. Baba had said Iranians ate dried fruit and nuts for dessert. He had felt that foreigners had brought over shirini, such as baklava from Turkey and cream puffs from France, and they had taken root in Iran like the kedu from the Piruz garden.

I walked into the shop and asked for five shirini.

"Which type, Khanum?" asked the pretty girl behind the counter.

She was wearing no hijab – only a hair net. Her hands had an intricate henna design which began at the wrists and meandered over her hands to her fingertips.

"You choose," I said, wondering why I was buying shirini after all these years.

The visual effect as she hand-picked the shirini was enhanced by her hand art. I paid, took the small paper bag filled with five rose water and rice flour shortbreads, and left the store. As I walked the short distance remaining to the bus stop, I was full of regret.

What am I supposed to do with this shirini in my hand? I thought. It was not a respectable box of shirini that I could offer to Fereshteh on my next visit. I had no interest in eating it myself.

There was an indent in the brick wall of the building I was passing. I lifted my hand that held the bag of shirini to place it on the brick ledge. Just then, a woman went by me, her chador billowing in the wind. She looked at me, puzzled. I felt ashamed and took my hand back. I could not leave the bag there, on the street, where the wind might blow it over, scattering the biscuit into a soggy mess.

Besides, someone might think I was leaving a bomb hidden in a small paper bag meant for shirini. That would cause unnecessary alarm.

I arrived at the bus stop, and so did the bus.

I boarded, holding my chador between my teeth, one hand holding my groceries and the other holding the stair rail for balance. All the seats were taken, but a man got up and offered me his seat. This was one of the advantages of being visibly pregnant. Next to me, a toddler was restless in his mother's lap. As the bus bumped along, the toddler became more and more aggressive until he was screaming and pulling at his mother's hair. The young mother continued to readjust her chador and hold it firmly under her chin without a word to her son. She faced the window, perhaps embarrassed. I took a shirini out of the small paper bag and handed it to the boy. He took it from my hand and gobbled it up. I handed him another and another until they were all gone. I folded the bag to show him it was empty. His head drooped onto his mother's shoulder and he fell asleep. The mother looked over, curious why her son had mysteriously become quiet. She noticed the crumbs on her chador and the grease-stained paper bag in my hand.

"Thank you, Khanum," she said to me shyly.

I nodded and smiled at her.

"We were visiting someone, and we stayed past my son's lunchtime and naptime. I did not feel comfortable asking for food, so I was hoping he would fall asleep in my arms until I reached home, where I could feed him."

"I never buy shirini, and today I stopped and bought a few for no reason that I was aware of. This shirini was your son's roozi."

If you look for it, there is wood everywhere. People are practically giving it away. Whenever I saw someone throwing away something made of wood, I offered to take it off his or her hands. Streets in my neighbourhood became cleansed of sticks and twigs. The firewood lasted through the winter and into the spring. Every time I went for a walk anywhere, I collected wood. I even got some from a local carpenter to build my cradle.

"Do you have any plans for that table among the rubble in the back of your store, agha?" I asked the tall carpenter, whose back was to me.

He turned around, and I saw Baba's beautiful green eyes looking at me.

"Ahmad Agha!" I cried, surprised that I remembered his name after all these years.

He was the beggar who had come to Khanum Piruz's door, and I had given him food in his bowl. The neat haircut and shave made him look younger, but the grey in his hair betrayed him. He recognized me, too. He smiled and bowed, with one leathery hand over his chest to show sincerity.

"Well, you sure have grown up," he said. "Expecting a little one yourself, I see."

"I am so glad to see you, agha."

"Glad to see you too, azizam," he said. "You have gotten prettier, if that were even possible. Is the Piruz boy excited about fatherhood?"

I burst into tears. I think I startled him, because he became nimble for a man of his age, bringing me a chair to sit on, a handkerchief to blow my nose, and a glass of water. He had to take my hand and physically push the glass into it.

"You got hold of it, *ghorban*?" he asked cautiously. "I am letting go."

I nodded. He went back inside, brought himself a chair, and joined me. He sat beside me and waited until I finished crying. I appreciated his patience – his unspoken permission to cry in his presence.

Once I had no more tears, we sat together in silence.

When he did speak, his words seemed natural – as if they had been there all along but I had not seen them.

"You have gone through a lot," he said softly. "You are welcome to tell me all of it, some of it, or none of it. I am moved that you felt comfortable to show your emotions to me. I want to reassure you that your trust is well placed. Take your time, dokhtaram. I will stay with you as long as you need me."

"You have Baba's eyes," I told him, not knowing why I wanted him to know that.

"I would be honoured if you were my daughter," he said, giving my hands a little squeeze.

"He died eight years ago."

"I am so sorry for your loss."

"My husband left me when I told him that I was expecting our baby."

"His loss. A life with you and a baby would be treasurable."

"The Piruz family kicked me out and kept my daughter. The Piruz boy loved me but was trapped by his mother."

"Sometimes we feel the control over our lives, and sometimes we do not. We do the best we can and trust God will lend a hand when he gets around to it."

I laughed. He put one arm around my shoulders, gave a quick squeeze, and then put his hands back in his lap.

"Which table did you say you wanted?"

I laughed again, falling into his arms with a whole new flood of tears.

"Go ahead, azizam," he said, patting my back. "These are tears of relief."

Ahmad Agha helped me carry the table to my home once we had reconstructed it into a cradle. Using the tools in his shop, he allowed me to work alongside him on the cradle project. Like Baba, he did not talk down to me or give me trivial tasks. In fact, he made me feel as though we were working as partners. We took the table apart. We drew a plan for the cradle, complete with a crescent moon cutout on one end and a blazing sun on the other. We cut out the pieces according to the plan and nailed and glued until it was complete. I used all the scraps for firewood. In fact, Ahmad Agha became the sole source of my firewood.

The cradle was complete, and we carried it to my home.

"Where would you like it, azizam?" he asked once we were inside.

"Beside the cot, please."

I placed the feather mattress on the bottom of the cradle. I lined it with some sheets and the orange pillow with matching blanket. The orange looked striking against the dark brown stain of the wood.

We stood back and admired our handiwork.

"It is the loveliest piece of furniture in this home," I said.

"I am proud of us too, jigar tala."

I looked at him, startled. He appeared apologetic in advance.

"Are you all right, ghorban?"

I nodded. "Baba used to call me jigar tala."

"He must have loved you very much."

"He loved my brothers, too," I felt compelled to say.

"I am sure he did. A father loves all his children."

Ahmad Agha periodically joined me for dinner. He would never show up empty-handed. Sometimes he brought a dish he had cooked. His enthusiasm for cooking reminded me of Abaas. Other times he would bring flowers or a baby gift, just as Farid had. It was fun to share my joy of having a baby with someone who knew my whole story.

We read about the lives and works of ancient poets. We chatted or simply sat in each other's company. Eventually, Ahmad Agha felt comfortable enough to share his story with me.

Seven years ago, Ahmad Agha's wife died. The funeral took place a month before Norooz, the Iranian New Year, which was on the first day of spring. His three daughters – Zahra, Azam, and Akram – were married and living in distant cities of Iran. It had been their tradition to come home for Norooz with their entire families. After their mother's death, the three sisters came home for the funeral but did not return for Norooz. That year their tradition of being together for Norooz was broken, and so was Ahmad Agha's heart.

His grief made him give up his carpentry shop. He handed the keys to his friend Samad, who was mourning the death of his own son. Ahmad Agha locked up his house and travelled to Tehran, where no one knew him. With no hope and no goal in life, he turned to begging. His daughters could not find him, because he did not want to be found.

Ahmad Agha returned to Karaj for the funeral of his friend Samad. Samad's family was thrilled to see him. They said he had helped Samad overcome his grief over the loss of his son. The responsibility of tending the shop every day had given him a purpose and the strength to live. Now he was at peace in heaven with his son. The family wanted to return the shop to Ahmad Agha, who was ready to accept it gratefully.

For the coming Norooz, Ahmad Agha called his three daughters, who were relieved to hear his voice. He invited them for Norooz, which was in a few days. He was ready to continue the tradition they had followed when his wife was alive.

"This year," Ahmad Agha had told his daughters, "instead of your mother, there will be another mother who will be more like a sister to you."

This sounded like a riddle.

The three sisters were eager to see their father, and they made the necessary arrangements. When Ahmad Agha invited me to join them, I was moved. The first day of Norooz is traditionally spent with immediate family. I felt homesick for my brothers, but I did not dare reach out to them. I accepted Ahmad Agha's invitation.

The day before the sisters' arrival, I spent the day at Ahmad Agha's home, where we made preparations for Norooz. We set the *Sofreh Haft Seen* – the seven S spread – on the low table in the family room. We covered it with a traditional handmade block-printed tablecloth with a paisley motif. The organic paint used for these cloths was made from crushed berries, seeds, and nuts. Then we placed on the table the seven items that start with the letter S, symbolizing ideals for the new year.

Sabzeh, the sprouts of lentils (wheat, or barley could also be used) tied with my yellow ribbon, symbolized rebirth.

Samanu, a pudding made from wheat sprouts, symbolized affluence. Baba, who was not a fan of wealth, said samanu stood for patience because it required great patience to pound the wheat sprouts and stand for hours at the pot stirring it until it thickened into a sweet pudding.

Senjed, dried oleaster, symbolized love. For Baba, senjed symbolized the coming together of people or ideas, since eating this wild olive fruit brought together everything in the intestine and ended diarrhea. My brothers groaned when Baba told me his interpretation of senjed, but I laughed. Bathroom talk was always humorous.

Seer, garlic, symbolized medicine and health.

Seeb, apple, symbolized beauty.

Somaq, sumac fruit, a spice to garnish kababs, symbolized sunrise and new beginnings because of its burgundy colour.

Serkeh, vinegar, symbolized patience, but to Baba it meant old age, indirectly meaning the hope of a long life.

We added other things that had become traditional: "Divan-e Hafez", a poetry book of Hafez, for me, and the Quran for Ahmad Agha; a mirror to reflect the past and look into the future; a goldfish to represent our need for God through the goldfish's need for water; candles for the sacred fire of the Zoroastrian faith; painted eggs for fertility; coins for prosperity; and bread for nourishment. Every Sofreh

Haft Seen had the seven objects, but every Haft Seen was different, as were the people who set it.

Once we were finished, we sat on the carpet cushions, sipping tea and admiring our work. I would not have set up the Sofreh Haft Seen had I been alone. I was grateful for the inspiration, as it made Norooz come to life for me.

Baba had explained the meanings of the Haft Seen to me, so I took for granted that everyone knew them. In the Piruz household, every Norooz another child would be of age to understand, so I repeated the Haft Seen meanings annually to the children, who listened to them like a story. I hoped that one day I would tell my niece, my nephews, and my own child.

On the day of the sisters' arrival, Ahmad Agha made the meal: white fish and sabzi polo, dill rice. I showed up right before dinner and set the table with herbs, goat cheese, and spring onions. I added a pitcher of water and the dishes. The sisters were expected to arrive at the Tehran airport and taxi to Karaj, as their father did not own a vehicle.

Ahmad Agha was jittery as the hour of his daughters' arrival grew closer.

There was the sound of a car pulling into the driveway and women's high-pitched chatter as car doors opened and closed. Ahmad Agha jumped from his seat and flung the door open. Three women immediately threw their arms around him and stayed there, laughing and crying. There were questions and answers, too, but from everyone at once, so it was incomprehensible to an outsider.

As each sister and her family walked into the house, the sphere of joyful chatter continued to flow inside. There were introductions of me to everyone and the grandchildren to their grandfather. Ahmad Agha was enamoured by the children and commented on how they had grown in the last seven years.

The sisters were tall and plump with kind brown eyes – like their mother, I assumed. Their families were similar in form, showing they shared the same lifestyle.

The three women would not leave their father's side. Ahmad Agha was confined to his seat on a cushion in the family room. His daughters surrounded him on the cushions and later at the dinner table, one on each side and one across the table from him. They would not let him out of their sight. I could imagine that if Baba suddenly called me after so many years and asked me to come home, I would be ecstatic too. There was so much to say and so much to learn from the years lost. It was difficult for the conversation to maintain a reasonable pace.

The sisters accepted me into their circle graciously. They were clearly an extension of their father's welcoming soul. Each sister spent time asking me about the baby, when it was due, how I was feeling with this pregnancy, and what preparations I had made so far for the arrival. I learned about them, too: how each had found a life for herself and her family outside of Karaj, and how they were fulfilled by their careers and their involvement with their children.

When the evening came to a close, everyone hugged and expressed their thrill over meeting me. Ahmad Agha walked me home because it was dark and cold. The sisters generously agreed it was a good idea.

We walked in silence. I was happy to give Ahmad Agha room to relax. The streets were quiet, since families were gathered in their homes on the first day of the year.

A few cats were running through the streets, occasionally knocking over a discarded object and making a clatter. The street lamps cast shadows of structures that always looked more mysterious in the night than the day. Shops were locked and barred. Close to my home, I felt compelled to tell Ahmad Agha how much the evening had meant to me.

"Thank you so much for including me," I said as we strolled in the lamplight, coming in and out of the beams.

"It would not have been the same without you."

"You know what I mean. You had not seen your family for so long, yet you shared their attention with me."

"You do not know your own worth."

"Well thank you. I had a really great—"

"Pari?" said a voice in the dark.

It was Khale Sara. She must have been waiting for me at my home. I could see only shapes as the darkness engulfed the night. We found a section of the street where there was enough lamplight to illuminate our faces.

"Who is this with you?" she asked rudely.

"This is Ahmad Agha," I answered her with a mind-your-manners tone.

"Ahmad, at your service, Khanum," he said, with a hand over his chest.

Khale Sara continued to stare at him rudely. I felt embarrassed.

"This is my aunt, Ahmad Agha, and she must have worried about me for a long time until we showed up. She is not herself right now."

"Do not defend me," Khale Sara began.

"Goodnight, Ahmad Agha," I said, interrupting her. "Thank you ... for understanding."

I wanted these two people who were important in my life to meet each other under a better circumstance. I wanted them to care about each other as they cared about me.

Ahmad Agha was wise enough to take his cue. He disappeared into the darkness after a bow towards Khale Sara and a wink towards me.

"What was that all about?" Khale Sara demanded.

"I could ask you the same thing," I said with a voice that matched her level of annoyance.

I walked past her, entered my home, and sat at the table, exhausted. The room was already warm from the fire Khale Sara had started in the stove. She walked in past the curtain and closed the door. I did not look her way or offer her a seat. She sat down anyway.

"I am sorry," Khale Sara said, but her voice did not show it. "I came as soon as I heard Abaas left you and you were pregnant. When I got here, you were gone, and then I saw you returning with a strange man."

"That man is my friend, and you were rude to him."

"What sort of friends are you making around this place?"

"You do not know anything about him, so I suggest you keep your opinions to yourself."

"What?!"

"This is the only cot," I said, getting up to change into my pyjamas, "so we have to share if you are staying the night."

"Sit down and talk to me, Pari joon."

Khale Sara was back. Her voice was calm, and her eyes looked genuinely concerned. She had spent Norooz alone until late into the night. I came back to the table and sat down even though sleep was begging to creep in.

"Last week I saw Abaas' mother, Khanum Tabriz, at the market, and she ducked behind the jars of olive oil to avoid talking to me. I let her go, thinking she had things on her mind and did not have time to socialize with me. Then, today, I passed her crossing the street. I said hello, so she had to acknowledge me. She looked wretched. I asked her if she had any news from you newlyweds, and she told me Abaas had moved to another town because my Pari had been dishonest with him."

I opened my mouth to speak but did not know where to start, so I continued to listen.

"Dumbfounded, I was left in the middle of the road until the honking of a car moved me to the other side. Imagine my surprise when I came to find you with a strange man coming home late at night. Give me some credit."

"You can give me some credit too," I said, starting my rebuttal. "Abaas' concern over how he would manage financially with a new baby overtook his excitement for becoming a father. He left the night I told him that I was pregnant and never returned, not even for his belongings. One husband abandons me for not getting pregnant and another abandons me for getting pregnant. Hard to know what people consider dishonest these days. I have been alone for six months, but I managed to feed us and keep us warm through the winter. No one in all that time came to say, "Kharet be chand mane." I met Ahmad Agha on one of my walks to gather firewood. He was kind to me and helped me build this."

I swung my arm towards the bright orange-and-brown cradle by my cot.

Khale Sara smiled at me with compassion. "Where were

you coming back from tonight, Pari joon?" she asked gently, accusation gone from her voice.

"Ahmad Agha invited me to his home for Norooz. His three daughters joined him for the first time after their mother's death seven years ago."

"Did you have a good time, azizam?" she said, smiling sweetly.

"Yes. They treated me like one of the family."

Khale Sara's smile faded, but I placed my hand over hers on the table and we understood each other.

"I am sorry I was not there for you. How do you feel?"

"I have not seen a doctor, and I am eight months pregnant. I thought this time would be different."

Khale Sara looked puzzled but stayed focused.

"Tomorrow I can take you back to Tehran. I will take you to see my doctor – Doctor Forsat. You cannot stay here."

"This is my home. It is where I belong."

"Pari joon, please come back to your father's house."

I realized that the long drive was not ideal for Khale Sara and she was suggesting the most practical solution. Leaving this home that I had built with Abaas and then lived in for the duration of my pregnancy made me sad.

The next morning, Khale Sara was sensitive during the packing, asking about anything she was not sure of.

"What are these?" Khale asked, holding up the bag of baby toys I had collected.

"Gifts for the baby from Ahmad Agha."

I took the cradle with the baby materials folded inside, the leather sewing bag, and the vase from Fereshteh. I had turned most of our clothing into baby materials. In my carpet bag, I packed my remaining clothes, my mother's wedding dress, and Baba's books. I decided to leave the herb planters and the food in the cupboards for the next tenant. I was tempted to take something of Abaas' to remember him by, but I realized the baby I was carrying would be the best souvenir.

Khale's Peugeot was packed, and our trip began along the dirt road. I asked Khale to pull up next to a local boy riding a bicycle. He stopped when we came close. I gave him a sannar to deliver a letter to Jaleh Khanum. The letter thanked her for her generosity and notified her that the suite was empty and available to rent.

"What was that about?" she asked.

"There are angels everywhere," I confessed to my confused aunt.

There are a thousand ways to kneel and kiss the earth.

—Rumi

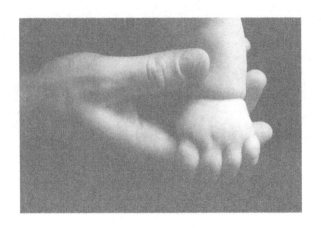

Chapter 19

Audel (1317 SH)

Khale Sara drove through Baba's gate, and we got out of the car. The three children ambushed me at the pond, all of them speaking at the same time. Even though the words were undecipherable, I understood they were happy that I had returned. When they noticed my belly, six little hands were immediately on me, feeling for a kick.

"Children," Khale Sara said, gently pushing them aside and leading me into the house, "let your ameh enter the house and take her shoes off before you let her know how much you missed her."

I noticed the absence of Kuchulu in the yard, but

Khale Sara had told me in the car that he had sneaked out through the open gate just as he had sneaked into the yard so many years ago. Perhaps I had not given him hope of my return by neglecting to say goodbye, or maybe he felt it was time to go. In any case, I had a baby to think about now. I said a little prayer for Kuchulu and walked into Baba's house – again.

I decided to redecorate my room to make room for the baby. I began with some leftover pale yellow paint I found on the third floor and painted my room, making it cheerful and bright. I set the cradle by my bed and redefined my dresser to take the role of a baby's changing table.

The three children wandered in just as I finished gathering up the paint sheets from the floor. They watched me in silence as I moved around the room, organizing things for the baby's arrival.

"Are you here to stay?" Shabnam asked, sitting on my bed, swinging her legs.

I was filling the drawers of my dresser with the clothes I had sewn for the baby.

"We do not like it when you leave," Saeed said shyly, watching me from his spot on the carpet.

From their point of view, I was the aunt that they had not even known about until I showed up four years ago. I was in the children's lives for two years, left for one year, returned for a few months, left for another year, and now was back again.

"I do not know," I answered honestly.

"I want you to stay, Ameh!" Reza pleaded, standing beside the dresser.

He was five years old now and accompanied his older siblings to Pishraft School.

It felt wonderful to be wanted, even if they were not the decision-makers in the household. I did not feel right making promises I could not keep. I came and sat on the bed beside Shabnam, and the boys jumped onto the bed beside us.

"I would like to stay with you always," I said as a compromise.

That seemed to satisfy them, and they went back to adoring my belly.

"You are going to live with us," Reza whispered to my belly.

My bedroom became more like a nursery. I placed Ahmad Agha's baby gifts around the room as decorations for now. I used an old yellow sheet and made new curtains to match the painted walls. As I was putting the leather sewing bag away, my water broke. My brothers were not expected home until late, and neither of the girls knew how to drive. I called Khale Sara at work on the desk set telephone.

She pulled into our front yard and helped me into her car. She looked very nervous, and my reassuring words only increased her anxiety, so I remained quiet.

I was taken into the delivery room, and the nurses prepared me for Doctor Forsat's arrival.

"What if Doctor Forsat does not get here in time?" I heard Khale Sara ask one of the nurses.

"Do not worry, azizam," the nurse said soothingly. "All of us here know how to deliver a baby. It is the most natural thing."

Khale Sara was led to the waiting room. I was tickled at the thought of her pacing with the fathers in that room. A contraction sobered me up.

I was ten centimetres dilated, and the doctor had not arrived. A midwife named Mona Khanum entered the room. In minutes my son came into the world, screaming with dismay at being removed from his cosy environment. He was cleaned, wrapped in a warm blanket to simulate his previous home, and handed to me. I held my tiny Audel and marvelled at every part of him. He had Abaas' dark eyes and my light colouring. I knew I was holding the best part of my husband.

We spent two nights in the hospital. On the third day, Khale Sara picked us up and drove us home. She jogged over to my side and opened my door. I handed Audel to her. Even with both hands free, the climb out of the car was a challenge for me. This second birth had taken more of my energy. I found myself thinking of Khanum Piruz. I understood how an eleventh child could leave her in a wheelchair for years.

I stood up and noticed Khale Sara was smiling at the baby, although she looked awkward holding him. She sighed as she handed him back to me.

The house was empty when we entered. We climbed the stairs to my room. I took great pleasure in placing Audel into the waiting cradle. His sleeping face peeked through the white sheet against the orange blanket. He looked tiny in the large cradle. Khale Sara and I sat on the edge of my bed in silence, our eyes on the rocking baby. Once we had caught our breath, we stood and went to the kitchen to get the tea tray ready.

"When are we expecting him?" Khale Sara asked, placing sugar cubes on the tray.

"He said he would come after lunch and leave before dinner."

"What time is it?"

"One twenty-five," I said, looking at the grandfather clock in the hallway.

We were expecting Ahmad Agha. He did not waste any time in arranging to come to see the baby. The tea tray was ready, and I heard Audel crying, showing a great sense of timing. His cry was more melodic than Vaziri playing the *tar*. It was more endearing than the song of a nightingale. I assumed I was the only one who heard it sound that way, but I was fine with that. I went to my room, picked up my baby's little body, and nursed him. His soft cheek against my breast comforted me. His chest rising and falling relaxed me. It was my privilege to be able to satiate him.

Abaas was missing out on seeing what I saw in our new son. Six-year-old Pantea would have loved meeting her little brother. I could not share this joy with Baba. Yet I was content, because I had Audel to care for.

Emptying one breast took so much energy that Audel fell asleep. I changed his diaper and pulled one of the hand-knit wool soakers over it. Changing him also served to alert him. I sat down and let him nurse on my other breast. Once he had his fill, sleep claimed him, and I carefully placed him back into his cradle.

As I entered the kitchen, I could hear laughter and the clinking of tea glasses in the living room. Ahmad Agha had arrived and was sipping tea with Khale Sara.

"Yes, I can imagine. It would be a challenge to work

among people who refuse to see past your gender and appreciate your talent."

"Would you like something with your tea?" she asked him.

"No thank you," he said in a shy voice.

For some reason, his usual confident voice had a hint of vulnerability.

"Enough about me. How are your three daughters? Have you seen them recently?"

"Thank you for asking. The older two are doing well, busy with work and family. My youngest is visiting from Mashhad next week with her son."

"Akram is her name?" Khale Sara asked, interested.

"Yes. She is a nurse like her mother was."

His voice drifted off towards the end, and Khale Sara was perceptive.

"Tell me, what was she like?"

"She loved to sing around the house. I miss her singing. She had a great sense of humour and laughed easily. She was always thinking of others before herself: her patients, her neighbours, and, most of all, her family."

"She sounds wonderful," Khale Sara said. "You must really miss her."

I walked into the room with a platter of shirini and saw Ahmad Agha nodding. They both looked up and greeted me. My wish had come true. They were caring towards each other as they were towards me. I sat and had a glass of tea with them. When Audel awoke, I took Ahmad Agha to meet him. Ahmad Agha knelt beside the cradle and talked softly to the baby as if he were old enough to understand.

"It is a pleasure to meet you, Audel joon. Welcome to

the world. You have a bright future ahead of you. You are very lucky because there are many people who love you – especially your mother. She worked very hard to keep you safe for nine months. No doubt she will work hard for the rest of her life, ensuring you have every door opened to you. I will try to be like a grandfather to you, and I know you have a wonderful aunt in Sara Khanum."

He smiled up at Khale Sara and me, and we smiled back in agreement.

At the gate, Ahmad Agha said goodbye to us with a hug and a kiss on our cheeks. That form of salutation belongs to close family, but I was accustomed to receiving it from him. I noticed Khale Sara's face looked flushed as she closed the gate behind him. Most men were timid around Khale Sara, only bowing with a hand on their chest. No one dared to hug her or kiss her on the cheeks.

We walked into the house and straight to the kitchen. It was the usual time to make dinner, but it was unusual for Khale Sara to stay and help. She took her cues from me. I planned on making *Khorok* – a stew with potatoes and carrots in a tomato sauce. I was using more meat in the meals here than in Karaj. I had taken lamb out of the icebox earlier and placed it in a stone pot with chopped onions and water. I placed the pot on the gas stove, and Khale lit it. I carried carrots to the sink, and Khale brought the potatoes. I poured tomato sauce into the pot.

"Do you not find them so unusual, his green eyes?" she asked as she washed the potatoes and carrots.

"Baba's eyes were green," I said, but she did not comment.

"How old do you think Ahmad Agha is?" she asked, peeling carrots and potatoes and handing them to me to chop.

"I do not know," I said, distracted.

"How old is his oldest daughter?"

"Zahra? She married at nineteen, and her oldest is fifteen, so I suppose she is thirty-five."

"Then he may be as young as fifty-five," she said, delighted.

"Why does that matter?" I asked, pouring the vegetables into the pot.

"I should go, Pari joon. Are you going to be all right until the others get back?"

"Yes, Khale, no need to worry about me."

"When are the girls returning? You should not be on your feet cooking."

"I do not know where they are to know when they are returning."

The grandfather clock chimed. I liked its melodic ring.

"Amir and Ali will be home in an hour, right?" asked Khaleh.

"Yes, and this stew cooks itself."

We said goodbye, and I returned to the kitchen. I was glad to be alone in the house. I placed the lid on the stone pot and turned the heat down to let it simmer. Audel, in his great wisdom, took that moment to call on me again. I was grateful for his thoughtful sense of timing.

I settled down to nurse when I heard the front door open. Many voices and footsteps came bounding in: children's high-pitched voices and fast steps, and adults' serious tones and lethargic steps. It took no time for the children to come bouncing into my room. They climbed all around me on the bed with wide-eyed wonder.

"Ameh Pari, is this our new baby?" six-year-old Shabnam asked, kneeling behind me and peering over my shoulder.

"Yes, azizam, this is Audel," I said, my heart swelling at the word "our".

"Is he the one that kicked my hand?" asked Reza, grinning with shrugged shoulders.

"Yes, Reza joon. He was in a hurry to come out and play with you."

Reza yelled hurrah and began jumping on the bed.

"Reza!" Shabnam scolded. "Do not jump on the bed or you will make the bed explode – or you will fall off the bed and cut your head open, and there will be blood everywhere."

My head turned to Shabnam in shock at her harsh description. She looked nervously at me until I smiled.

"That was not quite how I put it," I told her, "but I am glad you remember it is not right to jump on the bed."

"He cannot play yet, right Ameh?" Saeed asked, perhaps remembering that he had to wait for Reza to grow before he could play with him.

"You are right," I answered. "You will have to wait until he gets stronger to be able to keep up with you athletes."

They beamed proudly at my compliment.

"Ameh, what is in there?" asked Reza, pointing to the breast Audel was nursing on.

"Reza! That is rude!" Shabnam scolded.

"It is all right to ask," I said. "It is milk, Reza joon."

Reza quietly contemplated this new information.

"Is the other one juice?"

I burst out laughing, and the older two children joined in, whether or not they understood the humour.

"What is so funny?" Shole said, appearing at the doorway.

"Reza asked Ameh if—"

"You children need to go wash up for dinner," Shole interrupted.

The children groaned as they left my room. I promised them that I would bring Audel down to dinner. Shole waited until the children were gone before speaking.

"Is that the best name you could come up with?" she criticized.

"What do you have against the name Audel?" I asked, not really caring what she thought.

"First of all, Crazy Pari, it is not Iranian but Arabic in origin."

I was unmoved, so I stayed silent, gazing at the sweet face of my baby, who was drinking his fill. Shole was not satisfied.

"Why not a religious name, such as Mohammad, after your father, or Ali, after your brother?"

"Religious?" I asked, feeling confident in my argument. "We refer to God as Khoda-e Audel, meaning 'the impartial, just, and fair God'. My son will grow up to be all of that."

Shole chose cruelty over reason.

"Even the name Amir, which means 'leader', would have been better. Maybe it could have served your brat better than Ali's sidekick of a brother."

"Dinner is ready," Amir said from the doorway. "Nasim sent me to tell you."

Shole spun around and saw her brother-in-law inches away from her. His tall build, dark features, and deep voice unsettled her. Amir remained looming over her, until she backed away.

"Oh, Amir, I did not see you there," Shole said in a singsong voice. "Hurry along now, Pari joon."

Shole scurried away, and Amir's glare followed her.

"She does not know anything about you," I said to my brother.

Amir turned back to me with one arched eyebrow.

"What *did* you name him?" he asked.

"Audel."

"That is a fine name," he said with a blank expression, and he left.

I finished nursing Audel and carried him down to the dining room with me. I was told that the sofreh was for backward people, so now dinners in Baba's home were eaten at the dining table. The adults stayed on practical topics, such as car arrangements, house maintenance, and necessary purchases. Only the children spoke of the family's new baby.

"How do you like your school?" I asked the children, turning the attention back on them.

"It is all right," said Saeed, who was more interested in Audel's tiny toes.

He had finished his dinner and knelt on the floor beside the sleeping baby. The orange blanket unfolded enough for one small foot to pop out. I watched Saeed take off one of his own socks and hold his foot next to the baby's. Saeed's face was filled with awe at the comparison.

"I like my school, Ameh," Shabnam said, moving one seat over so she was next to me.

"What do you like about it?" I asked.

"I like reading poetry," she said.

"Really?" I said, pleased that we shared this joy. "That was my favourite part of school too. There are many poetry books that belonged to your grandfather. We could read some together if you like."

"I would like that very much," Shabnam said.

"Why not ask her what you really want to know, Pari joon?" Shole said.

"Shole!" Ali threatened.

"Shabnam joon," Shole said, ignoring Ali. "Is Pantea Piruz in your class?"

I felt my heart tighten and a familiar ache resurface. I wanted to pick up my baby and run as far away from this house as possible. It was difficult to know that my first baby was next door and I could not hold her. I repeatedly told myself she was being cared for, but I could not be sure. Besides, I wanted to be the one doing the caring.

I looked up from my plate and realized the room had become silent. Shabnam was staring at me, knowing something was wrong, but she stayed silent.

"Ali joon," Shole said in a syrupy voice. "Do you know what Shabnam's teacher told me?"

No response.

"She told me that she is very proud of our little girl. She thinks Shabnam is destined to become a psychiatrist. She overheard Shabnam advising a friend, saying, 'You do not really hate that girl in your class. If you saw her lying on the street, bleeding from the head, you would run over and help her.' Her teacher thought that was insightful of our Shabnam."

Shabnam was looking down at her plate. When she glanced up at me, she looked embarrassed.

"Ali joon, do we not have the most wonderful little girl?" Shole swooned.

"Amir and I will go to the family room and wait for our tea there," said Ali, gesturing to his brother to join him.

The two men stood and left the room. I quickly got up, picked up Audel, and headed for my room. Nasim stood up and blocked the doorway.

"You had better not think you will get out of any of the work around here because a baby dropped out of you," Nasim whispered.

"You mean *all* the work, as before," I corrected her.

"Watch yourself, Crazy Pari," Shole said. "We let you do chores so you did not feel like a burden in this household."

"What did you girls do so you did not feel like a burden?" I asked. "Well, I already know what you did, Shole. Your three children are proof of that. What about you, Nasim?"

Nasim's face grew red and distorted.

"You have some nerve," she said, taking a step towards me.

"You do not intimidate me," I said, looking down at her. "You sting; you get swatted at. Go get your husbands some tea like they asked you to and let me be."

I pushed past her with one shoulder and went to my room. My boldness was a welcomed surprise.

I heard a knock at the door and then saw Shabnam's head peeking in.

"Yes, jigar tala?"

I patted the bed beside me, and she ran and hopped onto it. I was rocking Audel even though he had fallen asleep. I suppose the rocking was soothing me.

"I am sorry, Ameh joon," she said with the same embarrassed expression as before.

"What do you have to be sorry about?"

"That was your advice I gave to my friend at school."

I shook my head. "You remembered the advice, you understood it, and you used it to help your friend. There is no need for an apology. I got that advice from somewhere and helped you. Your friend may use it one day to help someone else. That is life. We share wisdom."

Shabnam hugged me, pinning my arms to my sides. She released me and ran from the room, singing goodnight as she went.

Part 3

If you are irritated by every rub, how will you be polished?

—Rumi

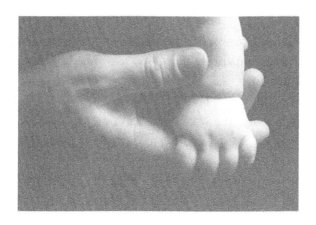

Chapter 20

Dissonance (1318 SH)

Again I had a household to maintain, a baby of my own, and other children to care for. I set the breakfast table, packed the school lunches, and saw each child to the door. My brothers left for work; and the girls, for shopping. I cleaned, cooked, and bought groceries every Wednesday, thanks to the icebox. I rested with Audel in the middle of the day and even had time to read when the children were quiet and dinner was stewing on the stove. Like clockwork, the girls arrived an hour before their husbands. They changed into housedresses and chatted with the children to ensure they were not mistreated. They sampled the dinner in the pot, made a few displeased comments, and then settled on the carpet cushions, sipping tea until their husbands returned from work.

It made me wonder how they managed in my absence.

Baba's homemade radio was remembering that it had been almost a year since Germany invaded Poland. As a result, Britain and France had declared war on Germany. People around the world were fighting for their lives and fighting for peace. Listening to the radio helped me put my life in perspective.

Audel was going to have his first birthday in two weeks. I was looking forward to a fun party with his three cousins. All three children were in school for the day, but when they arrived home, they would be surprised with balloons and streamers and cake after dinner. I was sure they would be excited to help Audel blow out his one candle.

I made Audel's doctor appointments for Wednesdays so I could have him vaccinated and do the grocery shopping on the same outing. This Wednesday, I had my annual physical check-up with Doctor Forsat. The nurse had told me not to bring Audel.

"We do not offer free care for children here, Khanum," the nurse had said. "That is not our job."

On Tuesday night, as everyone prepared to go to sleep, I heard Shole's voice in the hall. I hurried into the hall to catch her before she retired to their room for the night.

"Shole, I have a doctor's appointment tomorrow. Can you watch Audel for a couple of hours?"

"Nasim and I have plans," Shole said, walking away and signalling the end of the conversation.

"It will be when he is napping," I called in haste before she walked into her room.

"Is tomorrow not Wednesday?" Shole asked, looking curiously over her shoulder. "That is grocery day, right? You always take your brat along on grocery days."

"His name is Audel. The doctor's receptionist told me that I need to find another arrangement."

"So find another arrangement."

"You are my other arrangement," I said, swallowing my pride.

"That brat has been nothing but trouble since you brought him into this house."

"That is not true," I said, trying to keep my frustration out of my voice. "He has not woken you up once. I know because I wake up before he does. I watch him until he wakes and put him to my breast before he has a chance to cry."

"You have grown into quite a confrontational terror," Shole said, turning to look at me, her eyes narrowing.

"I learned from the best," I said, ignoring her shocked expression. "You need to be here when I leave for my physical at one o'clock in the afternoon."

I walked into my room and closed the door before she could say more.

Shole turned up ten minutes late, and I had to rush through my instructions to her in case Audel woke before I returned. While I spoke, Shole rummaged through her shopping bag, which contained her purchases of that morning.

"Did you hear me?" I asked once I was finished.

"Uh huh," she answered distractedly.

I had to hope for the best and left the house.

Doctor Forsat confirmed that I was healthy, and I headed for the market. I got the meat first, and then the produce, and I literally ran to the last shop to pick up eggs and milk. I filled my basket with eggs, and just as I reached for a jar of milk, a man's hand reached for the same jar. Our hands touched, so I pulled mine back. Without looking at who it was, I picked another jar.

"Pari?" a woman asked.

I looked over and saw it had not been a man, but Khanum Tabriz, with her large hands. I became alarmed. In my mind's eye, I saw Khanum Piruz – spherical, uptight, holding Pantea. I saw Audel sleeping peacefully in his cradle when suddenly two large hands snatched him up. I heard myself gasp at the thought. I put down the milk and eggs, my eyes searching for the exit of the store.

"Please, Pari." Khanum Tabriz said gently. "Do not leave because of me. Here, let me get these for you."

She overpaid the store owner with one large bill and handed the parcel to me. I took it from her, stuffed it into one of my cloth bags, and offered her a smaller bill that would cover the cost more closely. When she made no move to take it, I placed it on the counter next to her.

"Thank you, Khanum, but I am in a hurry and must go."

I weaved through the shoppers towards the exit.

"He is turning one soon," she said in a strained voice, trying to keep up with me.

Her words filled me with distress, which quickened my pace. How much did she know about my Audel?

Khanum Tabriz followed me down the street until there were no more shops but only kagel homes on either side. The street turned from paved to dirt. Soon she was at my side, breathless. Her long legs made up for her lack of stamina. Her wheezing filled me with guilt. I was responsible for making her walk at such an uncomfortable pace. Still I continued. I tried telling myself that I was being paranoid, but losing Pantea had left an imprint on my heart and on my brain. The adrenaline pushed me faster.

"I want to see my grandson," she said, exhaling heavily.

I looked sideways at her strained face and said nothing. She was not my concern. I was glad Audel was not with me, but at the same time, I knew I would feel much better once he was.

"Are you listening?" Khanum Tabriz raised her voice. She shook her head with regret. "What is his name?" she asked in a soft voice.

I reminded myself not to trust anyone who yelled in one sentence and talked softly in the next, but my upbringing forced me to answer her question.

"Audel," I said, and I felt vulnerable now that she knew his name.

"That is a wonderful name," she said, sounding delighted.

Her compliment did not ease my nerves. My negative emotions towards this woman grew into boldness.

"I have been caring for my son on my own for almost two years," I said, wanting to add "You misinformed my aunt about me. I have always been loyal to Abaas."

"Yes, I know," she said, sounding sincere. "I am sorry. I would like to help by giving him his first birthday party at my home. Please let me do that for him."

For him or for you? I thought.

Khanum Tabriz stopped, hands on her knees and

panting loudly. Relieved, I continued, in an attempt to put as much distance between us as possible.

"Goodbye, Khanum," I said over my shoulder with a quick bow.

"You will not keep me from my grandson," she panted.

I did not dare run until I turned the corner. Thirty metres down the road, my sprinting legs became liquid and I crumpled to the ground. I knelt there with my head hung low and my body trembling violently.

I remembered lying on Khanum Piruz's bedroom floor with Farid's face inches away from mine. He looked so lost, and I felt sad for both of us. That day, he lost me and I lost my child.

I remained kneeling in the middle of that empty dirt road until my body stopped betraying me. I reminded myself that Audel was at home, comfortably sleeping. Standing slowly, I noticed my legs were under my control again. I ran the rest of the way home with bags flailing about. Only one foot was still wearing a flip-flop upon arrival at our gate. Wheezing, I bolted the gate behind me with considerable difficulty. My sore hands seemed to have a mind of their own, and it took some convincing to get them to cooperate.

My distress peaked when I heard Audel's cry. I ran up the three wide steps and through the front door. I dropped the grocery bags on the floor when I saw Shole dangling Audel by the armpits. She thrust my screaming baby towards me, his arms and legs floundering. I took him and folded him into my arms.

"Where is his blanket?" I panted. "He feels vulnerable without it."

Shole was almost out of the room, but I heard her groan, "That is your thank you?"

Audel's face looked unusually red and swollen. Tears were still streaming down his face. His nose and quivering mouth were foaming. His diaper had soaked his clothes, resulting in chilled arms and legs. I blamed myself. I cuddled him until he was calm and then cleaned and nursed him. I lay beside him on my bed and rocked his cradle until he fell asleep. Then I fell asleep.

I woke up to Audel's cry for his next feeding. I realized it was dark outside. As I sat on my bed nursing, the grandfather clock chimed nine times. I had slept through dinner.

Shabnam stuck her head timidly through the door.

"Hi, Ameh. You are awake?"

"Yes, azizam. How was school?"

"Good," she said, sliding in and closing the door behind her.

"Why so secretive?" I whispered, amused by her drama. "You have school tomorrow and should be asleep."

"Ameh, are you leaving us?" Shabnam asked, bursting into tears.

"What are you talking about?" I asked in surprise, motioning for her to jump on the bed next to me. "Come here, ghorban."

I held Audel with one arm and held her sobbing body with the other as she made herself into a ball. She was mumbling a whole story, but I could not understand all of the words. Once she lifted her head and used the handkerchief that I gave to her, she paraphrased.

"Maman is telling Baba that you want to move away," Shabnam said with a shudder.

"Why would I do that?" I asked, not completely oblivious to what the reason could have been.

"Maman says you do not think she cares about you or Audel."

"Why would I think that?"

"Maman says you want to be impenendent of us with your share of the inerence and go live on your own like before."

"I do not recall thinking that, so your maman could not have read my mind. I know I did not say it, so your maman could not have heard me. I wonder why she would say that to your baba."

I was trying to get her to think for herself.

"Is maman pretending?" Shabnam said with a gasp.

"If you mean she is making it up, then yes, Shabnam joon."

"But why?"

"You will need to ask her that," I said, rising to change Audel.

I walked to my dresser/change-table, picked up a towel, and headed for the bathroom, carrying my baby. The indoor plumbing that Ali had installed once his twins were born made the task of changing a diaper on this floor much easier. I took the old diaper off, washed Audel's bottom in the deep concrete sink, wrapped him in the towel, and made my way back to my room. Later I would return to wash the soiled diaper, which would devotedly wait for me in its tub.

Shabnam had fallen asleep in my bed. Her room was next to her brothers' room, on the third floor. Ali had cleared out the clutter from those rooms and decorated them for the children. The boys had each other, but Shabnam was alone and lonely.

I put a fresh diaper on Audel, pulled on a wool soaker, nursed him on my second breast, and laid him in his cradle to sleep until morning. It was too warm for the orange comforter. I covered him with a sheet. Then I returned to the washroom and washed the soiled diaper.

My exhaustion overpowered my hunger, so I crawled into my bed next to Shabnam, trying not to wake her. Our bunking together had become a regular event. I did not mind her kicking in her sleep. It was better than the alternative: hearing her scream from a nightmare. No one seemed to have an objection as long as she was quiet.

Let yourself be silently drawn by the stronger pull of what you really love.

—Rumi

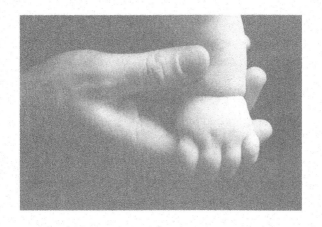

Chapter 21

Derelict (1319 SH)

Days passed, and I waited, knowing that soon I would be having a conversation about my living arrangements with the adults in the house.

It was bedtime, and I was returning from the bathroom with Audel in my arms. As I approached my room, I heard Shole and Ali in my doorway, trying to convince Shabnam to go to her room. Shabnam wanted to stay and hear my fate, which meant her fate. I entered my room, walking past the three of them.

"Oh, there you are, Pari joon," Shole said in the ultra-sweet voice of a lyncher.

I diapered Audel while they continued to coax Shabnam into leaving. I sat on my bed to nurse Audel on my second breast, a blanket over my shoulder for Ali's benefit. My brothers were not comfortable around me when I nursed.

Shabnam ran to the bed, leaped, and landed beside me.

"Shabnam, get off that bed and go to your room," Shole said with ineffective authority.

Shabnam pushed in closer to me, looking at her parents defiantly.

"See, Ali," Shole said, as if reinforcing an earlier argument. "Your sister is a bad influence on our daughter. See how she blatantly disrespects me."

I remembered a similarly painful accusation from Khanum Piruz a lifetime ago.

"Did you want to talk to me?" I asked to get the ordeal in motion.

"Pari," Ali began, "I want to offer you your share of Baba's asset as your inheritance."

"It is nine hundred toman," Shole added, her excitement fading with Ali's glare.

"Why would I need that much money?" I asked, toying with them.

"Well, Pari joon," Shole said, her voice dripping with honey, "you do not want to live in this old house for the rest of your life."

I lifted Audel to my shoulder to burp him.

"Why not?" I asked, having fun. "It has been serving you and your sister for almost a decade."

"Pari," Ali said sternly, "You need to use this money and come up with a plan. Your future is not here."

"You would send your little sister and her child away?"

I asked, knowing his weak spot. "What would the relatives think? What would people say?"

Ali's face became distraught, and Shole worried that they were losing momentum.

"Imagine what you could do with nine hundred toman, Pari joon," she said nervously.

Audel relieved himself by burping, reminding me of his great sense of timing.

"Yes, I know the value of nine hundred toman," I said, placing Audel inside his cradle and covering him with the sheet. "I am ready to sleep now, since I will be up early to make everyone's breakfast."

Ali walked away, motioning to Shole to follow him. Shole reluctantly followed, even though she had hoped for a resolution that night. Shabnam had fallen asleep, and neither parent seemed to remember the importance of her sleeping arrangement.

A few days later, I got a visitor. I was in the kitchen making lubia polo, and the boys, Audel and Reza, were sleeping in the family room among the cushions. Reza was home sick from school.

I opened the front gate and saw Fereshteh standing there with a bouquet of daisies.

"I remembered they are your favourite," she said with a grin.

We hugged and we laughed and we cried.

"You are here; you are really here," I repeated, forcing myself to believe it.

"I knew where your father's home was, and your mother-in-law told me that you moved back to Tehran."

"Khanum Tabriz?" I asked, trying not to sound unnerved. "Where did you see her?"

"Take it easy," Fereshteh said, looking worried. "She came to collect her son's belongings. Jaleh Khanum must have found a new tenant and called her to clean out the place. I showed up and startled her. I had not heard from you, so I came looking for you. She told me that you had a healthy boy and you were both safe at your father's home."

"She said that?"

"Yes. Is something the matter?"

"Forgive me. I left in a hurry. I am thrilled that you came."

"I do not come into Tehran often, and when I do, I am always in a hurry. This visit is long overdue."

We walked inside and straight to the kitchen, where I prepared the tea tray.

"Khanum Tabriz did tell me that you named him Audel," she said. "What a meaningful name."

Reza walked sluggishly into the kitchen from his nap. He had a fever which broke about noon. When he saw Fereshteh, he ran and hugged one of my legs while watching her suspiciously.

"Wow, he has grown!" Fereshteh said, and we both laughed.

"This is Reza, my nephew."

Fereshteh knelt down and introduced herself as my dearest friend.

"So where is the little darling?" she asked.

"In the family room," I said, trying to move around the kitchen with the weight of Reza on my leg. "Reza joon, please show Fereshteh Khanum where baby Audel is sleeping."

Reza let go of me and marched to the family room, periodically glancing back at Fereshteh, who followed. His mission relieved him of his shyness.

Fereshteh saw Audel and knelt over his sleeping body, cooing and throwing kisses in his direction.

I brought in the tea tray and saw Fereshteh was crying.

"Why are you sad, Fereshteh joon?"

"This is the third time a man has not kept his promise to you." She wiped her tears and came to sit next to me. "I feel so sad for my friend."

I felt sad for *my* friend. Fereshteh had carried all of my burdens through the years. In Karaj I had told her about the weakness of Farid, the loss of Pantea, the challenge of getting my diploma, and the cruelty of Mahmood. I patted her hand and beamed as brightly as I could.

"I have done all right."

"You have been strong for as long as I have known you. On my wedding night, when I was falling apart, you came to my rescue. When I was living in Karaj and needed a friend, you came to visit me every week, even after Abass left. Now I realize that."

"You were not alone in Karaj. You had your grandparents."

"They were not like you – a friend, close to my age, going through the same things in life."

"Well, not quite the same things, fortunately."

"I am sorry," Fereshteh said looking as though she were about to cry again.

"Look at me!" I said quickly. "I am doing fine. God hands you your life in pieces, and you are supposed to figure out what to do with them. You can lie down and give up or you can do your best."

"You have done well, Pari joon."

"You have, too, my friend. Tell me about the boys. They must have grown so big,"

I longed to see them and their playful ways.

"Yes, they are five and seven and take most of my time. You know me. I am devoted to driving them to football practise and violin lessons and whatever else their passion demands."

"Your children are the most important project in your life, right?"

We were silent in each other's company for a while.

"When they were toddlers," Fereshteh began, "Niku had this awful habit of walking and leaving a trail behind him after dirtying his pants. I wish he would have stood in one spot."

She placed her tea glass on the table as she continued her story.

"One day, Nima was on the cushions with a fever, and Niku had a bad case of diarrhea. I had been alternating between wiping a wet cloth over Nima's limbs to keep the fever down and cleaning up Niku's trails. As I was scrubbing yet another mess on the floor, I muttered that I wished I were dead."

"I know how frustrating it can be."

"Later that day, as I spoon-fed Nima some awsh, he asked me, 'Do you still wish you were dead, Maman?'"

"Oh, Fereshteh," I said, touching her arm in sympathy.

"I placed the bowl of awsh on the table, held my baby in my arms, and told him that I would never want to be apart from them. I apologized and assured him that my words were due to fatigue. Nima thought for a moment, and do you know what he said to me?"

"What, Fereshteh joon?"

"He said, 'We can help you, Maman. Maybe we cannot make stew, but we can make sandwiches.'"

"You are blessed."

"We both are."

I poured more tea.

"How is your living arrangement working out here?" Fereshteh asked unwittingly.

"Challenges never end," I confided.

"What is it?"

"I have been asked to leave Baba's house and take my baby with me."

"What sort of a person would ask this of you?"

"My brother, Ali. He offered me nine hundred toman as my share of the inheritance."

"What can you get with just nine hundred toman?"

"This is their offer."

We sat in silence, neither of us sipping our tea. We watched as Reza snuggled next to the sleeping baby.

"Are you not concerned your baby will get sick from Reza?"

"I am still nursing, so Audel has my immunity," I said.

"You are so smart," Fereshteh said.

I finally read the biology textbook, I thought to myself.

"Do you still have your diploma certificate?" she asked, changing the topic.

"Yes."

"Go get it for me, plus your birth certificate."

I went to my room and took both documents out of the small tin box under my bed. I kept my important papers in it. There were notes from Baba, on which he had drawn funny pictures. There were three wedding greeting cards from Khale Sara. She made her own cards with poems that held messages of love and encouragement. There was a collection of drawings – well, scribbles really – that Pantea had done. No one in the Piruz household took notice of the children's creations, so I kept my child's.

I returned to the family room with my birth certificate and diploma and handed them to Fereshteh. I suppose I should have been curious why she wanted these documents, but my mind was occupied with the sentimental memorabilia.

We tiptoed to the kitchen so as not to wake the two sleeping boys. I cleared our tea tray, and we sat at the table, on which there was a pile of green beans. Each with a small knife in hand, we proceeded to clip the two ends of each bean.

"Have you given any thought to what you might do with your nine hundred toman?"

"I want to buy a piece of land – maybe in Narmak, where it is less expensive and not far from here. I want to begin by building an *ab anbar* on it."

"What about a house?" Fereshteh asked.

"A house, too, in time. That money could afford only the land and the ab anbar."

"Why an ab anbar?"

"The people around there do not have easy access to water. They would be welcome to get their water from my ab anbar, and as they did, they would say the traditional Khoda pedaresho beyamorze. Since the ab anbar would be built from Baba's money, it would be appropriate that every time someone took water from it, they would say a little prayer for him."

"I agree."

"I will have to figure out how to raise funds to build a house on the lot."

"You will come up with an idea."

"Perhaps when Audel grows up, he can get a job and help me," I said, and we laughed half-heartedly.

As if on cue, Audel woke up crying.

"Ameh, Audel is crying," Reza announced the obvious.

"I will get him," Fereshteh said.

Reza stumbled into the kitchen after his second nap. I sat him at the kitchen table with a glass of juice. I unbuttoned my blouse as Fereshteh returned with Audel and handed him to me.

"That one is the juice," Reza said with a smirk.

I told the story to Fereshteh of Reza's theory about breasts, and she laughed.

Nursing was my favourite activity. This act that no one else could replicate belonged to me alone. I had the power inside me to satisfy my baby. The experience changed from one tiny hand resting peacefully on my breast to a demanding hand impatiently tugging at me. After the first teeth erupted, he even drew blood from my nipples due to his impatience. Audel had turned one, so I was in the process of weaning him off nursing.

Fereshteh and Reza visited at the kitchen table while I took care of Audel's needs.

The time came when Fereshteh had to leave to pick up Nima and Niku from school. She still had a long drive ahead of her.

"I will be in touch, Pari joon," she promised as she climbed into her car.

I knew it would be a long time before I got to see my friend again.

Come, seek, for search is the foundation of fortune: every success depends upon focusing the heart.

—Rumi

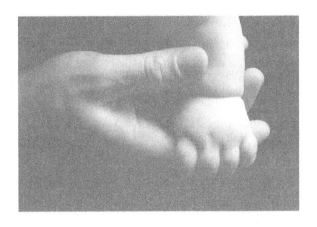

Chapter 22

My Own Home (1319 SH)

The following spring, my ab anbar was built in Narmak – an eastern, more modest district of Tehran. Khale Sara took care of the legal papers for the purchase of the land, and Ahmad Agha did the construction. I dreamed it, and it happened. People from the neighbourhood came and took water. As I had suspected, they spoke their thanks with the traditional phrase that was Baba's rightful prayer: "Khoda pedaresho beyamorze."

During the construction of the ab anbar, Khale Sara acted like a love-struck teenager, fluttering around Ahmad Agha, waiting with anticipation to do something for him.

She would drive to the construction site with lemonade, cut melons, or even ice cream for him to have as a break. Of course she would sit with him and share the moment, under the pretence of needing to take the dishes away afterward. They would chat about the past, the present, and the future until they finally got to the topic of their future together. By the time the ab anbar was ready, so were they.

A wedding was planned to take place in Karaj at Ahmad Agha's home. His daughters were overjoyed by the news and came for the ceremony with their spouses and children. My brothers and their families plus aunts and uncles that I saw only at weddings and funerals all attended. It became a family reunion as well as the start of a very special life together.

Once again, Ahmad Agha left his store to a friend. He moved to Tehran to live with Khale Sara. I was fascinated by how naturally two strangers' lives blended seamlessly. Their affection was constant. They gazed into each other's eyes even when they were talking about the most mundane activities. Khale Sara had found a man she could respect enough to share her life with. She fulfilled her promise to her sister and wore Nargis' wedding dress.

"Any thought to when you are moving out?" Shole asked as she stopped in the doorway of my room.

It was the morning after Khale Sara's wedding. Ali had not mentioned my leaving again, but Shole was persistent.

"I have to figure out my finances," I replied, dressing Audel for our Wednesday shopping.

To preserve Audel's safety and my independence, the Wednesday shopping took place after Audel's nap instead of during it.

"I would think that if you had not spent all that money on an ab anbar, you would have had enough to build a house."

"Yes. That is what you would think," I said, walking past her with Audel.

For weeks I dreaded seeing Khanum Tabriz in the market, but I did not. Slowly I came to believe that she did not intend to take my son away from me. Audel toddled beside me, holding my hand. If my hands were busy, he would hold my skirt. The shopkeepers were always glad to see him. They would comment on how he had grown and offer him a treat.

"How old are you, pesaram?" a senior man asked.

Audel held up two fingers proudly, and the man chuckled. I was immediately transported to the time I saw my little girl holding up her two fingers in response to the same question. The memory was bittersweet. As always, I pushed the thought of Pantea out of my mind and filled my attention with the present. It was self-preservation.

Some evenings when the house was quiet, I indulged myself in writing to Pantea and telling her my latest news. I told her of her little brother, of the building of the ab anbar, and of Khale Sara's wedding. I pretended that the letters actually reached her and she would know that I had not forgotten her.

Audel and I arrived home after the children were home from school. I could hear their voices chirping around the house and Shole snapping at them. Audel ran into the kitchen and immediately had three cousins ready to play with him. Shabnam had brought the mail in, and there it sat on the kitchen table. An overstuffed white envelope stood out among the pile. I proceeded to unpack and put away the groceries from the cloth grocery bags.

Shabnam handed me the overstuffed envelope.

"This is for you, Ameh," she said.

"For me?" I asked, not accustomed to getting mail.

"A man came while you were gone and left it for you. He said he was the custodian of Movafagh Secondary School down the road."

Who would be sending me a letter from my secondary school and having it hand-delivered?

I folded the grocery bags and sat at the kitchen table with the envelope. I turned it over and over in my hand, looking for a clue. It had my name on it, but I still could not understand why it was for me.

"Ameh, will you make more cream puffs?" asked Reza.

"Later, azizam," I answered him, preoccupied.

"Hoorah! She said yes," said Reza.

"No! She said tomorrow," said Saeed.

"No! She said not right now," said Shabnam.

I tore open the envelope, and inside I found a large bundle of cash tied with a string. Now I was sure that there had been a mistake and this envelope had been delivered to the wrong house. I checked the front of the envelope and reread my full name. I wondered if there was another Pari Pushtekar, but then I saw my birth certificate and diploma inside with the money. I took everything out and found two more documents with my name on them: a teaching contract and a maternity leave certificate with the date of return stamped on it. There was a letter enclosed, and I recognized the signature at the bottom; it was that of Shahram Nemat, the superintendent of schools.

According to the teaching contract, I was on maternity leave until the end of the summer. The money was my pay for the length of my maternity leave. In the fall, I was to 'return' to teaching mathematics at Movafag Secondary School – the very school I had graduated from three years ago.

"What is it, Ameh?" Shabnam asked, startled. "Why are you crying?"

I had not been aware that I was crying.

"These are tears of joy, azizam," I said, smiling at Shabnam to reassure her. "I got a little help from a friend, in return for dressing up his bride one night long ago."

The first person I contacted was Ahmad Agha.

"Salaam, jigar tala," he said playfully.

"Salaam Ahmad Agha," I said, smiling into the phone. "I heard you recently became available for employment."

"You heard right, ghorban. At your service."

"I want to build a house on my land," I said, hardly believing my own words.

"*Bah, bah!*" he exclaimed in delight. "When do I start?"

While I used my three months to prepare for teaching, Ahmad Agha used his to learn how to build a house. He employed the expertise of a local builder, while I called Agha Nemat to mentor me.

I had been listening to Baba's radio and hearing about the struggle the Shah was having in keeping Russia and Britain out of Iran. The last report said there were rumours that the Shah had been exiled and his young son given the throne.

"Have you heard anything new about the Shah's attempt

to stand up to Stalin and Churchill?" I asked Agha Nemat as he gathered his books at the end of one of our sessions.

"Reza Shah would not have backed down," Agha Nemat said.

He sat again at the kitchen table. He held his packed briefcase to his chest with both arms. Periodically he pushed his large glasses up the bridge of his nose, only to have them slowly slide back down.

"They wanted the Shah to allow access through Iran so they could reach Germany.

"There were no other routes," I said, repeating the remarks of some shopkeepers.

"The Shah spent the last sixteen years improving the highways and buildings. He was not going to let foreign tanks tear them up because it was the easiest route to Russia."

"The war ending may have been more of a consideration than newly paved roads."

"I also want this war to end, but they should have been more creative instead of taking the easiest route by force. The world is a big place with many possibilities."

"What will happen to him?"

"Reza Shah? Who knows? He is exiled to South Africa, and his son is sitting on his throne."

"So it is true!"

"Sadly, yes. Yesterday that boy could not tell the difference between the letters of the alphabet, and today he is the Shah!"

"He will learn," I said, devoted to the idea of learning.

"Yes, yes, I am sure he will learn … all that the British want him to learn."

"What do you mean, 'the British'?"

"And Russia. They could not get Reza Shah to cooperate, so they gave power to his impressionable son. Now they will use him as their puppet."

This was the first time I heard Agha Nemat sound cynical.

Everyone in Baba's house knew I was building on the property in Narmak, but no one knew when the home would be ready for me to move in. Two factors affected the move-in date: Ahmad Agha's expertise, and sufficient funds.

The children and I were reading before bedtime on the cushions. Audel had already fallen asleep in my lap. The mood of the other three was melancholy. Shabnam was the first to speak. She whispered so she would not wake Audel.

"Khale, when you go, we will not see Audel any more. He will grow up not knowing us."

"You said I have to wait until Audel is older before I can play with him," Reza said. "And now you are taking him away, so I cannot play with him at all."

I wished for Audel to grow up among his cousins as well. I consoled them the same way I consoled myself.

"I will make sure you cousins get many chances to play together. Every time you meet, it will be like a big party. It will be better than living in the same house."

The children were not convinced. I suppose they knew as well as I did that without a car and their parents' cooperation, visiting each other would be difficult.

I tried a different approach.

"You three are Audel's older cousins," I told them. "You have a very important job. He depends on you to teach him how to ride a bicycle, throw a ball, and know right from wrong."

"I know how to throw a ball, Ameh," Reza said, volunteering enthusiastically.

"I will teach him how to ride a bicycle," Saeed promised in a serious tone.

"You do not even know how to ride a bicycle yourself, dummy!" Shabnam said, shutting down his idea.

"Gentle," I said to her, and I turned my attention to Saeed.

"Of course you can teach Audel," I stated to comfort him, noticing his shamed face brighten. "He will not be old enough to learn for a few years. In the meantime, I can teach you so you can be ready."

Saeed nodded with a grin.

"First we need to get Saeed a bicycle," Shabnam added, joining the land of the constructive.

I smiled at her. She had potential.

"Can I read to him?" Shabnam asked.

"Of course you can," I answered.

My heart was melting at their generosity.

I would visit the site in Narmak periodically, whenever Ahmad Agha wanted to consult me before a decision had to be made. He would pick up Audel and me in Khale Sara's Peugeot and drive us there. Along the way, we would talk the way we used to in Karaj. It was a welcomed break in the day for me and a great opportunity for Audel to nap in the car.

On the way back, *bastani sonati*, saffron ice cream sandwiched in wafers, was a certainty for the three of us.

The first ice cream shop in Iran was opened by a man

named Akbar Malayeri as soon as Reza Shah came into power. It became known as Akbar Mashti *bastani* and grew famous as high-quality ice cream. He did not make European ice cream, because he knew what Iranians preferred. Our bastani had rose water, saffron, and pistachios.

There was only one shop close to the site that served this treat, and Ahmad Agha had discovered it. The shop belonged to Agha Javad – a round man who looked as if he indulged in his merchandise more often than he should have.

"So how are the mathematics lessons?" Ahmad Agha asked once we were on the road and Audel was asleep in the back of the car.

"Great," I answered. "Agha Nemat is very patient and full of practical advice for teaching methods."

"So you feel confident?"

"I will know better once I am inside the classroom and actually teaching them."

"Anything new on your Baba's radio?"

"They said that in the early hours of the morning, tanks came through and made their way to Russia through Baghdad and the Caspian. Now they can transport supplies from Britain to the Red Army. Hopefully Germany will be stopped."

"Yes. I hope for that too. What a treat that they knocked out the German diplomats so they could have easy access to the huge oil fields to help their cause."

I detected sarcasm.

"Those poor Iranians did not have a chance," I said in agreement. "Their armies could not stand up to two countries. I heard the death toll is up to a thousand – and not just defenders, but civilians too."

"Yes. Several ships were sunk and planes were bombed. How many men did the British and Soviets lose?"

"The two countries combined lost sixty men."

"Wow! One thousand of us and sixty of them," Ahmad Agha said, shaking his head disgustedly. "Hardly a fair fight, huh?"

At the end of three months, Ahmad Agha and I were ready to fly solo in our respective endeavours.

Everyone has been made for some particular work, and the desire for that work has been put in every heart.

—Rumi

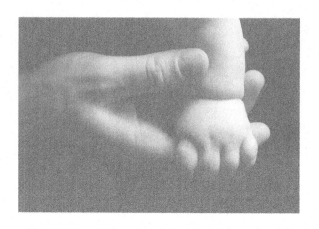

Chapter 23

Advocate (1319 SH)

On the first day of school, I wore a navy skirt and jacket and carried a leather briefcase that Khale Sara gave me for this occasion. I wore flat shoes, since I was walking the half kilometre to school, plus I did not want to tower over my students any more than I had to.

I shared the street with children going to school – some running, some skipping, and some dragging their feet and raising dust. The children were showing their individual moods in their gaits.

When I reported to the office, the secretary, Khanum Felfeli, gave me my teaching schedule, class lists of student names, and a set of keys. It was clear that she did not recognize me – perhaps more as a result of the unlikelihood of the situation than my appearance. I recognized the first-period room assignment. It was my old classroom. I politely thanked Khanum Felfeli and turned to leave the office, but she stopped me. I thought she had recognized me after all, and I turned to face her in anticipation.

"I will call a student to show you where your classroom is, Khanum," she said.

I laughed at my presumptuous self in my mind. "Thank you, but that will not be necessary," I said. "I know the way."

She looked puzzled, but I gave a grateful nod and left the office.

The rooms were numbered in order. It felt strange to be walking down those halls as a teacher. Once I reached my assigned room, I felt a great sense of responsibility. I had heard that Khanum Sadaf had transferred to another school and I was her replacement. I was walking in the footsteps of Agha Nemat and Khanum Sadaf – two teachers I admired. I was determined to make them proud of me.

I turned the key in the lock and entered the classroom. Immediately I felt at home, as if my life had been leading up to this moment. The room was sparsely furnished: wooden benches with ink holes and one large wooden desk. The wall opposite the door was covered with tall windows, and the two adjacent walls were mounted with blackboards so I could face the students either way. On top of my desk were the textbooks I was to use and a cup full of writing utensils. A bouquet of daisies in a vase with beautiful green Minakari (enamelling) told me Fereshteh had been here. There was a note attached to the vase that read, "Have fun teaching – Love, Fereshteh".

I set my papers and briefcase down beside the vase as my first class began showing up. I referred to my schedule and noted that my session-one class was grade-eight math. The desks filled quickly as I observed each girl entering the room. The various faces and sizes only somewhat showed their uniqueness, but they all looked older than grade eight students. Some were confident looking, and some seemed to be petrified. Some were chewing gum arrogantly and looking straight into my eyes as if to say, "You cannot tell me what to do."

I briefly felt intimidated.

I stood at the front of the classroom, and a few seconds after the flow of students ebbed, the school bell sounded and session-one began. I picked up my class list and leaned against my desk, facing the girls.

"Good morning, girls, my name is—"

"Good morning, teacher!" The entire class responded in unison.

"Well, thank you for that warm greeting. Since I would like to learn each of your names and get to know you, I thought it fair to give you my name, which is—"

"Good morning, Khanum Pushtekar," said a large woman in an outfit similar to mine.

She marched briskly into my classroom, her hand extended long before she reached me. When she took my hand, she shook it so hard that my head and shoulders shook with the same frequency.

"Good morning, Khanum …" My voice vibrated to the rhythm of my hand.

"Khanum Mehre," she announced louder than she needed to. "I am the principal of Movafagh Secondary School."

"Very pleased to meet you," I said, withdrawing my hand from her firm grip.

"Welcome back to teaching. I hope you had a fine break with your new baby."

There was a soft hum among the students as they realized I was somebody's mother.

"Yes, thank you," I said, remembering Audel with affection.

"I will be in my office behind the secretary if you should need me," she said, and without acknowledging the students, she turned and left.

I was about to continue when Khanum Mehre peeked into the classroom, having forgotten one thing.

"Pardon me, Khanum Pushtekar. Please give my best regards to Agha Nemat when you see him next."

She was gone before I could answer. There were giggles from some of the students, and I could not blame them for being amused.

"Now you know my name, and yes, I have a two-year-old boy named Audel. To help you, I will write my name on the board, and then I will do roll call to learn your names."

I had just picked up a piece of chalk at the board when another voice sounded behind me. I turned around to see a tiny woman with very large spectacles standing in the doorway and almost giggling.

"Khanum Pushtekar? I am Khanum Shoja, the head of the math department," she said.

This woman was the complete opposite of the principal.

Her high-pitched voice begged to be tuned. She crouched as she approached me, making her look even shorter. She gave me a handshake so soft that it felt as if it melted in my hand.

"Salaam, Khanum Shoja," I said, not appreciating this second interruption.

"You know they gave you all the failures from last year," she said, as if only she and I were in the room.

"I do not understand what you mean," I lied, embarrassed for my students. "If you will excuse me, I need to start my class."

"I am telling you," she said, with one hand beside her mouth, supposedly in confidence. "You will have a difficult time teaching this bunch. They have failed previous years, some of them two or three times. Look, the breasts on some have popped out. They will be nothing but trouble. It will not look good on your record either to have so many failures."

Now I felt embarrassed for this woman in front of my students.

"I will take my chances," I said politely, trying to dismiss her.

"I am here to tell you that you do not have to. If you talk to Khanum Mehre and ask her, I am sure she can give these to a junior teacher. If you want, you can pick through them and give the poorest ones. A teacher referred by the superintendent deserves better at our school," she announced proudly, standing up straight.

"I believe you pick through melons. We are talking about students, yes?" I asked. I reconsidered when I saw her assaulted expression. "Thank you, Khanum Shoja, for your advice," I feigned gratitude, trying not to show my indignation. "Now, if you will please excuse me."

She looked confused but quickly welcomed me to the teachers' lounge at break to meet the other teachers and have a cup of tea. When she scurried out the door, I could not contain the sigh of relief that escaped me. When I faced my class, gone were the giggles, the confidence, and even the arrogance. Every face looked bleak and defeated.

"You did not take her seriously, did you?" I asked with a forced chuckle.

"She is right. How can you teach us?" said a student.

"No one else has managed it in all these years," said another student.

"You do not even look like a teacher," said the student with the gum.

"What does a teacher have to look like?" I challenged.

"Certainly not like a Coco Chanel model."

Everyone laughed. At least their faces relaxed some.

"Let me tell you something," I said, taking a seat on the edge of an empty bench. "You are intelligent. You are capable – every one of you. Do not ever let anyone tell you who you are and what you can or cannot do. This is a new year and a new beginning. You believe in new beginnings?"

There were some half-hearted nods.

"I am making a promise to you today. I am willing to work hard for you if you are willing to work hard for me. I will help you look good, and you help me look good. In the end, you will pass the year and we will show them that we are not failures."

There was applause. I felt goose bumps on my arms. I refocused.

"All right. Now the work starts," I began. "I will give you my undivided attention thirty minutes before and after school. Anyone who is struggling can come and see me then. Every problem can be understood with enough explanation."

I did roll call, we opened our books, and I gave them their first lesson on rational expressions. The following classes went more smoothly and with fewer interruptions.

At the sound of the bell, I picked up my briefcase and, with a warm goodbye to my students, went to my session-two classroom. The school was organized such that the students had set classrooms and the teachers travelled to different rooms according to their teaching schedules.

At break, I did visit the teachers' lounge and introduce myself to the other teachers. I wanted to make a good first impression and initiate collaboration. The tone in the lounge was negative. Teachers were not coming there to relax but to vent about their students, the parents, and the education system. I did not feel comfortable there, so I did not visit very often.

My afternoon classes consisted of boys. They were little gentlemen, rushing to wipe the board for me, asking me if I needed anything, and advising each other in support of me.

"You need to remember your pencil for tomorrow," Firuz said to Arash.

"Khanum Pushtekar just explained that, Babak. Come here and I will help you with it," said Omid.

The next day, I showed up thirty minutes early, and so did my entire first-session class. I was both thrilled and overwhelmed. It was not easy to give individual attention to twenty-two students at once, but it worked out organically. At my desk, Dori needed me to explain how to factor by substitution, but she already knew how to cancel. Farshid was next in the queue and needed me to show her how to cancel. Once I showed Dori how to factor by substitution, I sent her to Farshid so she could help Farshid with cancelling. I showed Bahar how to factor by parts. As she got up to go back to her desk, she called to the class.

"Come to me if you need to learn how to factor by parts."

There was a great feeling of cooperation in the room, and it fuelled itself. The queue to my desk moved fast, and everyone was engaged in learning from me and each other.

I was forced to leave Audel in the care of the girls, who put up a fight and lost. Audel was independent in using the toilet, feeding himself, and dressing himself. Shole was under the scrutiny of Shabnam, who reported directly to her father if Audel was neglected. Shole did argue that her daughter needed to do her homework, but she had to back down when Shabnam proved with her marks that she could handle both responsibilities. I would return home to find Shabnam and Audel cuddled on the carpet cushions, reading. Saeed and Reza were often nearby with their toys, listening to the poem or story.

Exam day arrived for my first-session students, who were nervous but prepared. I did not admit to them my own anxiety. I kept the tone light until they entered the exam room with the other students from other classes. While they were inside, I paced the hall like a man waiting for his wife to deliver a baby – or so I had heard.

Time was up, and the double doors to the exam room flew open. Students rushed out, discussing the questions and looking relieved. My students rushed to me and they all spoke at once, but I got the general consensus. They had done well.

"Khanum Pushtekar, why are you the only teacher here?" Mahnaz asked.

"Were you scared we were going to fail?" Talat followed.

"No, you donkey," Dori snapped at her. "She is the only one who cares about us."

"Gentle," I reminded. "You worked hard, and you feel good about it. Go and celebrate."

"Yes, we can celebrate with some *basatni*," Farshid said, and everyone cheered and followed her.

Talat stopped and turned to me.

"Would you like to join us, Khanum?" she asked with a grin.

The other girls stopped and turned to me, waiting for my answer. I knew I should get back to Audel, but I could not turn down a student's ice cream invitation. I supposed that a teacher did not get one of those very often.

"I was part of the winning team, right? Of course I will celebrate with you."

Cheers from the girls assured me that I had made the right choice, and we headed to the nearest Akbar Mashti.

A week later, I picked up my students' marks in a sealed envelope and confidently brought it with me to class. All my girls were eager to find out how well they did, and so was I. I broke the seal on the envelope and read the marks printed on the sheet. The scores were out of twenty, and there was not one over four. There were groans and even tears as they heard the numbers. I was discouraged that all the work I had seen had not given these girls the results they deserved.

"This cannot be true." Mahnaz was the first to say it.

Everyone turned to look at her with hope.

"We knew those questions, and we answered them correctly."

"Mahnaz is right!" said Talat. "There must be a mistake."

At first I thought they were not willing to face reality, but as I listened to them recall the questions in detail and agree on the same answers, I began to wonder if there had been a mistake. I went to the office and asked to see the principal. I was led into her office.

"Salaam, Khanum Pushtekar. What can I do for you?" Khanum Mehre asked, standing and pointing to a chair.

"Salaam, Khanum Mehre," I said, sitting down. "I need to see my students' exams, please. I believe my students should have gotten much higher marks."

Khanum Mehre looked disturbed but remained professional.

"They would be filed away unless they are still with Khanum Shoja, who marked them."

"Please. I believe there has been a mistake with the marking. Can I see the exams?"

"We can call Khanum Shoja before we jump to conclusions," Khanum Mehre advised diplomatically.

She picked up her phone and called Khanum Felfeli.

"Please have Khanum Shoja report to my office immediately with Khanum Pushtekar's session-one math exams."

The two of us waited awkwardly. There was a knock at the door, and in walked Khanum Shoja, holding a stack of exams. I stood up when she entered. She looked startled and held the exams tightly to her chest.

Pari

"I … I do not understand," she stuttered. "Is there a problem?"

Khanum Mehre pointed to the seat next to me, and we all sat down again.

"Khanum Pushtekar feels her students should have done better than the marks showed and would like to view the exams."

"Those students are not capable of getting good marks. They have failed so many years previously. This was to be expected."

"May I?" I requested, extending both arms so she would give me the exams.

Khanum Shoja's eyes darted nervously between the principal and me. Khanum Mehre nodded sombrely towards her, and slowly, she handed me the pile of exams. I placed the pile on the principal's desk and opened the first exam, which had been scored a zero. I looked at the first question, and it was correct, with all the steps shown. I looked at the next few questions, and they were correct too. I handed the exam to Khanum Mehre who paged through the exam, noting the detailed work of the student on every problem.

"The first three questions are correct on this exam, yet the score reads zero," I said in dismay. "Khanum Shoja, did you look at any of these questions?"

"What was the use?" she burst out. "I was not going to waste my time. I am telling you, these girls have failed every year."

"Then why bother coming to work at all?" I said, all inhibition gone. "We can save ourselves the effort and give our students their marks from last year."

"You have made your point, Khanum Pushtekar," the principal said politely.

"I will mark these exams," I said to Khanum Mehre, "and give you the correct results. These young ladies gave up their mornings and after-school time to achieve these marks."

Khanum Mehre did not object. She nodded, and I left. What was to become of Khanum Shoja was not my concern. In fact, I stopped going to the teachers' lounge altogether.

As the weeks went by, my first-session students were elated about math and learning. They would embarrass me with gifts, invite me to their volleyball games, and offer to wash my car (and be disappointed that I did not have one). I knew I had advocated for them, and they were grateful, but I was only doing my job. Besides, I felt embarrassed when I was thanked, not knowing how to respond. Finally, I managed a shy "*khahesh mikonam*".

I walked home from school on the dirt road, past the curtain houses and along the homes with iron gates. The sycamore trees lining our street stretched their arms towards each other, weaving into a green canopy. The sunlight streaking down through the branches produced long beams all around, as if to say, "God is here now, in this grove." This sight appeared beautiful to me again – this light and shade.

I was almost at our gate when I heard a familiar voice.

"Ameh, another letter for you," Shabnam called, running out to meet me from the front yard.

She handed me a flat envelope and stood in front of me, so I had no choice but to open it right there.

"More money?"

"Let me see," I said, setting my briefcase down and opening the envelope.

I did not expect it to be money, as Khanum Felfeli routinely handed me my pay cheque in an envelope. I looked inside, and there was a note from my old math teacher.

> Dear Pari Khanum,
>
> So you reprimanded the principal and the department head of math all in one go. I am so proud of you. I do not think you need my mentorship any more. If you can make that session-one class of yours learn, then you can teach anyone.
>
> Yours truly,
> S. Nemat

"What is it, Ameh?" Shabnam asked. "Why are you smiling?"

"Someone whom I admire now admires me," I said.

I tucked the letter into my pocket, picked up my briefcase, and, with an arm around Shabnam, walked through Baba's iron gate with the pretty copper and brass flowers lining the top.

Wear gratitude like a cloak and it will feed every corner of your life.

—Rumi

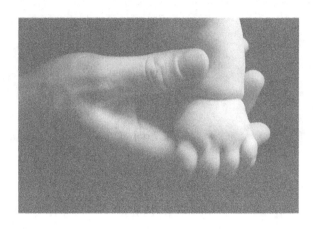

Chapter 24

Independence (1323 SH)

Looking back, I saw that time had gone by quickly. I had taught school for four years, every year more fulfilling than the last. Shabnam was a year older than I was when Baba became a morgh-e behesht, heavenly bird. Pantea was the same age as I had been when I became married to her father. I prayed that she was happy.

Three years ago, the Allies signed a treaty stating that they would pull their armies out of Iran six months after the war ended. The war was still being fought despite the high death toll, and millions of dollars' worth of supplies went through the route in Iran.

The young men and women, still with idealistic views, continued to rally and protest their opposition to the foreign occupancy. They were jailed, tortured, and even killed to make an example for the others. The others, however, remained idealistic and motivated, so the stream of the young continued to disappear.

Another school year was ending, Audel was about to turn six, and our house was completed. We decided to celebrate Audel's birthday at our new home. Ahmad Agha came Friday morning to pick us up.

In earlier weeks, Ahmad Agha had taken our belongings to the house with multiple trips in the Peugeot. I sent Baba's radio, Baba's books (leaving some for Shabnam), the two Minakari vases, my box under the bed, Abaas' leather sewing bag, and Audel's cradle, although he had been sleeping in a cot in the boys' room for years. I did not need anything else. The girls made it clear that we were not to take any furniture. I told Audel that I knew how to make a soft bed on the floor for us, using our clothes, until we could afford furniture.

The girls declined our invitation to Audel's birthday party. They said they were going to have a private celebration of their own. They did allow us to take Audel's three cousins to join the fun.

That morning, when Ahmad Agha drove Audel, his cousins, and me to our new home, he was like an excited child. He was participating in the children's games and singing along when he knew the words. I was sure I was the only adult in the car.

Ahmad Agha carried my large carpet bag in one hand and opened our gate and front door with the other. Khale Sara was waiting inside the door, and they were both watching us intensely. When we stepped inside, we saw one huge room with three corners – furnished! There was a dark brown stained dining table with six chairs in one corner. Carpet cushions and a Persian floor carpet occupied the second corner. Pretty white cupboards, a sink, an icebox, and a gas stove made up the kitchen in the last corner. Audel dropped his football on the floor and ran to his room. He had seen that room on numerous visits to the house while it was under construction, but today we were moving in.

"Maman!" Audel yelled from his room. "There is a bed in here! We do not have to sleep on the floor."

Ahmad Agha and Khale Sara laughed. I ran to Ahmad Agha and threw my arms around him. He chuckled as he patted my back in acknowledgement.

"I cannot believe you did all this for us. A father could not have done more."

"You are like a daughter to me. I love you and Audel."

"Yes," Khale Sara said, wrapping her arms around the two of us. "*Behistun ra eshgh kand o, shohratash Farhad bord.*"

Khale Sara was reciting Ferdowsi, a poet who took true events in history and turned them into Persian love stories. Shirin, the betrothed to the king, was falsely promised to Farhad if he could carve stairs into the Behistun Mountain. Ferdowsi wrote, "Love carved the mountain, but Farhad gained the fame."

"It was love that created this home," admitted Ahmad

Agha, and with a childish whine, he added, "but I do not mind getting some of the credit."

"And you shall," I assured him.

"Look, Maman!"

Audel was riding his new bicycle on the wide brick path that encircled our house.

"I am watching you, azizam," I called to him through the kitchen window.

The bicycle was a gift from Khale Sara and Ahmad Agha. I had bought a bicycle for Saeed, and he had kept his promise and taught Audel how to ride. Saeed was standing near the imaginary circle that Audel was tracing around the house with his bicycle. He applauded Audel every time he rode by. Saeed beamed with pride when he glanced over at me, and I grinned back at him from the window.

Audel and his three cousins ran around our property, weaving through the small fruit trees and flower beds that Ahmad Agha had planted. He had tried to replicate as much as possible Baba's garden, with jasmine and honeysuckle flowers, and mulberry and walnut trees. He even installed my father's pedestal fountain inside a brick pond in the front yard. He must have gotten the idea from Khale Sara, since he did not know about its existence. The pond sat on a mustard-coloured brick front yard – an extension of the path that wrapped around the house. Ahmad Agha's attention to detail showed he was trying to do everything he could to make me feel at home in this new place.

The two-bedroom brick house had barred windows and a brick floor. It had a flat roof to sleep on in the summers when it was too hot inside. The property was surrounded by a brick wall and iron gate. The length of the wall had coiled barbed wire on the top so no one could climb over it.

Ahmad Agha respected Baba's wish to reuse as much as possible. The materials used were from homes that were being knocked down or renovated. He often needed to wait for materials to become available.

In the time it had taken for me to get my finances in order, Ahmad Agha had been building each piece of furniture and setting it aside until the house was ready. Days before our move, he brought the furniture in and arranged everything according to Khale Sara's taste. It became a home more extravagant than any I could have imagined for myself.

"Can I have a drink of water?" Reza asked, stumbling in from outside.

"Yes – straight from our own ab anbar," I said triumphantly.

"There is the pitcher, Reza joon," said Khale Sara. "Help yourself."

The birthday party had been a success. The children enjoyed the awsh, the cake, and the football game afterward. I carried dishes to the sink and put food away while Khale Sara washed dishes. It was a blessing to have indoor plumbing.

"Are you children coming inside soon?" I asked Audel, who had also come in for water. "The sun is about to go down."

"Ahmad Agha just joined the game," Audel said between gulps. "We cannot disappoint him by stopping now."

He placed his glass by the sink and ran outside.

"I am so happy to see you in your own home," Khale Sara said.

"Yes, this feels like home."

"You will be all right at night here?"

"Of course, with bars on the windows and coiled barbed wire on the top of the walls." I winked at her in good humour.

"Ahmad joon did not want to spare any safety measures."

"I appreciate that," I admitted sincerely.

"Narmak is not like Shemiran."

"I know, but it does not seem as bad as its reputation. We will be fine."

Khale picked up one of the vases on the windowsill and turned it in her hand, admiring the blue Minakari.

"I remember in Karaj you had this one, but I did not know they can multiply," Khaleh joked.

"A friend gave me both. The green-enamelled one she left on my desk on my first day of teaching. They need daisies."

As we finished in the kitchen, the football players came inside. Their game had naturally ended with the sunset. Khale Sara and Ahmad Agha drove their niece and nephews home.

Audel and I fell into each other's arms on the carpet cushions. Audel's head was on my shoulder, and I stroked his light curls away from his eyes.

"Did you have a good time, azizam?" I asked.

"Yes, Maman, thank you," he said, and then he giggled.

"What did you remember?"

"How did you know I remembered something?" Audel asked, in awe.

"Mamans know everything."

"Wow!" my baby said, still gullible about my proclamations. "We walked down the street to Agha Javad's shop with three sannar in each of our hands from Ahmad Agha. Reza and I spent our three sannar each getting a bastani sonati, and Shabnam got *douq* with her three sannar. Saeed, after some deliberation, spent two sannar on a lemonade."

"Saeed loves douq," I said, puzzled. "He had enough money. Why did he settle for lemonade?"

"Maybe he wanted to save one sannar, but his eyes could not leave Shabnam's douq. At last, he spoke. Pointing at the '150 millilitres' written on both bottles, he concluded that they both had the same volume of drink, but through his genius, he had saved one sannar."

Audel began giggling.

"What did Shabnam say to that?" I asked, guessing this was the punchline.

"She said, 'Yes, you saved one sannar, but my douq does taste one sannar better.'"

We rolled back onto the cushions, laughing. I loved that Audel found Shabnam's comment funny. His sense of humour had matured. There was a time when he would call me to find him hiding under a blanket that shook with his excited giggles.

"I wonder if Audel is under this blanket?" I would say, circling the blanket.

"Nooooo," he would scream, and then he would giggle some more.

His cousins would shake their heads and roll their eyes.

Yesterday is gone and its tale told. Today new seeds are growing.

—Rumi

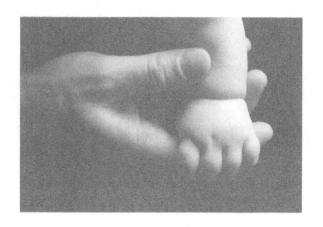

Chapter 25

Redemption (1323 SH)

Shemiran was too far to walk to from Narmak. I took a bus to Baba's house, Khale Sara and Ahmad Agha's house, or Movafagh Secondary School. I felt a little more connected to the world through Baba's radio and his books.

Audel and I spent that summer contently in our new home, with occasional visits from Khale. On Fridays, if she and Ahmad Agha came together, they would kindly pick up the three cousins too. Fridays were the social highlight of the week for both of us.

As a result of our isolation and free time, Audel and I became close, as Baba and I had been. We cooked together.

Audel showed the same enthusiasm as his father had for cooking. We shopped together. I would ask Audel's opinion or pause and let him contribute to the conversations with shopkeepers. We tended the garden together, having metaphysical conversations during weeding and watering. Tasks that did not utilize the brain lent themselves very nicely to abstract, mystical, and spiritual topics. After consistent watering, our garden faithfully grew from dry and dusty to lush and green.

The evening air was heavy with August heat. Audel and I slept on the roof most nights under a starry sky. We pointed out constellations to each other and wished upon shooting stars. The patio bricks were cool on each side of the house at different times of the day. During the first half of the day, we used the western patio to escape the sun's heat, and in the evening, we used the eastern patio.

Summer holiday was almost over. As usual, I was feeling both excited and nervous about returning to school. I turned on the radio for a distraction. The announcer was talking about the war. Almost four years prior, Japan had bombed Pearl Harbor, and last week the Americans had gotten even by dropping two atomic bombs – one on Hiroshima and, three days later, one on Nagasaki. Tens of thousands of Japanese people were killed, and many were injured.

"Today, August 15, Japan formally surrendered," said the announcer, hardly able to keep the excitement out of his usual monotonous voice. "The war is officially over! Time to buy shirini and spread the cheer, *hamvatana*!"

Khale Sara and Ahmad Agha picked up the three cousins and came to our home to celebrate the end of the war. The drive was only fifteen minutes, but the Peugeot pulled in an hour after I heard the news. The cousins jumped out of the car and continued to jump on the spot with excitement.

"Ameh!" Reza yelped.

"People are going wild, Ameh!" Saeed cried.

"The streets are crazy with people, cars, motorcycles, and everyone cheering," Khale Sara said, staggering out of the Peugeot.

"Every time we stopped at a light," Shabnam squealed, "people would shove boxes of shirini into the car – and from the other side, bouquets of flowers!"

"I think the bakeries and flower shops are doing great business tonight," Ahmad Agha said, looking tired after the drive.

"I hope the Allies honour that treaty they signed and we can have our country back in six months," I said.

Despite the abundant sweets from the car, Ahmad Agha gave the children three sannar each for their trip to Agha Javad's store. It had become a tradition that all four children looked forward to when they visited. Ahmad Agha was not about to alter a tradition just because a war had ended.

At eleven and twelve years old, Reza and the twins thanked Ahmad Agha soberly with a respectful nod, whereas my Audel pulled at Shabnam's hand impatiently. I gave a gentle reminder to Audel, and he remembered his thank you.

We three adults slumped onto the cushions, sipping tea and discussing how ending the war was going to change Iran's economy. The radio was on, so we could hear follow-up news as they announced it.

The sky had grown orange outside.

"Where are those children?" Ahmad Agha asked, and he got an elbow jab from his wife.

"Not to worry, Pari joon," Khale Sara said. "Shabnam is with them."

I nodded and went to the kitchen for more tea. Khale Sara followed. I could not help worrying. The children should have been back by now. It was going to be dark soon. I stood at the sink, watching the water fill the samovar; Khale stood beside me, instinctively quiet.

"Maman, look!"

It was Audel. A heavy sigh of relief escaped me, and Khale Sara patted my shoulder. We both went to the door to see what he was excited about.

There stood my son, surrounded by his three cousins, barely holding a huge white cat in his arms. The cat was drooping out of Audel's embrace from so many corners that finally he jumped right out. He stood for a moment on the spot.

"Kuchulu?" I asked.

"Yes, yes, yes, Ameh," Reza screeched.

"You agree it is him?" asked Saeed.

"We are sure of it, Ameh. Look at him!" said Shabnam.

I knelt on the floor and called him. He jogged over, and I felt as if no time had passed. I was eleven again, and this cat had found me. How he had made it from Shemiran to Narmak would remain a mystery.

"Is this really your cat, Maman?"

"I think so, azizam."

"Then can we keep him?"

I paused and considered his cousins.

"Shabnam joon, what do you think?"

Audel's mouth dropped open.

"We had our turn with Kuchulu," she said, smiling at Audel, who looked relieved.

"Yes. It is Audel's turn now," said Reza.

Saeed nodded, so it was unanimous. When I gave my consent, the four children cheered and gathered around Kuchulu to pet him. With a peace of mind, I carried the tea tray to the cushions. As I passed the children seated on the brick floor, I saw Reza put an arm around Audel's shoulder.

"Did you know that this cat saved me from drowning when I was little?"

"Wow," Audel gasped, looking up at Reza.

"I will tell you the whole story," Reza began.

I registered Audel for grade one at our local public school, Shokre Elementary. We developed a routine: I took the bus to work, and Audel walked to and from school alone. The boys attended school during the second half of the day, but I taught full days. Audel was alone for hours each day.

At the start of the school year, I would come home to find Audel sitting at the kitchen table, doing his assignments – a habit Shabnam had modelled for him. In Baba's house, Audel would sit next to Shabnam, admiring her as she worked on her school assignments. Shabnam would reward his admiration by giving him a blank sheet of paper to scribble on, later draw on, and eventually practise his letters on. He had read Shabnam's first-grade readers before he turned five. He was over-prepared for grade one, so he finished his assignments quickly and was bored.

The first day I came home and found him with a black eye, he said he banged into the door, and I believed him. When more cuts and bruises got similar excuses, I became suspicious.

"He is a young boy," Khale Sara would say. "Boys get

bumps and bruises more often than little girls. Trust me; you and your two brothers were the ideal examples."

One day I needed to take Audel to the clinic to have three stitches on a cut just below his eyebrow. I knew it was painful, but my baby did not make a sound. Only the tears that rolled out of the corner of his eyes betrayed him. He did not even complain about missing an eyebrow, refusing my offer to draw one in. Instead he went to school with one eyebrow, holding his head high.

"Audel, who is hurting you?" I asked, confronting him. "These cannot all be accidents."

Audel looked uncomfortable, but I could tell he was collecting his thoughts, so I waited.

"It is my own fault," he began. "The boys are bigger than I am, and they say I cannot join them because I may get hurt. I join them anyway, because it is too boring at home."

"What do you join?" I asked, my mind racing through unthinkable possibilities.

"Football."

"Football?"

"Yes. They are bigger than me, so they play faster and rougher. The boys my age stand and watch, but what fun is that?"

Relief washed over me as I realized my son was not doing anything illegal.

"Who are these older boys?" I asked, ready to advocate for my son. "What are their names? I need to speak with their parents. This cannot continue. Children need to feel safe in their community."

"You see?" Audel said, frustrated. "That is why I did not tell you before."

I saw myself through his eyes and realized that I had overreacted. I took a deep breath. I remembered Khale Sara overreacting in Karaj when I came home late with a strange man, and now I understood how she felt.

"What can we do so this does not happen again?" I asked, ready to hear ideas.

"How would I know?" Audel said with a shrug of his shoulders.

"No idea for a solution? We have to come up with something, or I will need to ask you to stay inside until I get home."

"What?" Audel shrieked. "That is too long to stay inside!"

"You can play with Kuchulu."

"I do, but then he wants to nap."

I wanted to suggest that he nap with Kuchulu, since he was only six years old. That would be another battle.

"I could ask the boys my age if they want to have a game of our own."

Audel was used to playing football with Reza and Saeed, but they had been gentle with him. These older boys offered the same level of play but with no mercy. Audel knew that if he wanted to play football, he would have to settle for playing with boys his own age.

"That is a good idea. You can offer our yard."

The possibility cheered him up, and we went in to make dinner.

The next day, I arrived home from school to find Audel sitting on our front step, with Kuchulu napping peacefully at his feet. My baby looked tragic, but I was selfishly glad he did not have any cuts or bruises. His elbows were resting on his knees, and his cheeks were in the palms of his hands. I loved holding those hands. They filled my hands. Of course, I was comparing them to Pantea's tiny two-year-old hands and his cousins' slender hands. His face was scrunched up, so he looked like an angry cat – a cute angry cat.

"You had a good day, azizam?"

"Yes!" he grumbled. "I sat here the entire time and watched the boys kick the football and have fun. How was your day?"

I heard the sarcasm – one of the less favourable things he had learned from Shabnam.

"What happened to asking the younger boys if they wanted to have a game in our yard?"

"Their parents will not allow them to go into someone's yard while they are at work."

"How about further up our street or the next street?"

"Their parents will not let them leave this street, and the older boys will not share, saying they came first."

"Well, that is inflexible."

"Like you not letting me play with the older boys."

"I …" I said, my feelings hurt a little. "You want to help me with dinner?"

"No."

I hated to see him like this. I wanted to make him happy.

"The boys may be too big now, but in time you will grow to be big and strong and able to handle yourself in a game with them."

"I want to play with them now," he whined.

"I know."

I went inside and changed out of my dress suit and into my comfortable white cotton dress. I washed and prayed. I removed the pots I needed and the food out of the icebox and cupboards. I began to make adas polo and a salad.

Audel ran inside.

"Maman, Maman! He is here again."

"Who, azizam?" I asked, looking over his head to the open front door.

"The man who comes around asking me my name and how old I am."

Terror struck my heart. It was a physical pain. I thought the worst I was facing were the boys in the neighbourhood playing rough. I had no idea that there was a child thief in the neighbourhood.

I ran through the door, through the gate, and into the dirt street. The street was empty except for a few parked cars and the scarce trees that grew here and there. I looked from left to right repeatedly. Suddenly from behind a tree, a man ran down the street away from me. I was not sure what possessed me to run after him. I must have given up on life itself. All I could think of was Audel.

The man wore an old tattered suit and an oversized pair of shoes that were impeding his running. I was sure to overtake him soon. His hair was shoulder length and flying in the air behind him. He looked over his shoulder a couple of times. The third time, he missed his footing and fell to the ground in a cloud of dust.

I reached him and instantly realized that I had no plan of action. Was I going to jump on him and claw at him with all of my strength or respectfully ask him what his business was coming to my home and asking my son his name and age? By the time I stood over him, he had lifted himself to his hands and knees. At that moment, I found my words.

"Who do you think you are?" I screamed at him, my hands flailing in the air, a new gesture for me. "You cannot wander around here talking to our children without an adult around!"

"Please, Pari," he said, glancing up and then quickly covering his head with both hands.

"Do not dare call me by my first name!" I warned him.

He knew my name. I do not know which registered with me first, his voice or his face.

"Abaas?" I asked, confused. He slowly got to his feet with one arm still protecting his head. "Is it really you?"

"Yes, to my shame," he mumbled, barely audible.

"Why did you run?" I yelled, anger rising again, at which he cowered. "We are still husband and wife. You did not divorce me."

He was standing but looked crumpled, with rounded shoulders and bent knees. His oversized clothes looked as if they were crying on him. He had cut his forehead – probably when he fell. Blood was trickling down the side of his face and pausing at his jaw. I had begun to slap the dust off of his clothes so aggressively that he winced. I told him to bend lower and held the hem of my white dress bunched against his cut. A wave of sentiment for him returned, and I welcomed it. I remembered a time long ago when my white cotton dress was of no use in saving my father.

"Why run?" I murmured, dropping the skirt of my dress and stepping back to see him more clearly.

"I was ashamed," he answered. "I had no right to come looking for you, but I could not stay away any longer. I wanted to see Audel so badly hurt. I left you when you needed me, and I am back now that you do not."

He gestured with a limp arm towards our house.

I looked at him for a long time. He had not changed except for the long hair and the ragged clothes. There was the familiar face, albeit unshaved. There was the voice that lulled me, the dark eyes that moved me, the man I was determined I wanted as the father of my children. He was standing right in front of me, but he did not think he deserved me.

"You are wrong," I started, and he looked down, embarrassed. "But not in the way you think. I did not need you then. I managed to live in our rented shack for most of my pregnancy, through the winter and into the spring with the help of many generous people. It was not as difficult as you thought. I was in Baba's home for years afterward, not needing anything. Now I need you. Audel is alone when I am at school. He needs adult supervision for several hours until I get home. That is what I need from you now."

Abaas stared at me in disbelief. A smile crept across his lips, but he straightened up and became serious.

"So – you want me to take him to school," he stated formally, "and stay with him until you get home. I can do that."

"What I need most is for you to be around when he plays street football with the neighbourhood boys, so they do not maim him."

"I can do that too," he said eagerly.

I stared at his lit face and recognized hope in his eyes.

"I know you can."

"I am sorry for leaving, Pari joon," he said, shoulders drooping with every word.

"That is all in the past," I said, linking my arm in

his and leading him back home. "We have a son to think about now."

His handsome smile lifted me. The memories of those few months together came back in a flood: the intimacy, the magical kiss, and the evenings sitting in the moonlight after dinner, reading poetry.

Our new routine was perfect. I went to work without worrying about Audel. Abaas would walk Audel to and from school. He would supervise the street football after school and even participate sometimes. When I returned home, the house would be clean and orderly, dinner would be simmering on the stove, and, at the kitchen table, Audel would be working on his assignments.

One day I came home to find Audel listening to his father reading from his first-grade reader.

"Baba … naan … daad," Abaas read.

"Good, Baba," Audel encouraged his father proudly.

"Baba … ab daad," Abaas continued.

"That was smoother," Audel pointed out.

I remembered Baba telling me how he had taught five men to read and write when he was very young. I was moved to see my son following in his grandfather's footsteps.

Audel noticed I had come in and ran over to give me a hug. He took my hand and pulled me to his father to show their progress. Abaas looked at me with a sheepish smile, and I felt my pride swell in my throat.

"When I get better, perhaps we can take turns reading the works of Saadi – or your favourite, Molana," he suggested.

"That would be a real treat for me," I agreed.

The two of us enjoyed the most important project of

our lives. We supervised Audel as he brushed his teeth and read him a bedtime story. We tucked him into bed and then pulled our chairs outside under the moonlight. There on the cool east side of the house, we sat together and shared the events of our day.

Abaas was no longer swept away by dreams of having a business that grew into something great. He had accomplished that, yet it had left him empty. He had sold his company and set out to find us.

"You were right, Pari joon," Abaas said, staring at the moon.

"About what?" I said, squeezing his hand.

"You said you had it all – the fortune – and it did not mean anything."

"I am glad you found us," I said.

I leaned over, and we kissed.

"Me too."

This is love: to fly toward a secret sky, to cause a hundred veils to fall each moment. First to let go of life. Finally, to take a step without feet.

—Rumi

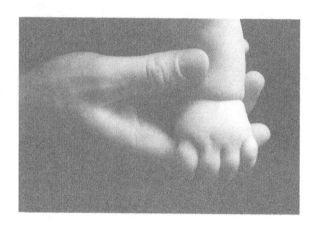

Chapter 26

Senjed (1343 SH)

It was the last day of school, and everyone was in a good mood. The bell signalled the end of the day. I walked by the office to say goodbye to Khanum Felfeli and Khanum Mehre.

"Have a great summer, Pari joon," Khanum Felfeli called back.

She had finally remembered me as the student who had returned to school and graduated with her peers. In the absence of students, she referred to me without the formal "Khanum". I liked it.

Khanum Mehre stood up, came out of her office, and shook my hand.

"It was another successful year, Khanum Pushtekar," she said politely. "You live up to your name every year."

"Thank you. That is kind of you to say. I could say the same for you."

"Thank you. We will see you next year as the new head of the Mathematics Department," Khanum Mehre said, formality in her voice but a smile on her lips.

"I will do my best to live up to your expectations," I promised.

"Of course you will."

With a casual wink, she returned to her office.

I walked outside and towards the bus stop. In the parking lot, I saw Khanum Shoja, who was now officially retired. She was putting boxes into the trunk of her Wolseley. Her purse was on the top of her car, and her keys were dangling from her mouth. I waved goodbye, and she nodded back, causing her keys to jingle.

On the bus, I planned Friday's dinner in my head. Khale Sara and Ahmad Agha were coming, as usual. I had even more time to make something special for dinner, since I would not be working until next fall.

At the first family gathering, shortly after Abaas returned to us twenty years ago, there was Khale Sara, Ahmad Agha, and Khanum Tabriz. Since Abaas lived with us, I was comfortable having Khanum Tabriz join us.

* * *

Khanum Tabriz arrived first. After the customary greetings and introduction to her grandson, Audel took her hand and led her to the kitchen table, where he was working on his school assignments. She listened with interest as he explained his work to her. I placed a glass of tea and sugar cubes next to her, and she beamed at me gratefully before returning her attention to Audel.

Audel accepted new people into his family as if they had always been there. He did not seem to have a need to know why they had not been there before. He simply enjoyed their company now.

When Khale Sara and Ahmad Agha arrived, Abaas and I greeted them at the door. Abaas recognized Ahmad Agha first. Apparently they had met years ago and Ahmad Agha had saved Abaas' life. Abaas retold the incident over a glass of tea before dinner.

"I had agreed to march with some friends to protest the British occupation in Iran," Abaas began. "As we were marching, Ahmad Agha pulled me aside and advised me against marching."

"Yes, I remember. You were a tall boy whose arms and legs dangled like a marionette's."

Everyone laughed.

"I saw your innocent face and wanted to help you."

"I remember you told me to go home, saying I would only find trouble in this protest."

"You were stubborn and did not listen to me."

"It is true. I continued to march and chant with the others, '*Marge bar Engelis*!' As we approached the British Embassy, the leader turned to us and said, 'Hold your tongue until we pass the embassy building, and then we will resume chanting.' Ahmad Agha tapped me on the shoulder and said, 'See, these people do not mean what they say. We are here to break up the embassy, yet we are being quiet as we pass them?'"

"Ahmad joon, I am surprised at you!" Khale Sara exclaimed. "That leader was not a coward or inconsistent in his ideals. He was acting out of respect. The British Embassy is considered British soil. Iranians are respectful, even to their enemies."

"Yes, we are too polite," Audel added with a deep sigh. "I have to always check that I am not sitting with my back to anyone."

We laughed. Audel had finished his schoolwork and sat on a cushion beside Khale Sara. Kuchulu trotted over to be petted.

As Abaas began to speak again, I caught a smile exchanged between Ahmad Agha and Khale Sara. I felt like a child who had discovered the reality of a situation. Ahmad Agha had used any means to get Abaas out of that dangerous march.

"Ahmad Agha continued to follow me," Abaas went on. "He advised me to go home until I gave up and went home. The next day, I heard the news of the protest on the radio. The police had intervened, killing five people, sending several more to the hospital and many more to prison."

"And knowing the prison in Iran at that time, you were lucky if you made it out," Ahmad Agha said with a shrug.

There was a wave of nods throughout the room.

"You saved my son's life, Agha," Khanum Tabriz said, humbly thanking him.

Ahmad Agha bowed towards her with a hand on his chest.

"You saved my son's life too," I said. "Without Abaas, there would be no Audel."

"We could not do without Audel," Khale Sara said, pinching his cheek.

Audel squirmed away and continued to pet the purring Kuchulu.

Kuchulu had waited until Audel was settled in secondary school before he laid down, head pointing towards the qiblah. We missed him terribly, but we were glad he had returned to live the rest of his life with us.

* * *

Abaas had opened up a small tailor shop on the main business street in Narmak. He had regular customers and made a good profit. Abaas was surprised that I had kept his leather sewing bag and accepted it gratefully. I would bring my marking home, and he would bring sewing projects home so our evenings together could be longer.

The bus stopped, and I got off and walked home. I walked past the gate, the pedestal fountain, and the front door to find Abaas relaxed on the cushions, sewing a man's jacket. As usual, the meal was simmering on the stove, the house was tidy, and my man was waiting for me to join him. I changed my clothes, prayed, and settled on the cushions next to him. He put the jacket away and pulled a book off the shelf.

"How was your day?" Abaas asked.

"Great, right down to the bus ride home. How was yours?"

"The highlight was finding this for you. I have been

saving it, wanting to read it to you when you came home today."

I lay beside him, closing my eyes and resting my head contentedly on his chest.

"Go ahead, Abaas joon. I am listening."

"'The minute I heard my first love story,'" Abaas read to me from Molana, "'I started looking for you, not knowing how blind that was. Lovers do not finally meet somewhere. They are in each other all along.'"

"Thank you, my love," I crooned.

We read for a while, and then Abaas put the book back on its shelf.

"Audel is coming for dinner tonight," he said as we got up to wash.

"Oh good."

"He said he has a surprise."

"Another surprise?" I complained jokingly. "The last surprise needed to be housebroken."

"You know you love Lulu."

"Yes, I have gotten over the initial shock of owning a dog."

"He told me this one has only two legs – and do not bother guessing a chicken."

"Too bad. Fresh eggs daily would have been nice."

We washed our hands in the kitchen sink. Abaas left the room to change his clothes for dinner, and I began to set the table.

I was excited. Did Audel have a girlfriend? He was now twenty-six years old. He had finished his engineering programme and landed a respectable job on the design team at the airport. All that was left was for him to bring home a nice girl so I could have a grandchild. I missed having a little one around the house. Lulu did not fulfil me as a new baby would.

"Is it a girl?" I asked, entering the bedroom.

Abaas shrugged and left the room. I took that as a yes.

Instead of my usual housedress I decided to put on a nicer dress for her.

While I was still changing, I heard a knock at the door. Another knock sounded, but I did not hear Abaas' footsteps.

Where is that man? I wondered.

I slipped my feet into my pretty slippers that I reserved for when we had guests and hurried to the door just as they knocked a third time. I pulled it open and saw Audel beaming, with a stunning girl next to him. She looked nervous, so I quickly averted my eyes and invited them in.

"Come in. Come in. Welcome," I said. "Please keep your shoes on; the floor is cold bricks throughout."

Audel charmingly led her to the table in the kitchen while I busied myself with getting the plates for dinner. Intentionally, I tried to give her space to relax and become comfortable with us.

Audel did his part to make small talk about his work and asked me about my last day of school.

"What are your plans for the summer holiday, Maman?"

"I had not given it any thought, Audel joon," I answered, hoping that I was going to be busy planning my son's wedding.

"How did you find Audel?" I asked the young girl, pouring water into the samovar.

Audel had not even told me her name, but I was in no hurry. We had all evening.

"He found me," she said, guarded. "I do the accounting for the Mehrabad International Airport. Audel works in their design department. We met at one of the company meetings."

"How wonderful," said Abaas, finally making an appearance.

"Abaas joon," I called to him, "please put this salad on the table, and Audel, you can get the sabzi basket."

"Is there anything I can do to help?" asked the young girl in a sweet voice.

I liked her already.

"Sure, azizam," I said. "You can fetch water in this pitcher."

I handed her our glass pitcher, and she reached to take it with both of her slender hands. She had such dazzling eyes. They were the greenest that I had ever seen. I became lost in them.

"Merci, Maman."

Did I hear her right? Could it be? Was she my Pantea? The last time I had seen her, she was two years old.

I let go of the pitcher, and it fell to the floor. The sound woke me.

"Oh, I am so sorry," I said, but my eyes could not leave her face.

"I have been looking for you for so long," she said. "No one would give me a straight answer."

I stepped into the glass and hugged her. I hugged her so hard. I heard her sob in my arms – or maybe that was me. I stroked her long hair and wished I could give her back all the years she did not have a mother. I did not dare ask how they had treated her.

"Pantea," I said, stepping back to look at her, "forgive me for not being there for you."

She laughed through her tears. "They kept you from me."

I was grateful she knew I wanted to be with her. Abaas and Audel were trying unobtrusively to sweep up the glass under our feet. I held her face in both of my hands.

"You look lovely," I said.

"I am proud to be your daughter."

"So you are not Audel's girlfriend."

"No." She grinned.

"I am so glad."

"Ameh Malize gave me a stack of letters and said they were from you. I read them all – some several times. You were very descriptive, and it gave me a picture of your life."

Malize kept my letters? I was lost in thoughts of the past when I felt Abaas' hand on my shoulder.

"You knew?" I asked Abaas.

"Yes," said Abaas, looking guilty. "That is why I let you answer the door. We wanted to surprise you."

"You did," I laughed. "The best surprise ever."

"I dreamed of this day," Pantea said, as if she knew exactly the words I needed to hear.

"I always dreamed that when you were grown up, you would come looking for me."

"I have so many questions," she said.

I smiled at her.

"Now I know my plan for my summer holiday," I said, addressing Audel's question from before.

I gazed into my daughter's beautiful emerald eyes.

"I will answer your questions, as I have always wanted to."

Grief can be the garden of compassion. If you keep your heart open through everything, your pain can become your greatest ally in your life's search for love and wisdom.

—Rumi

Glossary of Persian Terms

Pari: fairy
joon: dear (casual)
jaan: dear (formal)
baba: father
Pushtekar: perseverance
khale: maternal aunt
Khanum: madam
agha: sir
Piruz: victorious
shirini: (literally) sweets; pastries, cookies
Takht-e-Jamshid: Persepolis
sofreh: a large cloth spread on the floor for a meal to be eaten
    off of; also used at a wedding
Rahim: merciful (a name given to God)
roozi: blessing from God
Gole Gandom: flower of wheat
kedu: zucchini
khoresht: stew
jigar tala: (literally) golden liver; (figuratively) my dear
azizam: dear
ghorme sabzi: stew of green leafy vegetables such as parsley,
    leak and cilantro
"Tasliat migam": "My condolences"

"Akharin ghametun bashe": "May this be your last grief"

"Khoda pedaresho beyamorze": (literally) "May God rest his
father's soul in peace"; (figuratively) "Thank you" (with
relief of being free of an unwanted situation)

Ye-ghol-do-ghol: a schoolyard game played with five stones

jari: typically a rival relationship between two women who
are married to two brothers

"Dast-e shoma dard nakon-e": (literally) "May your hand
not hurt"; (figuratively) "Thank you"

"khoshbakhteem": "We are fortunate (to have visited
with you)"

khahar: sister

kuchulu: tiny

Movafagh: successful

naan taftoon: taftoon bread

naan barbari: barbari bread

naan sangak: sangak bread

noghl: a white confection made of sugar and rose water
that has been boiled into a syrup, with an almond or
pistachio centre

batel: nulled, invalid

maktab: place of learning – usually a room in a mullah's
house

deh bala: northern village

pesaram: my son

awsh: hearty soup

shirin polo: rice with carrots, almonds, and saffron. A
traditional wedding dish.

Khafesho: (literally) the command "Choke!"; (figuratively)
shut up

baleh: yes

gache zende: fresh plaster

"Panah bar Khoda": (literally) "I take refuge in God!";
(figuratively) "Good grief!"

Pishraft: progress

nani: baby swing

kagel: mixture of mud and straw before cement came
into use.

"Akh": "Oops!"

Ab hosi: water pond

Molana: Iranian poet, also spelled Mawlana; in English he
is known as Rumi

kilim: a rug made using flat weave – a less extravagant rug

Maman-bozorg: grandmother

adas polo: lentil rice

"Khodaya": "Oh my God!"

Ayee: poop, in baby talk

aroos: bride

kaleh pacheh: stew made with sheep head, tongue or tripe

besavad: illiterate

lubia polo: green bean rice

ameh: fraternal aunt

sabzi: mixture of herbs: Parsley, Basil, Spring onion, Persian
Leek, Mint

mahr: dowry

mobarak: congratulations

momen: believing; religious

toman: unit of currency, equivalent to a US dollar

sefid kardan: polish copper

tadeeg: rice crust

seezdah: thirteen

ab goosht: mutton in stock

Minakari: "Mina" means "heaven"; Minakari is enamel ornamentation of the surface of metal with an intricate design

dokhtaram: my daughter

ghorban: (literally) one for whom one would sacrifice one's life; (figuratively) sir – term of endearment

Norooz: Iranian New Year, observed on the first day of spring – the Vernal Equinox

Haft Seen: (literally) seven S – the seven symbols of Norooz that start with S

"Kharet be chand mane": (literally) "What's your donkey worth?"; (figuratively) "How are you?"

sannar: unit of currency equivalent to less than a US penny

ab anbar: water well

"Khahesh mikonam": "You are welcome."

"Bah, bah!": "Good, good!"

bastani: ice cream

sonati: traditional

morgh-e behesht: heavenly bird

douq: yogurt-and-mint drink

hamvatana: fellow countrymen

Shokre: gratitude

"Baba naan daad, Baba ab daad": "Dad gave bread, Dad gave water" (from first-grade reader)

"Marge bar Engelis": "Death to England"

Baba holding me. We are in our yard with
the fruit trees and flower bushes.

Agha Rahim with his
three children. I am
with the little dolly.

Grade 3 school photo.

Piruz family excluding the twins. Clockwise,
Agha Piruz, Sana, Mina with soother,
Khanum Piruz, Shakiba, Soghra, Malize holding
baby Darius, Curosh and Saba, hiding.

Playing volleyball with my students at
Movafagh Secondary School.

Epilogue

Farid remarried and his second wife gave him four sons. All four sons were imprisoned for illegal activity, shaming the Piruz family. All of the Piruz children, save one, became labourers despite Khanum Piruz's efforts to have them become professionals by sending them to private school. Pantea was the only Piruz who satisfied her grandmother by becoming an accountant at the Mehrabad International Airport.

Mahmood remained childless until the end of his life. Word traveled and people were no longer willing to give their daughters to him.

Ali and Amir, along with their wives, remained in their father's home and lived a secluded life outside of work. The three cousins, Shabnam, Saeed and Reza, were constant in Pari's life and great mentors for Audel. They each found their passion in life and pursued their dreams to the fullest.

Pari enjoyed a full life surrounded by her family and her students.

About the Author

Parvaneh was born in Tehran, Iran, December 1964. She was the tenth of thirteen children. Her family immigrated to Canada in 1973 and switched from city to farm living. The farm was over one hundred acres of land with sixty machine-milked cows. Challenges were overcome by family support and cooperation. Parvaneh has taught piano, preschool, elementary school and presently, mathematics at the local secondary school. She and her family live in Vancouver, Canada.

CPSIA information can be obtained
at www.ICGtesting.com
Printed in the USA
LVOW03s0204220817
545862LV00001B/1/P